To Janice

TEMPTING AUZED

THE CLECANIAN SERIES: BOOK FOUR

VICTORIA AVELINE

Victoria Aveline

First paperback edition July 2021

Cover design by Mayhem Cover Creations

ISBN 978-1-7346788-3-3

www.victoriaaveline.com

Tempting Auzed

The Clecanian Series: Book Four

Victoria Aveline

1

"You need to get up, mijita."

The words rang through Alex's mind as softly as a sledgehammer. She winced and tried to draw her hands to her face, but they wouldn't respond.

"Princesa, the clock won't wait for you."

Alex groaned at the annoying saying, a favorite of her father's. "Five more—"

All at once, clarity hit. The gritty sand stinging her cheek was not her jersey-sheet-covered mattress. The chilled water lapping at her ankles was not her down blanket. And the soothing voice urging her to wake was not her father's. It couldn't be.

Still, the moment of confusion had stinging tears building behind her lids.

The world around her spun, and an accompanying wave of nausea forced her to remain perfectly still.

Where am I?

Alex's eyes flashed open. *The rapids! Lily!* She jerked her head back just in time to retch cloudy water onto a large log lying next to her.

Her ears rang with the struggle to expel the contents of her stomach. With great effort, she dragged herself to her hands and knees and waited for the dizziness to stop. It only increased until she collapsed onto her side, her thrumming head cradled in her hands.

Everything was too intense. The sound of water made her skull feel like it was being compressed to the size of a grape. Blinding light from overhead speared through her tightly shut lids and caused a furious buzzing to rattle in her ears. She could barely think straight, and whenever she did, the use of any bit of brain power made the dizziness worse.

Need to get somewhere quiet. Inch by inch, Alex crawled away from the river on hands and knees. She didn't know how long it took her to find the sheltered niche carved into the hillside. Or even how she'd been lucid enough to realize that the curtain of vines concealing the muddy alcove could be moved. But the primal part of her mind set on survival took over and urged her to settle onto the cool, wet earth in the dark.

The damp shelter buffered the noise from outside, and the curtain of vines concealed the painful light. Pulling her knees into her chest, she shut her eyes again and tried to focus on the memory of her father's voice. She might have imagined him, but even if she had, the sound was right. The voice familiar. Concentrating on it, the pounding in her head lessened a fraction. Before she knew it, the world had grown blissfully quiet once again.

***

Time no longer existed to Alex. She'd wake up, attempt to move, and fail in an extraordinary display of dizziness often accompanied by dry heaving that renewed her headache. Then, after a while, exhaustion would overtake her, and she'd fall back to sleep. Had days passed? Or hours?

The last thing she could remember before finding the shelter was the current of the rapids dragging her under and a stabbing spike of pain to the back of her head.

One thing she was becoming concerned about, in her moments of lucidity, was her increasingly dry throat. Lily's words about how long a human could survive without water replayed in her mind. After they'd escaped from the bunker they'd been held in and ventured into the alien forest, Lily had made it a point to show Alex how to treat water so it was safe. There was no way in hell Alex would be able to accomplish that right now, though. She could barely keep conscious long enough to recall her surroundings.

What if she'd been held up for days? How much longer could she go without water? Did she dare drag herself back to the stream and drink directly from it? Before she could decide, her vision faded.

***

Noise in front of Alex had her lids creaking open. She didn't even have enough energy to be afraid that something other than her was making noise. Through her blurry vision, a small yellow object on the ground came in and out of focus.

Alex noted her rapid heartbeat and excessively dry mouth and somewhere in the back of her foggy mind wondered if she might be dying.

Something small and fast scurried past the yellow object, dashing out of sight behind the curtain of vines. Maybe it was adrenaline kicking in, but her vision cleared for a brief moment and the yellow object revealed itself to be a cup hollowed from a plant of some kind. The fast creature, whatever it had been, was nowhere in sight. With much more effort than it should've taken, Alex dragged herself over to the cup and peered in.

Was that water? Sweat trailing down her forehead, she tried to focus on whether or not she should drink, but the harder she focused, the more muddled her mind became until all she could think of was an argument from *The Princess Bride*. Vizzini and Westley sitting across from each other, sparring over which glass was poisoned. Would a small forest alien have poisoned the water hoping she'd drink it and die so it could move in on her body? Or was it trying to help for some reason?

Memories of the movie slipped away from her, and Alex realized she must truly be dying. It was one of her favorite films, after all, and there was no way in hell a healthy version of herself would've ever forgotten details about it.

Tentatively, she sipped the water, intending to test a drop or two. The liquid forked a hydrating path through the dry valley of her throat, and she couldn't keep herself from downing the rest in one greedy gulp. She fell onto her back, yellow cup in hand, and whispered, "Iocane powder. Inconceivable," before drifting to sleep...or possibly to death.

***

Her mind came back to her more readily the next time she woke. She turned her head, now only pounding a little, and found the yellow cup resting near the vine curtain where she'd seen it before. Feeling a bit better, Alex forced herself to sit up. Perspiration dotted her forehead with the effort, but she was able to do it, and that was all that mattered. Before grabbing the cup, she searched her small muddy cave, hoping to find the creature who'd left it. She was alone.

She sipped the water and ran her hands over a tender area near the base of her skull. She winced in a breath as a sharp pain speared through her mind. Sure enough, when she brought her fingers to her eyes in the dim light, she could make out dried red flecks mixed with thick congealed blood.

Alex dragged in a calming breath. Dried blood meant it wasn't actively bleeding. It was healing. There wasn't anything else she could do, unless she could somehow get herself to the river to clean it.

She finished off her water and placed the empty cup back where she'd found it. Fatigue swept through her, and she sat up straighter, attempting to fight off sleep for a little while longer. Lily would know what to do in this situation. A memory of the utterly defeated look on Lily's face as Alex had let the current carry her away flickered in her mind. Had she survived? A lump in her Alex's throat swelled. She and Lily had escaped the aliens who'd imprisoned them and survived for weeks together in the forest, and the thing that had finally torn them apart was a crumbling ledge. Alex had barely stepped on the edge of the cliffside overlooking the river before it had collapsed, dumping her and Lily into the unforgiving rapids.

The lump in her throat grew painful, and her eyes stung with tears. Her gaze traveled to the curtain of vines, and she wanted to kick herself for being so stupid. She began to cry.

Why had she crawled in here? *Sure, Alejandra, your survivalist friend got to shore and is probably looking for you, so why not go hide someplace she'll never fucking find you!*

Silent, fat tears streamed down her cheeks. Her battered body knew the pain that accompanied sobbing the way she wanted to would be too unbearable. How far had she floated down that river before dragging herself in here? Was Lily close by or miles away? Between the uncertainty concerning how long she'd been drifting in and out of consciousness and the unknown of the river, it was unlikely she'd ever find Lily.

Beyond the vines, the two milky-white moons lit the humid forest. The familiar buzz of the insects that had always hung around their camp could be heard. Weeks alone with Lily, talking and coming to terms with their abduction, now felt like a dream. Better than this lonely existence. Afraid, starving, and blanketed in mud.

A flash of tiny lights, like a thousand miniscule fireflies all grouped together, shot past outside. Alex froze and stared at the area where they'd disappeared. Just when she was sure whatever it was had gone, it darted past the entrance again. Alex had the distinct impression the creature was trying to peek inside on its mad dashes.

The vines in the left corner lifted, and two large, glowing eyes stared back at her.

Alex's frantic heartbeat made the ringing in her ears return in full force and her vision waver. She begged her mind to study the creature logically, reminding herself it was probably the thing that had been bringing her water, but her brain didn't want to hear it.

Stars floated in front of her vision, and the small animal blinked its bright-yellow eyes at her as though just as curious about what she'd do as she was.

In a move that was rather unhelpful on many levels, Alex's dizziness overcame her, and she slumped onto the wet ground, mind going quiet before her cheek hit the mud.

***

With her knees pulled into her chest and her eyes fixed on the entrance, Alex waited determinedly for her little savior to return. She spun the gold band on her right-hand ring finger, a nervous habit.

When she'd awoken last, she'd found her small cup of water as well as some very fuzzy and very dead insects. In all their time together scrounging for food, Lily had never made her eat one of the fat, flying bugs that had kept Alex awake at night—but only because they hadn't been able to catch them.

The thought of how disappointed Lily would be if she ever

learned Alex had turned down food of any kind in a situation like this spurred her to eat the bugs. Not wanting to know if they tasted like chicken, she'd swallowed the four smashed bugs whole.

And now she waited. Alex didn't know if there was a way to thank this creature, but she wanted to try. It was intelligent; the handmade cup made that clear enough. The damp smell of her cave mixed with the dirt hole turned bathroom in the corner would be enough to push any creature to stay away, but it had kept coming back. Why?

A flicker of light from outside caught her attention, and she slowed her breathing. It dashed by once, twice, then settled in the far corner just like before. This time when its round yellow eyes met hers, she gave a tight-lipped smile, making sure not to expose any teeth and scare it.

"Hey there, little…thing," she whispered on a croak, her voice strained from disuse.

Two bat-like ears came into view on its long face. The animal was furry, kind of, but its fur was wiry, and each strand was tipped with a glowing blue light as if it weren't hair at all but millions of strands of blue fiberoptic threads.

"Thank you for the water. I think you saved my life." Alex gestured toward the cup, keeping her movements slow.

The creature shuffled farther in, and she studied its features. It had a stretched, flexible nose, sort of like a fluffy trunk. Its long arms, legs, and tail reminded her of a spider monkey, but the webbing under its armpits was more flying squirrel than anything.

If she forgot about her life-and-death circumstances and thought about the creature as something created for a movie, she could admit it was cute. Haphazard tufts of glowing hair sprouted from its large ears and chest, making it look like an overworked cartoon character who'd guzzled one too many cups of coffee.

With three spindly fingers, it snatched the cup and darted outside.

"No! Wait!" Alex rose and tried to follow but only managed to stumble through the vines until she sprawled facedown in front of her cave.

Quick thumps against the top of her head had her craning her neck. The small creature was jabbing her with its long trunk like an accordion. When she only squinted up at it, it shoved at her head with its small, three-fingered hands until she unsteadily made her way back to the cave.

The frantic creature followed, forming itself into a smooth ball and rolling after her. It paused by the entrance in its round form, waiting to make sure she wasn't planning on moving again before rolling away. Alex rested her head against the muddy wall and calmed her breathing.

Before long, the creature had returned with another cup of water and some slimy, wriggling insects.

"This is gonna sound beyond ungrateful, but couldn't you have killed them again?" Alex grimaced as one particularly fat slug with stubby legs meandered back toward the exit. Her little furry friend swept the bug farther toward her and sat back on its haunches, peering at her with delight.

Alex lifted the fat bug between pinched fingers and waited for her wave of nausea to pass before slurping it down. She contained her wince and forced a grin, then nodded toward her little friend. "Slimy, yet satisfying."

Over the next few days, Alex started to feel better and better. Whenever her harried nurse allowed it, she would take short walks outside, washing in the river and using the forest as her upgraded bathroom. She'd search for signs of Lily before her headache forced her back into her shelter. Her new friend had become more comfortable with her as well, now sleeping next to her rather than spending its time wherever it used to.

Alex peered down at its sleeping form, curled into a tight ball in her lap, and stroked its thick yet surprisingly soft fur. Each time she ran her hand over it, its illuminated hair would light up in a wave behind her moving fingers. The faint scent of pineapple wafted off the creature and made her smile. It was odd to smell something so familiar from such an unfamiliar creature, but it filled the gnawing hole in her heart just enough to help her not think about how desperately she missed home and her family. Almost like having a bit of home with her. Sliced pineapple topped with some Tajín would always be waiting for her whenever she visited her tía's apartment.

Pain sliced through her chest at the memory that had squeaked through her barriers, and she sucked in a breath. *Don't think about it. Don't think about it.* She concentrated on the curled-up ball in her lap instead.

"You need a name, friend," she whispered.

Alex refused to ponder her life now or how she hadn't yet allowed herself to feel the full weight of what had happened to her. It was easier to not think about it. Years of practice burying and ignoring negative emotion kept her from devolving into hopelessness. That and her new alien sidekick. She was stranded alone on this alien planet and the one friend she had—besides Lily, of course—was this tiny thing who'd somehow known she needed help.

"You're the only thing keeping me sane, little one."

The creature rolled under her palm in what she'd learned was an affectionate snuggle.

Alex grinned. "How about Wilson? You aren't exactly a volleyball, but we'll ignore that."

She curled onto her side, pulling Wilson close, and worked through what the hell she was going to do next.

2

"Are you sure we should be going this way? You look even more nervous than you did at the river." Alex knew Wilson couldn't answer her, yet he seemed to know what he was doing, always pulling or urging her in one direction or another.

She trusted her new little friend, but as his eyes grew wider and wider and the forest grew darker and darker, she found herself wondering whether he now realized he'd made a mistake. Maybe he hadn't understood how slowly she moved compared to him. He kept rolling away at high speed, only to return, knock against the back of her legs, and roll away again.

Five days ago, when they'd left her muddy recovery room, Alex and Wilson had walked along the river while the shore had still been exposed and then trampled through the overgrown bank when the shoreline had eventually disappeared. Using the knife-making skills Lily had taught her, she'd managed to manufacture a small blade. Although she wanted to believe that Lily would be able to track her if she somehow got close enough to her trail, the intermittent rain flooding the river and washing all signs away made her doubtful. So, every so often, when they stopped for breaks, Alex would carve a sloppy message into a heavy piece of wood high on the bank of the river. It was a long shot, but at least she was leaving some kind of trail.

Her soft, gray Henley had gotten shorter and shorter with every note as she'd cut pieces off to use as flags. She'd tried to place her notes in plain view, but she remained pessimistic as to whether anyone would ever see them.

On the third day, after slow, miserable trekking due to her constant headaches and bruised body, they'd made it to a fork in the river.

Dense forest had loomed on one side, and a brighter forest leading to black, craggy mountains lay on the other. Alex had stood, miserably staring in each direction until Wilson nudged her toward the ominous tree line.

It hadn't taken much convincing. Alex was no rock climber, and if there was one thing she'd learned from movies about climbing mountains, it was that the higher you got, the colder it was. In the dark, warm forest, at least she wasn't in constant danger of hypothermia. She'd been living in the forest for weeks anyway; the landscape in this section would just be more of the same, right? Better to dance with the devil you know.

She found herself regretting not thinking harder about her choice now. This part of the forest wasn't only dark, it was sunlight proof. They'd slept near the river the last two nights, and if she guessed at the time based on when she'd woken, it should be about midday, yet there was absolutely no sunlight or sky to be seen. For all she knew, she could be sleeping through the days and it was actually night right now.

The ground sloped farther and farther downward as they hiked, but the treetops didn't sink along with the ground. Their expansive canopies remained at the same height, while the ground dropped lower and lower until they towered over her, taller and wider than the largest redwoods. Maybe even than skyscrapers, but it was difficult to perceive how tall they really were from the ground.

The ceiling of the forest was just that, a solid ceiling of veridian and teal leaves, blocking out the sky and sealing the forest in its own humid microclimate. The air was thick and perfumed by the fragrant scents of the luminous plants and flowers that were the only light source down here.

Prickly yellow vines shone brightly as they wrapped around the massive trunks of the trees and put off a bitter citrus aroma. Large radiant blossoms in a rainbow of colors littered the ground and lit their way. Even the insects and animals glowed.

Gauzy, luminous thread hung from the low branches of the trees like ethereal Spanish moss. Wilson scampered along the branches of those trees. Whenever he paused, he almost disappeared against the moss. Perfectly camouflaged. He'd probably urged her in this direction because this was where he was from. Was he leading her to his home?

Looking around this magical place, she could almost pretend she was merely reviewing a movie for her job at the paper. And yet she didn't have the words to describe the unearthly beauty of the place the way she normally would in her weekly article. An out-of-place chuckle lit in her chest. If she ever made it back to Earth, she'd end up being that whackjob who wrote a whole book about her abduction experience. Mind wandering, she clambered over a fallen branch the size of a mature tree trunk. How many of the people who claimed they'd been abducted actually *had* been?

A large floating worm bobbed by in the distance, and Alex took a moment to study it from a copse of seven-foot-tall, neon-pink-speckled mushrooms. A four-winged bird with sparkling aqua wings swooped down from the treetops, targeting the worm.

It opened its small beak to scoop the wriggling creature out of midair, but suddenly the worm changed. Sharp stripes lit up behind the worm, revealing that the wriggling object rested at the tip of the nose of a creature twice the size of Alex and not floating at all. Its body was massive and rough, and its nose was long and pointed like the horn of a rhino. The little worm at the tip was a flap of skin used to lure prey. Before the poor bird could change direction, the creature swallowed it, gulping it down while the glowing stripes on its body shimmered with joy.

Alex slapped a hand over her mouth and scuttled away toward the thinning river. Wilson leapt onto her shoulder and wrapped his warm, fuzzy body around her neck, nuzzling her cheek with his long snout. He always seemed to know what she was feeling. Maybe he was psychic. Had that been how he'd found her and known exactly what she'd needed to heal? Had she sent out some kind of psychic cry for help that her little savior had responded to?

Alex scratched his large, fluffy ears and continued on more cautiously. Wilson used his flexible trunk to pluck a nearby insect from the air. He crushed it between two long fingers and handed it to her before catching another for himself. Just like taking a pill. She swallowed, grimacing as its wings scratched a path down her throat. How much longer would she have to eat bugs? Forever?

Since she'd started eating them, her weight had managed to hold steady and her energy was getting better each day, but still…they were bugs. Wriggly and flavorless, unless they were sour. Memories of Sunday dinners at her brother's house infiltrated her mind. She sighed and allowed herself to remember them for a moment, if only to try to somehow taste Cynthia's cooking by focusing on it hard enough. *No more Sunday dinners.* Her chest expanded, and she gulped. Immediately she shut down her thoughts. She neither had the energy nor safety to break down right now.

The trees in the distance looked no different than they did here. How far were they going to venture?

"Okay, Wilson. Where are you leading me? I need to find *people*, no offense."

Initially, when she and Lily had fled from their alien captors, she'd been positive she never wanted to run into another alien again. But after a few weeks, the fear had worn off, and desperation for real food and a warm bed had settled in its place. She and Lily had decided to go searching for a city before being violently separated, so that was what she'd try to do now. The people of this world couldn't all be bad, right? They couldn't all want to lock humans up and run experiments. At least that was what she kept telling herself.

Wilson hopped off her shoulder and spread his arms, gliding to the ground. His large, yellow eyes met hers before he curled into a ball and rolled farther along the river and out of sight.

Alex followed, trying not to think about how she may be wandering aimlessly all because a little alien wanted her to. He'd return on occasion, handing her small fruits and nuts and sometimes water. She consumed the foods gratefully but paused before sipping the water.

She'd been too worried to voice it aloud or even concentrate on it, but her stomach had started feeling a little funny yesterday, and it hadn't gotten any better. Lily had warned her again and again about drinking unpurified water, but dammit, she wasn't Lily. She couldn't just MacGyver a fire out of sticks.

Alex sighed and drank the water. "I'm in it now anyway."

Without warning, the forest grew silent. Alex froze, scanning desperately for Wilson. Half of the millions of glowing objects in the forest had gone dark as well; only the plant life remained illuminated.

Bad. Bad. Bad. This is really bad. Not knowing what else to do, Alex crouched low and held still. Something had scared the creatures of the forest into hiding. Her insides turned to liquid and bubbled, grumbling and breaking the silence around her. *Fuck.*

Scurrying noises in front of her had every muscle shooting tense. Wilson rolled through a collection of tall razor-sharp grass and unfurled by her feet, looking as terrified as she felt. He wrapped three fingers around her wrist and urged her forward, his now-dimmed eyes shooting in every direction. Just as she began to move, a heavy vibration rattled through her palms pressed flat against the ground. The hair on the back of her neck rose. Something very large was nearby.

Wilson froze in place too, his long trunk trembling. Another vibration, more intense than the first, rattled under her palms. Something snapped in Wilson, and he heaved her wrists, trying to drag her in the direction of the river. Alex resisted for a heartbeat before dashing toward the water.

Don't look back. They always die whenever they look back. If you look back, you're gonna trip on something and fall, and it'll get you. Alex now understood the urge every movie character who'd looked back had felt. She shouldn't do it, but not knowing what was following her or how far away it was, was almost more torturous than being chased.

Thunderous footfalls vibrated through her legs, and she tried to pick up speed. Up ahead she could see Wilson flapping his short arms around from a large rock sticking up in the middle of the river.

Heart thundering in her chest, she strained to reach the

water. A flash of black sailed overhead and landed with a bone-jarring crash in front of her. An eight-foot-tall monster blinked each of its three inky-black eyes at her. Its thick, four-legged body and large, round face squared off between her and the river. Without another thought, she screamed, spun, and dashed in the opposite direction.

Crashing through glowing leaves, she slipped and slid through the forest as fast as her feet would carry her. She could feel the hot breath of the creature wafting against her shoulders. Was it toying with her?

A small opening in a knotted grouping of roots at the base of a tree came into view to her right, and she dove, scraping her hips along the roots as she struggled to squeeze into the dark space. Alex pressed her body as far back from the beast as she could. Its meaty arm and claw-tipped paw swiped at her between the roots, only inches away from her chest.

Unseen creatures squirmed under her legs and hands, unhappy about an intruder suddenly invading their space. After a few more missed swipes, the creature slid its arm back through the opening. Alex could hear her heart pounding in her ears. Between the gaps in the roots, she could just make out bits and pieces of the horrid creature's face. What was it waiting for?

A large yellow frill of skin that she'd thought was some kind of marking on its back lifted and collared its neck like a satellite dish. Her blood turned to ice in her veins as its smooth black face contorted, opening wider and wider until a cavernous, round mouth was visible. Rows upon rows of sharp teeth dripped with saliva. The hulking chest of the creature expanded as though readying to roar, and Alex instinctively slammed her hands over her ears.

Instead of the lion-like sound she'd been expecting, a pulsating shriek filled her mind, slicing and stabbing inside her skull until she was screaming in agony. She forced her eyes open despite the pain, desperately searching for an escape through her blurry vision. Sticky, hot wetness from her ears dribbled down her wrists.

The sound cut off abruptly. Alex saw the creature take another large breath and knew she'd be dead by the end of its next roar, the insides of her brain liquefied by the terrible sound wave.

A flash of silver and black darted above the creature suddenly. It stumbled back, and Alex could just make out an oozing slice in the yellow skin around its neck. The skin now lay rumpled against the sides of its face. As though it was only just realizing what had happened, the monster let out a fragmented shriek, still painful to her ears but not quite as debilitating. It lumbered away, shaking its head in pain.

Alex lowered her trembling hands and peered down at the bright-red blood on her palms. She took a few deep breaths to battle the nausea building in her gut. She clutched her head in her hands as a series of sharp, painful stabs pulsed and enhanced her ever-present headache. Straining her ears, she tried to hear...anything. Was the forest still silent? Or had she lost her hearing?

"Testing, testing," she whispered. With a sigh of relief, she nodded. The sound was tinny, but she could hear it.

Steeling her resolve, Alex forced herself to move toward the gap in the roots. There was no use hiding here like a sitting duck. Maybe Wilson was still—

She yelped as a shining black arm shot through the roots once more. She retreated back into her alcove, her vision temporarily wavering from the shock. Covering her ears with her hands again, she studied the arm. Her hands dropped at what she found. This wasn't a claw-tipped paw…it was a hand. A very large hand, but humanoid nonetheless. Five normal-looking fingers led to a thick forearm, all clad in some kind of black material.

"Come on. The sefa will be back soon. We need to leave," whispered a deep male voice from outside. He flexed his fingers.

Alex lifted her hand, then paused. A man had somehow found her here. Was it just a coincidence, or was he one of the men who'd orchestrated her abduction and imprisonment? And how could she understand him? She'd been able to communicate with the men who'd abducted her. They'd put a translator in her ear. Did this man have one too?

Did she have any other options? She had no idea where Wilson was, and even if she did, how much longer could she survive out here with beasts like the sefa running around?

Praying she didn't live to regret it, she took the outstretched hand and allowed herself to be tugged out of the knot of roots. When she was back on her feet, she pulled her hand away and stared up at the man. There wasn't much to see—rather, there was a lot of him to see; he was massive, after all—but he was covered head to toe in a black suit of some kind. She couldn't discern any hints of his features.

"Are you hurt? Can you run?" he rumbled in a tone that made her stand a little straighter. He stood stiffly, unmoving, and although she couldn't see his eyes, she felt as if they were inspecting her.

A pained roar rang out, and they both snapped their heads in its direction.

"I don't really have a choice, do I?" Alex said, taking a deep breath and preparing to run.

The man gripped her elbow and sprinted in the opposite direction of the sound. His steps were quiet and quick. Alex felt like a blundering elephant in comparison.

"I slashed its ruff so it shouldn't be able to kill with its sound waves anymore, but it won't stop until you're dead now that it has your trail," he explained while leaping over a downed branch the size of a large tree on Earth. "You need to move faster."

Alex heaved in deep breaths behind him, surprised she was moving as fast as she was. He didn't even sound winded. "I'm not...the bionic...woman." The furious shriek of the sefa grew closer. They weren't going to be able to outrun it. Correction—*she* wasn't. "Just leave me. I'll hide again," she panted, looking for another concealed spot and finding none.

He stopped, turning his head this way and that, and a lingering dread set in. She'd made the offer, but she really hoped he'd refuse to leave.

22

The sound of the sefa crashing through the trees was only a couple of yards away now. With a frustrated roar of his own, the man snatched her around the waist and leapt onto an overhanging branch high in the air. One second she'd been on the ground, and now she was dozens of feet from it. How had he jumped so high?

Before she could think about his feat of superhuman strength too much, he backed her against the broad trunk of their tree perch, then spoke in an odd language. The black material of his suit folded away until the most handsome man she'd ever seen crowded her. The suit coalesced into a small square of fabric stuck to his shoulder. A faint shimmer glinted all around them as if they were standing in a giant bubble.

The roar and the sound of the sefa crashing through the trees quieted, the rustling footsteps halting. Had it stopped its pursuit? Or just temporarily lost their trail? She wanted to ask the man what had happened, but between the adrenaline spiking her fear, the sefa lurking somewhere below, and his newly revealed visage, Alex was momentarily lost for words.

His golden-blond hair was tied into a knot somewhere behind his head, and his light-green eyes flicked over her face as she studied him. She opened her mouth to speak, but he pressed a large rough palm over her lips and whispered, "The more sound we make, the more energy is depleted. My suit isn't used to concealing two people. I don't know how long we have before it fails."

Alex nodded into his palm, ignoring the faint scent of warm spice on his skin. He removed his hand and placed it flat on the trunk just above her shoulder. His gaze angled to the forest floor, and she took his distraction as an opportunity to explore the rest of him. Straps leading to the pack on his back accentuated his large shoulder muscles. A short-sleeved maroon uniform top spanned his broad chest. It was tucked into black pants at his narrow waist.

She found herself drawn to his sturdy, unflinching demeanor. He stood with muscles taut, not in anger or fear but in preparation. Something about it screamed competence and skill.

Her attention drifted to the forearm near her ear, and she followed the progress of the corded muscle as it traveled to his impressive bicep. Thin iridescent tattoos curled and twisted upward, enhancing the perfection of his arm, until they disappeared under the edge of his thick shirt. A long, sheathed blade was strapped just below his shoulder, and a damp spot of purple blood seeped through the sheath fabric and marred his smooth, pale skin.

The forest floor remained quiet, and Alex began to calm. Had they done it? Escaped?

She tried to keep her attention dutifully focused on the problem at hand, but she found her gaze continuing to wander toward the man. Maybe she was so enthralled by him because he'd just saved her life. Or maybe she'd been stuck with Ray for too long. This guy was no Ray, that was for sure.

Her boyfriend back on Earth was good…fine…acceptable for the time being. But she'd known for a while now that he wasn't the one. Small hints of his controlling side had been making an appearance more and more often. Not to mention her tía Vero *hated* him. She couldn't imagine ever being with someone her family didn't like long-term.

Movement from below drew her eyes downward. The sefa prowled through the trees, pointing its wide mouth in different directions. Did it use its mouth to hear too? The man had told her they'd be shielded, but Alex found herself inching away from the creature anyway. Even standing above it, unseen, it still oozed an otherworldliness that made her skin crawl. How long would they have to wait here before it abandoned its search?

The shimmer surrounding them flickered, and a line of alien symbols scrolled by. The flicker continued to pulse intermittently like some kind of warning. *Danger, Will Robinson.*

The man exhaled through his nose with a tight jaw and eyed her. He glanced to the shimmery bubble, then to her, as if trying to tell her something. When she only stared back, his brows fell in resignation and he stepped toward her. He pressed his body into hers. She sputtered. This was no time to *get fresh*, as her best friend's mother liked to say. He looked down his straight nose at her and tilted his head back toward the shimmer. It was no longer flashing.

Ah. Not getting fresh, just conserving the battery. Got it.

His rich smell and the warmth radiating from his big body cocooned her. All at once, her brain became too aware of his muscled stomach and chest plastered against her torso. And farther down, where his hips pushed into her low belly, she thought she even felt—

From just below them, the sefa let out another shriek. The sound didn't pound inside her head like before, but it was still incredibly loud. Before she could guard her ears against the attack, the man had flattened his palms on either side of her face. She glanced up at him and saw the shadow of a wince. She lifted her own hands to cover his ears. His eyes widened briefly, the flecks of gold in his irises seeming to gleam. They stood like that until the shriek ended, awkwardly clutching each other's faces instead of their own.

The sefa must've realized they were close by because it was prowling in small circles below.

When it finally quieted, the man let his hands drop and whispered, "The suit won't hold for much longer. I need to kill it."

"Kill it?" Alex balked. Sure, he was a big guy, but that thing didn't even need to be close to do harm, and from what she could tell, he only had a knife. Before, he'd managed to injure it with a surprise attack, but how the fuck was he expecting to kill it? "How?"

One side of his mouth dipped, and his lids narrowed a hair as though he were insulted, but then his focus returned to the sefa. The flicker along the sides of their shimmery confines started flashing once more. He peered down toward the animal now pawing at the base of a small grouping of tall grass. "I'm not sure, but..." His determined gaze met hers again. "I don't really have a choice, do I?"

Alex let out a nervous laugh. He started to pull away,

drawing his deadly knife from its sheath, but she stopped him with a hand on his wrist. This guy was, in all likelihood, going to die, after refusing to abandon her.

He peered at her hand, then at her eyes, his dark-blond brows raised in confusion. Not knowing what the hell had come over her, she rose to her toes and kissed him. It was quick, and she didn't wait for him to kiss her back before moving away.

He stared down at her, his head still tilted slightly to one side. If anything, he looked more confused.

"What's your name?" she asked as the flashing around them picked up speed.

Taking a few steps back without tearing his gaze from her, he answered, "Auzed."

"Try not to die, Auzed."

His brows relaxed, and his features grew determined once more. With a silent nod, he turned, scanned the ground for the animal, and jumped.

3

Zed hit the ground just behind the creature. His bhadsit suit used the last of its charge to silence his landing but then retracted until it lay clasped to his shoulder, an innocuous piece of black material. The sefa spun toward him all the same, likely picking up on the thundering rhythm of his heart. Could it hear his blood rushing in his veins? Could it smell the female's scent on his lips?

He'd found her. She was covered in dirt, injured, smelly, and much too thin, but he'd found her alive. He still had trouble wrapping his mind around the fact that she and the other human they called Lily had survived out here for so long on their own, but there she was. Alejandra. And upon their first meeting, she'd pressed her mouth to his.

Why in the name of the Goddess had she done that right before he'd jumped into a fray? Had she been trying to get them both killed by distracting him so?

The sefa charged in his direction, its yellow frill flopping uselessly around the base of its skull. Zed dodged it, slashing into its side until the metal tang of blood hit his nose and warm liquid coated his hands.

She'd kissed him. Had performed that odd mouth play that humans seemed to enjoy with their partners. As he skidded past the sefa, mind focused on the kiss, its tail shot out, wrapping around his ankle and pulling his legs out from under him. Zed's knife went flying just as the sefa used its strong tail to throw him bodily against a large trunk.

Zed got to his feet and wondered if anything was broken or if it just felt that way. *She's going to get us both killed!* This was exactly why he'd had so much trouble controlling the males under his command these days. Human females were a confounding lot.

Although he'd never faced a sefa before, he'd certainly fought worse. It shouldn't be taking him this long to dispatch the creature. And he needed to kill it quickly so they could flee. Now that they were within Sauven territory, the murder of a sefa was illegal, the creatures held sacred by the people of the forest city.

He curled his fists, squaring off with the sefa while searching the ground for his weapon. He spotted it feet away beneath a pale white flower. The sefa thundered toward him, letting out its terrible pulsating roar that stopped most prey in its tracks. Covering his ears, he feinted right, but the beast knew better this time. It followed him, scraping its rows of teeth along his back and side just as he hurdled out of the way, landing in a clumsy roll. A long scrap of fabric fell from his shoulder, and he realized the sefa had torn his pack away.

A faint gasp sounded from the treetops. Did she really think he couldn't best this animal? Is that why she'd kissed him? As a parting gift meant to be of comfort in his last moments of life? It was an affront.

He jumped up and whirled around, ignoring the sharp pain in his side and stooping to snatch up his knife. Its pounding footfalls were just behind him. The sefa's foul breath wafted over his neck. Bending at the knees, Zed sprung into a backflip and landed, straddling the beast. Without giving it time to react, he angled forward and buried the knife deep into its middle eye. The other two eyes blinked out of sync as its brain slowly died.

Zed slid off the side of the crumpling sefa and took a quick swipe for his pack but was too late. The massive creature collapsed atop it. With a groan, he wiped his blade across his pants, then sheathed it. He straightened and watched the sefa's body struggle against death. The haunting final song which the creatures were famous for should be coming any moment now.

Just as he'd predicted, the sefa's great lungs filled with air and it released its final exhale along with a transcendent melody. Soft and calm, the song rode on its last breath, the gentle percussion sweeping over his skin and seeping into his bones until the melody stuttered out altogether. Zed found his chest tightening despite himself.

He dipped his head to the sefa and slid his eyes closed in a moment of respect. The creatures had been some of the few transported to this planet from their old world and were the last of their kind. Gently, he placed a hand over the sefa's torso and, in a hushed voice, recited something he'd heard his father say once to a dying mojak soldier far from home. "You have traveled so far, and yet your journey has only begun."

After another breath, Zed turned away. He glanced to where he'd left Alejandra and found her on her knees. Her dark brows were drawn, and silent tears carved tracks down her grime-covered cheeks.

With a deep, controlled breath, he moved to stand below her. Sticky blood oozed from his throbbing wounds and coated the inside of his arm. She was too high up for him to jump to without his suit and with the injuries he'd sustained. The sleek speeder he'd driven to travel here, now trapped in his pack under the heavy creature, was of no use either. It'd take at least three *uninjured* males to lift the sefa. "Jump down. I'll catch you." He lifted his arms, but rather than doing as he asked, she appeared shocked.

"I...jump?" She gave a pointed look to the red liquid dripping off his bicep and enunciated her words as she said, "You're bleeding."

He dropped his arms and tried to keep the annoyance off his face. He wasn't so injured that he couldn't catch her slight body. He placed his hands on his hips while continuing to stare up at her. So, she *had* thought he was going to die. The idea rankled for some reason.

"I can't jump up there right now, but I can catch you. If you don't want to jump, you could try to climb, I suppose."

He kept his voice even, though he wanted to command her to follow his orders the same way he did every day to the guards he oversaw. Auzed, or Zed to his friends—well, maybe more like his family, seeing as he didn't have many friends—was the head guard at the Pearl Temple. The title was prestigious, something every Tremantian soldier aspired to. He, and the guards under his supervision, protected the small number of females who still existed in their city and lived at the Pearl Temple. As such, Alejandra was now under his care as well.

"Climb? Are you crazy? There's nothing to hold on to. This is, like, the only branch," she argued unhelpfully.

Zed felt his ire rising and fought it back. He was tired, injured, and ashamed he hadn't just broken one law today by entering Sauven territory uninvited, but two, by killing the sefa.

For the last two weeks, various groups of soldiers and/or Temple guards had combed the forests searching for the two females who'd escaped an Insurgent facility and disappeared. First, they'd searched the Manta Forest and then lower into the dense Sauven Forest. The Queen had agreed that when they reached the ocean to the west, the Black Mountains to the north, and the city limits of Sauven to the northwest, their search would be over.

Auzed had believed the females to be dead, but he'd followed the Queen's orders to continue the search anyway. Then, a few hours ago, the Queen had contacted his small search party scouring the southwestern border of the forest and alerted him to the fact that one of the missing humans had been found alive and well and was with Verakko. The Queen had described the last known location of the other female, and he, along with two other guards, had sped to the Chisnop River immediately.

He'd sent his two guards to search the east bank of the river and the forest beyond, while he'd traveled into the heart of the Sauven forest. He'd failed to mention to his guards the Queen's additional private request to illegally search within Sauven territory for the lost human. He abhorred the idea of breaking any law, and he wasn't too happy the Queen had asked it of him, though he understood why she had.

After the Queen had revealed the humans' existence to Clecanian leaders worldwide, Sauven had been one of the cities to report they'd be forcing any discovered humans to participate in their marriage ceremonies, just as they did all their other citizens. Alejandra would be forced to do the same unless he could get her back to Tremanta, where there were already laws being put into place to offer the humans rights in concurrence with their culture.

Now look at him, begging the female he'd illegally rescued to allow him to help her further. If she only understood the state of his mood at present and how tenuously he was holding on to his temper, she'd obey without a second thought.

"Just jump, Alejandra," he pushed through gritted teeth, holding his arms out again.

"Okay, okay." She swept the matted mess of dark hair out

of her face and sat on the edge of the branch. He could see her mumbling to herself as she rotated a golden ring around her finger but couldn't quite make out what she was saying. Even through the dirt covering her face, he noticed her warm, brown skin pale a shade as she scooted forward and glanced toward the ground. She slid her eyes shut and was about to let herself fall when her lids sprung open again, "Wait, how did you know my name?"

"Jump!" he barked, his patience snapping.

A voice from somewhere overhead called down, "Now, now. There will be no need for you to jump. But you'll both need to come with us."

Zed winced. They'd been caught. He spun and saw a small contingent of Sauvenian rangers mounted on floating transport platforms. They hovered above, their angry gazes drifting toward the dead sefa.

A small tuey crawled into view over one of the ranger's shoulders and leapt, gliding toward Alejandra.

"Wilson!" she exclaimed, catching the tuey in a tight hug as it neared.

Vitriol boiled in his gut. He didn't know precisely how it'd happened, but the human had gotten them caught.

The rangers descended. He allowed two of them to haul him toward an apathetic male, who produced an extra-large transport platform from underneath his own. The plethora of achievement bands circling his thick tail identified him as the highest-ranking ranger among the group.

As they flattened Zed into a seated position on the

transport platform and cuffed his hands to a ring in the center, he wondered what his Queen would do upon hearing he'd been caught. His communicator, still strapped to his bicep, was plucked away by a ranger. Would she deny she'd given him the order and abandon him to his fate? Or would she confess and incur the wrath of the territorial Sauvenians?

He could hear Alejandra arguing in the background, but he tried to tune it out. The little tuey she'd befriended had brought these rangers to them. The human was the reason they were in this mess. If she'd only jumped sooner, they could've sprinted to the border half a mile away.

"I'm sorry for this, but it's procedure when a sefa has died," one of the rangers said to Alejandra as he gently guided her into position across from Auzed and cuffed her wrists next to his. The ranger handled her cuffs with care, making sure they weren't too tight before moving away. Zed's cuffs, on the other hand, had been tightened so much that he was sure he'd have lingering bruises.

She peered at him; the whites of her large brown eyes were marred by angry, burst blood vessels. That, along with her bleeding eardrums, were a product of the sefa's deadly roar. If he'd gotten there even a few minutes later, she would've been dead.

"Why—" she began, but he cut her off with a shake of his head.

He didn't want their guards to overhear anything before he figured out what his next moves were, and he also needed time to cool his temper. The logical part of his mind knew this wasn't her fault. He was just angry with the situation he'd been put in and that she hadn't helped their situation one bit. She'd actually stopped running at one point and asked him to leave her. What kind of male did she think he was?

The informant tuey glided down and settled in her lap, happy as could be. Then it opened its large yellow eyes and shot him a glare. He frowned back. *The feeling is mutual.*

4

∞

Alex took her cues from Auzed and kept quiet as the newcomers loaded them both onto a large floating platform and bound their hands with some kind of high-tech cuffs. These men were the most alien-like aliens she'd seen yet. They had graceful bodies and long, flexible tails. Their ears were pointed at both the top and bottom, and their wide, radiant eyes were just a bit too large to pass for human eyes. Their anime-esque size must help them see in this dark forest.

They began to glide away, but three tall, forest-green aliens with glowing geometric markings all over their bodies stayed behind, studying the sefa and glaring angrily in Auzed's direction. The other two remained with them.

The leader, a tall man with the same coloring and markings as the rest, rode ahead. Alex figured he was the leader because he'd been the one giving orders to his men. His long tail split into three near the end. Each tip expanded into a glowing orb. He gripped the edge of the floating board with his tail for the most part but occasionally used the bright light of its tip to guide their way through the darker stretches of their journey. The other guard rode ahead of them as well; their floating platform remained close to his.

While their two jailors rode their platforms standing upright, Alex and Auzed sat on theirs with their bound hands attached to a ring at the center of their platform. She didn't love being tied up, but she was grateful the connection at least ensured she wouldn't fall off the smooth floating board. She concentrated her energy on staring at her hands and not at the ground passing far beneath them.

Wilson migrated to her shoulders and squeezed its body around her neck in a comforting gesture. He hadn't abandoned her or been killed after all. He'd left to get help. Using his Sonic the Hedgehog super speed, he'd found these new aliens. At present, she couldn't decide if that was a good thing or a bad thing.

She chanced a glance up toward Auzed and found him glaring into space, fuming about something. The image of him skillfully dodging and slashing at the sefa played through her mind. She didn't like that the sefa had had to die, but watching Auzed fight had been mesmerizing.

"Dedeth, come here," the leader called to the ranger nearest them while peering at her. Their escort sped away on his board and joined his boss. They spoke in hushed tones while shooting glances in her direction.

She leaned toward Auzed and whispered, "What's going on? Who are you anyway, and how do you know who I am?"

Auzed's distracted gaze settled on her. "I'm from the city of Tremanta. A female named Lily was found and reported your last known location to my Queen. I was sent to find you before the Sauvenians. We're being detained for invading the territory of Sauven and killing one of their protected species in self-defense."

"She did it? She actually found some nice aliens?" Alex blinked. It was a lot to take in, and her head still hadn't fully healed. The pounding ache had only increased during their escape from the sefa. "So, Lily's safe? She's okay? Can I talk to her? Is she back in that place underground?" Alex asked the last with trepidation, hoping beyond hope this guy wasn't affiliated with the group who'd kept her, along with a handful of other women, locked in a bunker underground.

To her relief, Auzed appeared offended. "My Queen would never allow that to happen."

Alex let out a low breath and nodded. She had so many questions, but she needed to ask the right ones before the alien policeman returned. "What will they do with us?"

"I don't know. To you? Likely nothing." He barely contained a sneer as he glanced at Wilson. "We could've made it out of Sauven territory if your tuey hadn't led them to us. Did you send it to find them?" His words rang with accusation, but Alex couldn't bring herself to feel offended.

She gave a wry laugh. "Yeah, sure did. Because after recovering from a head injury that laid me out for who knows how long, I somehow learned to communicate with my buddy here. While I was running for my life from the three-eyed monster, I commanded him to go and tell the alien city I didn't even know existed to send someone to please lock me up." She raised a brow at him.

He grunted, looking mollified. "I was sent here to find you and bring you back to Tremanta as a Tremantian citizen, but they're going to push for you to be declared a citizen of Sauven."

"How is that decided? And why should I be a citizen of Tremanta? I'm a citizen of Earth, remember? I'll be heading back there as soon as I can anyway, so what does it matter?"

Auzed stared at her. It was clear there was a lot she didn't understand. His eyes flitted toward the guard, who was now heading back in their direction. "If you're deemed to be a citizen of Sauven, they'll force you into a temporary marriage with someone you don't know. If you live in Tremanta, you'll be around other humans and have the *option* of marrying or not. I just need time to figure out our defense. Keep your mouth shut and follow my lead when they speak to us," he hastily finished just as their guard returned to glide in front of them.

Married? She didn't want to marry anyone, especially not anyone from another planet. Auzed looked human enough, but these other people had tails. The tails themselves didn't bother her, but the thought of what type of machinery might be lurking in their pants did.

Alex furrowed her brows at Auzed but kept quiet. He hadn't mentioned the option of going home. Did they not have spaceships here? Those purple aliens who'd snatched her from her apartment had had a ship, but they might not be from this planet. Just an intergalactic transport? These aliens had these hover boards, but she supposed that could be the epitome of their technology. What if she was stranded?

Mouth gone dry, she gulped. No. If she could get here, surely she could get out. She'd just have to wait for aliens like the ones who'd taken her to come back, then hitch a ride. But if she was going to be stranded here for a while, she'd most definitely want to live in the city that wouldn't force her to get married, temporarily or not.

A sudden desperation to work through a plan before they arrived wherever they were going came over her. Auzed would help her, she knew it. He'd been nothing but helpful so far, if not a little grumpy, but who could blame him? He'd just risked his life, getting his back slashed open to help her, and had ended up being arrested for his efforts.

"We're here," he said, looking to the right.

Alex followed his gaze, and her breath caught. High above the forest floor, wooden, sloped-roof, multilevel buildings circled the trunks of trees as wide as skyscrapers. Their delicate arched entryways led to expansive patios overlooking the glorious city.

The buildings themselves had an odd style. Overall, they resembled luxury treehouses, but with Victorian gothic architectural elements crafted from organic building materials. She wouldn't have thought it, but it worked. The carved gables, colonettes, and finials blended with the natural wood tones and greenery of the trees they were set into and made the whole city look ancient and magical yet somehow tranquil.

The air up here was still warm but less humid. It smelled a bit *lighter* too, as though the competing scents of all the plants down below wafted toward the sky and dispersed enough to give the air a more subtle floral aroma tinged with citrus.

Enormous spiral staircases circled the trees, leading from one illuminated building to the next. Some of the trunks were close enough together that the structures spanned two trees, yet the architecture was so graceful it almost looked as if the trees had grown into each other.

No one back home would ever believe this. Her best friend, Jamie, was a Disneyland nut with a SoCal Select yearly passport. She'd probably keel over right here. Alex ignored the slimy voice whispering she'd never be able to describe the city to Jamie. She let the soothing fruity scent of Wilson, still wrapped around her neck, calm her.

Hanging from the tree's massive branches by impossibly thick, iridescent metal chains were glittering homes strung like teardrop Christmas ornaments in midair. People zoomed by on round platforms every which way, going to and from the suspended structures. The city went on as far as Alex could see, growing smaller in the distance until all she could make out was the bright shine of light from each of the numerous windows, twinkling in the background like billions of fairy lights floating in the darkness.

"The Swiss family Robinson has nothing on this place," she whispered as they passed a strange arena of sorts. Rows upon rows of seating were connected in a circle between four trees and were positioned around a large area of dead space at least three times the size of a football field. Without a floor to be seen, her mind jumped to quidditch.

All of the treehouse buildings were high up on the trees. It seemed as though the population of Sauven spent a majority of their time up here. How would it feel to live your life never walking on solid ground? Alex gulped as she peered over the edge of their platform to the glowing forest far below. A better question was, how many people fell to their deaths every year?

"I request a meeting with the regents," Auzed called to the leader, who was guiding their party toward the highest floor of a tall grouping of buildings. Unlike the stylish architecture around them, this building was plain and lined with mirrored windows. The effect was creepy. There could be a thousand people staring out at them, and they'd never know.

"Denied," the man in charge said without looking back at Auzed.

Anger flared in his mossy green eyes for a moment before he gathered himself. "Then I demand to speak with *my* Queen."

"You will be questioned before speaking to anyone."

Auzed growled, actually growled, and focused on his hands, the strong lines of his chiseled face deep in thought.

Their round platform pulled alongside an unloading zone, and she peered next to her at another large man being escorted off a platform in cuffs. What would an alien police station look like?

Their guard approached them and hunched over the area where their shackles connected. He held a small metal rectangle close to Auzed's cuffs, and they separated from the platform but did not open. The guard dragged Auzed to his feet, not caring that he was injured.

"Hey, be careful, would you? He needs to see a doctor," she reproached, tugging at her own cuffs only to find them still stuck to the ring. Wilson nimbly leapt onto the ledge, eyes focused on a group of pudgy orange insects. The bugs flitted around a dribble of sap leaking from the bark of the tree above the building's roof. Without so much as a backward glance, he scurried out of sight. She couldn't blame him. He had tended to her for almost a week now, after all. He deserved a bug feast.

The guard maneuvering Auzed lifted a glowing brow at her as though he hadn't understood her, then glanced questioningly to his boss.

The leader kept his gaze aimed at her and strode toward them. "Why do you care?"

Pinche pendejo. "I care because…" Alex trailed off at the warning look Auzed shot her. She snapped her mouth shut and glared up at the guard, then shrugged silently.

The man wore a tight vest that dipped low and exposed much more skin than she'd ever seen a policer office who wasn't on a calendar expose. His tight pants were stretchy, and his long tail wrapped around his right thigh as if keeping out of the way. Metal rings were stacked on his tail from the area where it forked and upward. The metal was a dark gray but shone with a rainbow of colors when he moved, like the chains holding the houses to the tree branches. The other guard's tail was positioned around his own leg in the same way but was decorated with a lot fewer rings.

The man squatted down and brought another metal rectangle to her cuffs. He was close enough that she could make out the odd wobbly borders of his large pupils as he gazed into her eyes. "Very well, human. We shall speak later."

There was something in his voice and in his stare that she couldn't quite place. Was he hitting on her or being protective of her? To her surprise, he used the metal rectangle to unlock her cuffs, freeing her hands. Alex stood, unease making her stomach feel hollow. She didn't like not understanding someone's intentions.

The man guided her with a palm on her back, while the other dragged a furious-looking Auzed beside her. Auzed glared not at the man whose fingers were cutting into his arm but to her guard. "Remove your hand," he spat.

The guy flushed a deep forest green and scowled at Auzed, but he did drop his hand.

A feeling of extreme wrongness overcame Alex as she was led from the dim, glowing exterior and into a remarkably sunny room. But how could it be sunny here? She squinted against the bright light as it ratcheted the pounding in her head. She hadn't realized until now how helpful the dark forest had been at keeping her head injury happy.

"What's the matter?" she heard Auzed call.

The guard from her side brushed past, shuffling in front of her. "What did you do to her?" he accused. His suspicious tone was directed at Auzed, and though she hadn't known Auzed for very long, she suspected he was currently glaring back at the other man.

"No one did anything. It's the light. I think I'm still recovering from a concussion. If we could get somewhere darker, I'll be good as gold."

A solid palm circled her arm and guided her forward. Chatter sounded around her, but a buzzing in her ears muffled it. She squinted at the matte green floor as the guard led her, trying with all her might not to hurl. Whenever she felt sick, the ghost scent of menthol always appeared out of nowhere. While concentrating on walking, her mouth curved into a sad smile. She could almost hear her mother's smooth voice saying, *"Ponte Vicks."* The thought speared through her, making her nausea vanish but leaving a familiar ache in her heart.

The man guided her into a soft chair and walked away. Blessedly, the bright light from above dimmed. Alex creaked her eyes open and found herself in a sitting room. The eggplant-colored walls were bare except for a few screens with sharp vertical symbols she couldn't decipher. She peered up to see where the daylight was coming from and found the entire surface of the ceiling was lit.

"Artificial daylight."

Alex glanced over to Auzed, still cuffed and standing while his guard gripped his shoulder.

The leader of the two scowled at Auzed as if he had no right to explain the light. "Yes. You happened to walk in during our vitamin-boost hour." He glanced back at her, and the harsh lines around his eyes softened. "We prefer the dimness of our sheltered city, but we need regular sunlight treatments to keep up our health."

Alex nodded. She'd read about people from different parts of the world needing SAD lights in winter, but being born and raised in southern California, she'd never experienced the side effects that came from lack of sunlight. How could people from this planet have such similar needs?

"I'll call for a doctor to come treat you now. He can work while we question you both." He turned to Dedeth. "Go contact Huten and tell him we have two detainees who need an exam and preliminary treatment. Also inform him he'll need to get the human language uploaded to his translator. You should do the same."

Dedeth nodded and shoved Auzed farther into the room before leaving.

"As for you..." The leader whose name she hadn't caught yet glared at Auzed. "You'll be coming with me to the fourth floor."

Alex didn't know what was on the fourth floor, but the tone of his voice hinted it wouldn't have padded chairs and pleasantly cushioned floors like this room did. "No, wait! I'm sorry, I don't know your name. Can't Auzed stay here with me?"

Auzed didn't appear angry at her outburst and instead

looked to the guard and waited for his response.

The man glanced between her and Auzed with an irritated curiosity before finally saying, "I'm Fierad. What is your connection to this male? You appear to be very familiar with him."

"Our connection is none of your concern. We're both Tremantian citizens. You should be contacting our government before questioning us." Auzed growled at the man.

Cool it, dude, Alex silently begged. Auzed's whole macho thing wasn't doing them any favors with this guy.

"She's a human, found within Sauven territory. Which means she's *our* citizen," Fierad argued, brazenly stepping toward Auzed.

"*I* found her. She's our citizen by law."

"Do you think the regents will care?" Fierad laughed. "She's *human.* You know how badly the people of our city will want her to stay. Our annual marriage games are days away. Merely having her in the crowds will bolster our people, not to mention the contestants. The regents will never just let her go to Tremanta without proof."

Marriage games? Alex pictured a bride and groom playing quidditch in that massive empty arena and contained a chuckle. Was this guy saying she was a top commodity here because she was human? But why? Was she some kind of exotic specialty item because she was from another planet? How aggravatingly human of them to think that way.

Fierad continued his rant, his green skin flushing darker

and darker as his anger built. "No, she'll be taken care of here, and you'll be sentenced for attempting an abduction of one of our citizens, slaughtering a beloved sefa, and illegally crossing our borders."

While Fierad was scary on his own, Alex found the silent fire burning in Auzed's eyes to be more so. She'd seen what he could do, and if she were Fierad, she wouldn't be pushing a man like that.

Auzed had helped save her life, and now he was going to be punished for it? It wouldn't surprise her if Fierad pushed for the harshest punishment he could either. She had to figure out a way to help Auzed. She owed him that.

So far it seemed like both these cities revolved around marriages and being married, seeing her as only an object belonging to one rancher's herd or another. Well, she knew which cowboy she wanted to belong to if those were the options. A thought came to her, and she tried to work through the string of lies she'd have to tell.

She interrupted the testosterone-fest building in the center of the room. "I *am* a Tremantian citizen." Alex stood and shot a smile toward Auzed, mentally trying to convey what she was about to do. "He's my husband. I mean…" The shock and anger that registered in his expression had her changing her lie slightly. "My soon-to-be husband."

Fierad stared at her for a moment, a hint of disgust curling his lip as her words registered. "You've promised yourself to him? When?"

Alex's mind raced. "He gets so worked up." She shook her

head playfully toward Auzed. "He neglected to elaborate before. He did *find* me, but not just now. Days ago. Let me go back to the beginning. I was being held in a bunker somewhere, but I escaped and ran into the woods to hide."

True so far. Alex thought, realizing she needed to explain away her current appearance without mentioning Lily. There were too many unknowns at present, and she didn't want to drag her friend into the lie.

"I was minding my business, surviving in the forest, but I accidentally fell into the river and was swept away. Luckily, he found me." Again, the truth—missing loads of information and jumps in time, but technically nothing she'd said was a lie...well, almost nothing. "He rescued me, and I was so grateful, I agreed to marry him when he asked," she said, standing with the intent to cross to Auzed. She second-guessed the action when she saw the fury flaring white hot in his stony expression. If she could listen into his thoughts, she was sure he'd be shouting, *Shut up! Shut up!*

Too bad. He'd saved her life. She could at least perjure herself to help him out. She stared at him, raising her brows. "Isn't that right, honey?"

A muscle twitched in his firmly closed jaw.

Fierad turned to him expectantly, arms crossed over his chest.

As though someone were pulling the words out of him, he finally spoke. "Yes. I didn't mention the details before because they don't matter. She's legally a Tremantian, and that's all you need to know."

"You agreed to marry him? Just like that?" Fierad wasn't buying her lie.

"He saved my life! Of course I did." She managed to put enough judgmental incredulity into her words to spark a look of hesitation on Fierad's face.

"Why were you found roaming the floors of Sauven, then?" he said to Auzed instead.

Auzed lifted his brows toward her. "Intended?"

Do I have to think of everything? "Oh, well, that's really my fault." Alex rolled her eyes in a self-deprecating expression of embarrassment. She searched her mind for a lie, scanning the room as if it held some hint as to what her excuse could be. Her mind snagged on something and she turned. "I was alone by the river getting some water, and I saw Wilson...the animal that led you to us. He was so friendly and so cute, but then something spooked him and he ran off into the forest, and, like an idiot, I chased him. I'd only walked a few steps in before that thing started chasing me." She gestured to Auzed as if the rest of the story were clear. "And of course, Auzed, being the great guy that he is, went in to rescue me. I must've stumbled across your border when I was running for my life. Auzed followed to help me. We had no other choice but to run away and then fight it off."

"You just happened to find her? What were you doing so close to our territory in the first place?"

Auzed looked down his nose at the man. "I received the information that there may be humans in need of help just as you did. Your regents made the information public, did they not? I went out searching and got lucky. Maybe if you'd done the same, you would've found her instead."

Fierad stared hard at her. She could tell by his gaze that he suspected there was more to her explanation, yet it also seemed he couldn't find anything particularly wrong with her story either. He spun on Auzed instead. "I am to believe you found her in this condition"—he motioned to Alex's raggedy appearance—"near our territory by happenstance and did not immediately take her back to Tremanta?"

"I had food and supplies. I called my Queen and apprised her of the situation, but Alejandra was terrified of returning to the city. Although she trusted me, she'd become convinced the people who'd taken her would be waiting in Tremanta to steal her away again. After the ordeal she'd been put through, her concerns were understandable, and so we waited until the Queen sent word that all guilty parties had been apprehended before deciding to return."

Ooh damn. That sounded believable.

"And if I call your Queen and ask her to corroborate this fabrication?" Fierad tilted his head with a knowing grin, clearly having made up his mind that they were indeed lying. He didn't wait for Auzed to answer before continuing on. "This female is ours, and you will be jailed for both your crimes and your lies."

"This *female* is named Alejandra," she interjected, tired of Auzed being the only man respectful enough to use her name.

A knock sounded at the door, and Dedeth entered with a burly green alien in tow.

Dedeth looked pleased as he gestured to the newcomer. "I've fetched the doctor." His face fell as he took in the tense scene.

"Shall I get you a glass of yubskani for doing your job?" Fierad barked, directing his irritation toward Dedeth, whose eyes grew wide at the unexpected insult.

"No, sir, I—"

Before Dedeth could finish, Fierad snapped, "We're going to retrieve Relli while they're being healed. He shot a cocky grin at Auzed and added, "She's half Swadaeth."

Whatever that meant wasn't good. Auzed had flinched, only making Fierad's grin grow.

"Fine." Auzed straightened his shoulders. "But as you know, I'm one of the Queen's head guards and have been made privy to private information. By law, I cannot be *swayed* without her express consent."

"No matter." Fierad shrugged before walking to the door. He pointed toward Alex. "*She* can be.

5

Auzed fumed. The human had lied, and now they were both in trouble. Dammit, he'd told her to keep her mouth shut and follow his lead, but she just couldn't do it. She had no idea what she'd done either. It was clear she believed she was helping, but she didn't know anything about this world. What being married meant and what lying to the proud people of Sauven could result in.

She was to be *swayed* by a Swadaeth, for Goddesses' sake! She'd be forced to admit the lie, and he'd be revealed as a criminal, having broken not one but three laws today. His honor would've remained in place if he'd only been found to have killed a sefa and entered Sauven territory in defense of a female. Even the Sauvenians would see he'd had no other choice. But to lie? He'd had a choice in that, and he'd chosen to break the law. There was no honor there.

Auzed had spent his life as a soldier, always following the rules. He'd been promoted to head guard, the youngest the

Pearl Temple had ever seen, and now he would sit in a cell, a dishonorable criminal. His decades of hard work gone like that. All because she had to go and "help."

What would his father think of him? Auzed sank into a chair, forgetting about his injured back and side, and shot to his feet again with a hiss of pain.

He inwardly seethed, pacing back and forth as the doctor checked Alejandra over, tending to what he could with the portable healer he'd brought with him. He could feel her eyes tracking his movements, but he refused to meet her gaze. Over his life he'd found remaining silent and retreating into his mind to be the best way to relieve the overblown spikes of anger he often felt thanks to his Traxian heritage.

As a half-Tremantian, half-Traxian male, he'd had to learn to manage the fiery emotions always blazing in him at the smallest thing. Being a soldier and now a guard had helped, years of strict training teaching him control.

He turned to continue his pacing but found his path blocked by the doctor.

"I was told you were injured," the male said unenthusiastically.

Without a word, Auzed winced and lifted his arms, unable to remove his shirt with his hands still cuffed, and presented his marred back to the male. The doctor tugged his shirt overhead until it bunched at his wrists. Zed's gaze landed on Alejandra's nervous stare. She tentatively crossed to him.

Her attention lingered on the doctor working behind him and then briefly on his bare chest. "What is a Swadaeth?" she whispered.

Auzed bit back the rude answer he wanted to give and instead took a calming breath. "A Swadaeth can *sway* individuals. It's a sort of mind control. Whoever they are will *sway* you to tell the truth." He hadn't realized there was a Swadaeth working here, or he would've denied the lie when Alejandra had first uttered it. Was there any argument to make her exempt from being *swayed*? If she were his wife...but she'd claimed they were not yet married.

Alejandra's eyes widened farther. "What? You guys have a mind reader here?"

Zed scowled. This female was so ignorant of this planet. How had she ever thought she could get away with lying about something like this? "Swadaeth don't read minds, they only influence you to do as they say."

"Can I..." She huffed out a breath in irritation and glanced at the doctor, possibly remembering she had to watch her words. Zed could feel the ripped skin of his back was almost mended.

The doctor stepped away. "Alright, I've done what I can, but I want to see you both after you're finished here for more internal scans and repairs. She'll need an elixir as well. Do you have any questions?" the doctor drawled in a tone of boredom.

"No," they both said in unison.

The doctor pressed the tips of his tail to his slightly bowed forehead, a customary greeting and farewell, then left. The electric whir of the door behind him ensured they were locked in.

As soon as the door slid shut, Alejandra spoke. "Can we just run?"

"Run where? I seem to recall you took issue with jumping from a great height before. Do you have access to transport that I don't know about?"

She quirked her lips downward. "Fine. Then is there any way for me to overpower the *sway*? Or lie through it or something? What if I say it's against my human religion or that my head still hurts, maybe?"

"Some can throw off a *sway*, but it takes practice. And most Swadaeth know when their *sway* has failed. You need to act like you've been *swayed* while fighting it off. And you've never even been *swayed* before." Zed chuckled in derision. "In other words, no. They will give you their command, you'll repeat the command, and that will be it."

"Thanks for the vote of confidence, bro," she said, throwing her hands on her hips in annoyance. "Do you have any ideas, or are you just gonna stand there pointing out problems?"

"*Now* you want me to come up with a plan? I told you to stay quiet and take my lead, and you mucked it all up!" Auzed barked a little too forcefully. To his surprise, she only jumped, but the flash of fear morphed into anger. She was a brave little thing, indeed. Her deep brown eyes sparked with determination. Though she'd just spent weeks in a forest— and looked like it—he could admit those eyes were enchanting.

"I didn't hear you spouting off any plan. All you were doing was making the guy in charge more and more angry. At least I did *something*! And by the way, I did it to save your ass, so a thank you would be nice!"

"Thank you?" he repeated.

Ignoring the obvious bafflement in his voice, she shot him a sarcastic smile and chirped, "You're welcome."

Auzed was lost for words. He'd never been spoken to like this by a female, and he'd certainly never spoken to a female with such a disrespectful tone. If she were another soldier, he would've challenged her to a fight. "You don't realize what your help has cost me, human. I—"

The door opened again, and Fierad strolled through, appearing way too smug. Zed's hands itched to smack the look from the male's face. It would only grow worse when Alejandra admitted to her lie. Their lie.

Behind Fierad entered Dedeth and then a tall female with dark purple bags under her eyes. Fierad had said she was half Swadaeth. Maybe she wasn't as powerful. She had a Sauvenian's long tail and coloring, but her glowing eyes weren't as large as a Sauvenian's and her ears were only pointed at the top, as opposed to the tapered points on the top and bottom that most Sauvenians had.

"Is this her?" the young female breathed. Relli, as Fierad had called her, appeared exhausted. Why was she working if it affected her health this much?

"Yes." Fierad nodded with a grin. "She needs to be *swayed* to tell the truth."

Relli moved to stand before Alejandra. Zed could not tear his gaze away. Everything he'd built, all the trust and respect he'd garnered, would be gone in the next minute. Relli shifted from side to side. Alejandra's nervous gaze followed her movements. "You want to tell Fierad the truth."

Alejandra's lids fluttered dreamily, and she muttered, "I want to tell him the truth."

Zed exhaled the breath he'd been holding, deflating.

Relli stepped out of the way, eyes still locked on Alejandra, and Fierad joyously stepped forth. Over his shoulder, he added, "The regents have been made aware of the human's existence, and they are on their way now."

That was it, then. King Bet and Queen Dasa, co-rulers of Sauven, would claim Alejandra as a citizen and mete out his punishment.

Fierad dipped his head until he was at eye level with Alejandra and grinned. "Have you promised yourself to this male?" He turned to smirk at Auzed while listening for her reply.

"Yes. I have promised myself to Auzed."

He and Fierad stared at each other for a moment, neither believing what they'd heard. Auzed quickly masked his surprise and donned a smirk of his own. "See?"

When Fierad faced Alejandra, who was still dazed and dreamy, his grin vanished and a maddened look of frustration replaced it. "When did you first meet Auzed?"

Alejandra blinked, her eyes glassy. "I first met Auzed three days ago."

"Where?" Fierad shouted, giving her a little shake.

Auzed growled and stepped toward the male. "Unhand my intended."

Fierad stepped back. "I don't believe this." His accusatory stare landed on Relli. "Are you sure she's under your *sway*?"

She pursed her lips and straightened. "This is what I do all day, every day. I know when someone has broken it."

"So, she belongs to this male already. Are they mated?" came an assertive voice from behind them. All turned to see the co-regents taking in the scene. Zed glanced back to Alejandra, who continued to stare into space. How was she doing this?

"Majesties." The Sauvenians in the room lifted the tips of their tails to their foreheads and bowed. Auzed only bowed, since he of course had no tail. Alejandra remained unmoving.

The king and queen of Sauven wore identically decorated white vests that ended near their ankles with long capes attached to the back. While Queen Dasa wore her hair in a tight braid against her skull, King Bet left his long purple hair loose.

Since no one else had bothered, Auzed answered, "No, we're not mated. But she has vowed to select me during the ceremony, and she's a citizen of Tremanta, Your Highnesses."

The co-regents looked at each other, exchanging a silent conversation. For the two rulers to come here together must've meant they were taking this matter seriously indeed. More often than not, the king and queen were off seeing to their separate responsibilities. The current queen saw to Sauven's international and intergalactic matters, making sure trade to and from the city ran smoothly and acting as the city's representative on The Intergalactic Alliance. The king remained in Sauven, seeing to the day-to-day needs of their people.

The news that had been disseminated mere days ago of the humans' existence must've been important enough to force Queen Dasa to return home. Auzed suspected many cities around Clecania were convening in much the same way. Working out a strategy to lawfully demand Tremanta send the large group of humans they protected abroad. To spread the wealth, as it were.

It was an uncomfortable notion, but humans were being thought of more and more as a resource and less as a sentient species with customs directly opposed to their own. And like any sought-after resource, it would only be a matter of time before the asking stopped and the taking began. The thinly masked desperate looks on the rulers' faces confirmed his worries. There was a war brewing.

"You have admitted to breaking our laws, Head Guard Auzed?" Queen Dasa asked.

"Yes. I entered your territory and slayed a sefa, to save Alejandra. There was no alternative."

"And do you cohabitate?"

They all studied him as, in an instant, he combed through the pros and cons of both answers, though he didn't know why they were asking. "We have not yet returned to

Tremanta. I found her days ago in the forest, but I insist on remaining with her while we're here."

"Gather yourselves while we convene and speak to your Queen regarding your punishment." King Bet turned his attention to Fierad. "Their interrogation is over for now. Bring them both to a nest. Disable transport and communications."

Queen Dasa slid her imperious stare to Auzed again, her voice filling with authority. "You will be comfortable while you're in Sauven, but you will remain in Sauven." She held his gaze until he nodded his assent.

A thought sparked, and he blurted, "We're supposed to visit your medbay first. The doctor requested it. And I also need access to my communicator so I may speak with my Queen."

The co-regents glanced at each other again, then the king answered, "I will send a messenger with a communicator, clothing, and other goods. They will supervise your communications until we have come to a decision." He focused on Fierad. "Take them to the medbay first."

And with that, the rulers left.

"You no longer feel my *sway*, Alejandra."

Zed turned to find Relli gently rousing Alejandra from her stupor.

She blinked, then her gaze focused on the female. Alejandra's gaze bounced around the room, and she fiddled with the gold band on her finger. "We good?"

Fierad glared at her—gone were the once-gentle looks

he'd bestowed her with when he'd thought she'd be eligible for marriage. He stopped Relli before she exited the room. "You take them to the doctor and then to an empty nest."

"But the regents said—"

"I don't care what they said. I have more important things to do than chaperone two criminals around the city," he barked, turning on his heel and walking out the door, Dedeth close behind.

Auzed bristled. He'd never seen a female treated so poorly for no observable reason. How had Fierad risen to his current status while behaving like that?

Relli griped under her breath, "And I don't have things to do?" She let out a sigh and flicked her tail at them. "Alright, let's go."

Auzed's head was clouded. He couldn't decide which emotion to land on. Relief? Shame? Caution? Somehow the human female had maintained their lie through Relli's *sway*. He shot Alejandra a sidelong glance. She caught his stare and shrugged, pursing her lips in a self-satisfied gesture that screamed, *Ha!* Despite himself, the corner of his mouth lifted. She'd broken the *sway* and faked her way through. Incredible. He'd do well not to underestimate her again.

"The tuey is waiting in the entry hall. My apologies. We had to cage it to keep it from running to you. How long have you been bonded?" Relli asked.

"Bonded?" Alejandra furrowed her brows. "I only met him a few…er, recently."

"Tueys are native to this planet and have some psychic

gifts. They're solitary unless they're looking to reproduce, but occasionally they choose to bond to a creature they feel connected with. As long as you treat *her*," Relli said pointedly, "well, she'll remain loyal to you forever and only leave your side to find a mate before she returns to you. She'll be able to sense when you're in trouble or when you're happy."

"Kevin's a girl?" Alejandra whispered under her breath.

"I thought you called her Wilson," Auzed said.

She glanced up at him and laughed. "Oh yeah, no, it's from a movie. Doesn't matter."

The hall opened up into the large entry, and as one, they glanced over to the commotion in the corner. A metal cage with bars on all sides had been placed out of the way, but inside the cage a round glowing ball flew around like trapped lightning. The box tipped and flipped over as the tuey continued to bounce around inside, ramming the walls in a desperate bid to break free.

"Oh, Wilson!" Alejandra cried, rushing over to the cage. Wilson unfurled and shoved its little hands out, reaching for her. Relli motioned for a guard to come and unlock the cage. When he did, Wilson happily zoomed around Alejandra's legs before leaping up to her shoulders and draping itself around her neck.

It was odd to see a female being so affectionate with an animal. His brother's mate, Jade, enjoyed spending time with their alien hound, Cebo, but he'd never met another female who liked having pets near them. It had something to do with the nomadic nature of a Tremantian female's life. Always moving from one husband to the next. They never let themselves get close to anything, or at least they never showed it.

Walking back over to join him, Alejandra grinned. "Ready to go, honey?"

Honey. She'd called him that before too. The term translated as a food that was sweet and thick. The byproduct of an insect, but the way she said it in a purr sent chills down his spine. He didn't like it.

Females didn't use pet names. They didn't like to keep animals. It wasn't how things were done. Not to mention his own odd behavior as of late. He didn't break the law. He didn't lie to authorities. And he certainly didn't get chills from a single word.

6

"I can't believe it!" Alejandra squatted up and down, then stretched side to side, testing her newly healed body. The doctor had fixed all her maladies inside and out, some she didn't even know she'd had, then had offered her something called the elixir. From what she'd grasped, it would give her an almost superhuman boost, adding decades to her life span.

Memories of her family had flashed through her mind, and on instinct she'd refused. Not until she knew for sure she couldn't get back to them. If returning were somehow possible, she couldn't bear to outlive them. Outliving her parents had been bad enough.

"Would you stop that?" Zed snapped in a hiss as she bent to touch her toes.

Alex rolled her eyes but did stop. Relli guided them to a floating board with a handlebar sticking up through the middle. Zed stepped onto it and waited for Alex to do the same, but she hesitated. "Maybe you could cuff me to this one too." She laughed, half serious. It was a long fall, and an irrational idea that her fingers might suddenly lose grip strength midflight kept popping into her mind.

Relli tilted her head toward them, already aboard her own platform, which was visibly without a bar. Instead, the three prongs of her tail were curled around one edge of the board, keeping her steady. Handles must be reserved for the tailless.

Not a care in the world, Wilson spread her arms and glided toward an empty platform, then, in a flashy display, jumped and glided from Relli's board back to the empty one as if to say, *See? It's safe.* Wilson settled herself on Relli's board and gazed at Alex expectantly.

She pursed her lips. *Show-off.*

"It's odd that you would marry a male you don't trust to keep you safe," Relli remarked, raising her brow toward Auzed.

There was something in her gaze, something Alex had seen during her interrogation—Relli had surmised the truth. She'd known Alex was lying about everything but had chosen to help her for some reason. Even now, her comment felt more like veiled advice than a random observation.

Auzed clearly hadn't realized the same, for in an instant he'd pulled Alex onto the board. She gripped the handlebar the way her childhood cat had clung to her clothing every time she'd threatened to give her a bath. To her relief, Auzed moved behind her, placing his hands on either side of hers on the handlebar and closing her in. No part of him touched her, yet his large body surrounding her made her feel protected all the same. The size of his hands gave her an odd little flutter in her belly. She tried to ignore the saying popping into her head about men with big hands.

Relli nodded and rode her platform ahead gracefully. When their platform began to move forward, Alex all but plastered her back against Auzed's chest. She felt his quick intake of breath and saw his knuckles whiten on the handlebar, but she refused to pull herself away. It wasn't her fault she'd never flown through the air on an inch-thick disk like the Silver Surfer. She could barely ride a longboard, and those were supposed to be easy to use.

"Even if you fall, there's invisible netting to catch you," Auzed rumbled from above her.

"Netting?" On instinct, Alex peered down before the word *invisible* registered. "I guess the population would hardly be this large if there weren't." She chuckled through the feeling of idiocy. Of course there was a net. It didn't make sense there wouldn't be.

His intention in pointing out the net becoming clear, Auzed said, "Now you may step forward. It's uncommon to see a female pressing herself against a male out in public."

She felt heat rise on her cheeks, and a twinge of defensiveness creeped into her voice. "We're getting married, though, *honey*," she said, stepping forward and instantly missing the warmth of his big body.

"Stop guessing at things you have no idea about," he growled low into her ear. Despite the annoyed tone of his voice, his hot breath made a shiver run through her. "The fact that we're planning to wed would make it even *more* unlikely you'd be touching me like this."

"What? Why?"

"You'd want me to prove myself to you during the Testing and then in the subsequent marriage. You'd only touch me otherwise if we were having casual relations, and even then, it would be very strange for you to do it in public."

Alex sorted through that explanation and tried to understand. Testing? Prove himself? Out of her depth, that's what she was. Woefully so. As soon as she got the big man alone, she'd need to learn everything she could. That was, if she wasn't able to talk to Lily first.

Their board descended to a teardrop-shaped home hanging in midair. To her left, the next nearest hanging home was much farther away than it had looked a minute ago. There'd be no way of leaving this house without one of these boards, not unless they wanted to take their chances with the net below.

Relli, Alex, and Auzed stepped onto the balcony that divided the oddly shaped house in two. Wilson bolted for the roof. Off to do some exploring of her own again.

"The nest is equipped with all the standard necessities. You're lucky there was one available. Most are occupied by visitors this week. They love to watch our games." Relli halted near the entrance to the home. "Have you ever been to the Sauven games before?" she asked Auzed.

"A few times with my family. They're enjoyable. Though I preferred exploring Sauven under different circumstances."

Relli nodded and shot him a look of sympathy. "If you need anything…I was going to say call, but you can't, can you? I guess just wait until someone comes and tell them what you need."

"Well, since you asked," Alex interrupted hastily, awareness of her stiff clothing and dirt-caked body seeping in, "I could use some clean clothes."

"Of course!" Relli replied. "The regents already put in an order for some basic things. But I'll need your measurements before I can order anything else." Her green cheeks flushed navy with embarrassment, and she added, "I'm sorry Huten didn't clean you. He really should have."

Alex recalled the odd sense of urgency she'd felt while being healed by their doctor, Huten. He'd kept darting uncomfortable glances at Relli until they'd finally left. After he'd put Alex in that medical tube and healed all sorts of old injuries lingering in her body, he'd practically shoved them out the door. She hadn't even known a shower was possible there. Although it made no sense to shower if she had nothing clean to change into anyway.

Auzed stepped forward, finally gracing the conversation with his input. His words held an undercurrent of outrage as he addressed Relli. "It's unthinkable that you're treated this way by these males. Why have they not shown you your due respect?"

Rather than looking consoled or relaxing at his soft words, Relli only appeared more uncomfortable. Her beautiful yet tired gray eyes strayed to the ground, and the tips of her tail flicked in agitation. "I… I'm… I have extended my marriage for over three years now."

"You're a demskiv?" Auzed blurted.

Relli flinched at the name but nodded.

The two aliens before her remained silent. Auzed, who'd just a moment ago seemed ready to joust for Relli's honor, now darted conflicted glances toward her while clasping his hands stiffly behind his back.

"Anyone want to fill me in?" Alex tried, her curiosity getting the better of her.

Almost too quickly, Auzed said, "We'll talk about it later." The urgent lift of his brows made it clear he felt the explanation would mess with their lie. Alex was about to brush off the look and reveal that Relli already knew they'd lied but then thought better of it. Holding her tongue, she walked over to the tall, emerald-green woman and smiled. "Well, I don't care what you are or what you do in your personal time. Thank you for helping us out today."

Relli raised her head and gave Alex a grateful smile that all at once turned conspiratorial. With a twitch of her lips, she bent down and whispered, "I've never liked Fierad anyway, and if what they say about humans is true, I know I'd want at least one human friend."

And there was her confirmation. Relli had been helping them, and as long as Alex lived, she'd be grateful. She moved to clasp the woman's hands but then recalled what Auzed had said about touching and pulled them back. "You have one."

With a swift tail-to-forehead farewell, Relli stepped onto

her board and gracefully flew away.

Her and Auzed's eyes met before his gaze traveled down her body. For a second she thought it might've been a perusal of interest, but then she recalled how disgusting she must look. She forced her shoulders to remain back to avoid hunching over in mortification. "Just you and me now, Auzzy." She put a heaping tablespoon's worth of sugar and cheer into her voice, a weak attempt to belay the talking to she figured she was about to get.

"Au-zed," was all he said.

"Just thought that since we're now…well, whatever we are, maybe a nickname was in the cards. You can call me Alex, by the way."

"Coconspirators. That is what we are now, unless you plan on following through with your lie and marrying me."

The tone of his voice indicated he knew full well she had no such plans, but she found herself denying it anyway. "No, I have a boyfriend back home, so it probably wouldn't be right." That wasn't really the truth. Things with Ray had been going downhill fast, and after caving to his most recent ultimatum—to give him a key to her apartment or break up— she'd decided she needed to dump him. She'd planned it all out too. A few final days together after he got back from his work trip, then she'd gently let him down. Before she'd had the chance, though, an alien had barged into her apartment and knocked her out.

Without a word, Auzed turned and prowled into the apartment as if expecting an ambush. Alex followed. The large room inside took up the whole floor of the house. Pillars decorated to look like trees, or maybe actual trees, held up the open room. Ornately carved tables and chairs were grouped throughout, providing a few different dining and sitting areas. The ornamentation was structured with harsh angles, but the gentle curves and cloudlike cushioning of the furniture softened it and made it appear artistic.

A seemingly haphazard collection of inlaid cabinets climbed up the far wall like a massive trailing vine. Auzed walked over and opened a few of the cabinets, searching for something. Finding what he was looking for, he produced a couple of glasses. Alex watched as he crossed to a golden bird-shaped faucet, its wings expanded over a hollowed-out stone basin.

When clear water flowed from the bird's long, pointed beak and into the two cups, she licked her lips. Thirsty—she'd just recalled how utterly thirsty she was, and hungry too.

Auzed offered her the glass, and she gulped the cool liquid down with one satisfying, painful swallow. Rushing to the sink, she filled and refilled the glass until her stomach was too full to hold anymore.

She panted and wiped a hand over her mouth then turned toward Auzed, who was staring at her and sipping his water. "How do they get water to this place?"

"Rain and condensation collect on the chain above us and falls into storage and treatment areas under our feet." His tone was to the point and emotionless. He continued to stare.

"What do we do now?"

"We wait."

"For?" This guy might look like a god, but he had the personality of a sea urchin.

Instead of answering her, he asked a question of his own. "How did you do that before?"

"You'll have to be more specific. I do a lot of things."

The skin around his eyes tightened with his frown. "During the questioning. How did you fool them?"

"Oh, that!" Alex spun in a circle and surveyed the lit ceiling. "You had such little faith in me, and look. I did it on my first try!" Alex had no idea how she'd done it, to be honest, but she acted smug all the same.

"How?" he grated again.

"I don't know, Auzzy." She sighed as she began searching through the multitude of cabinets. "I felt it and turned it down."

Auzed stepped toward her. "Turned it down?"

"Yeah. Turned it down. Said no. Pushed it back. Gave it the old one-two punch. Whatever you want to call it. I just didn't let it work. Don't know how else to say it."

"But what about after? How did you fool them into thinking you were being *swayed*?" Auzed urged.

Alex knew she shouldn't be so happy about lying to the alien police, but knowing she'd impressed the super-impressive, ridiculously hot guy in front of her made her shoulders straighten.

"Puh-lease. I was in all the school plays when I was younger and then I went to an arts college for my film studies degree. I can act. You told me I had to repeat, so I just mixed *Dracula* and *The Manchurian Candidate* and threw in a little Jasmine for good measure. I always thought Jafar was an underappreciated villain. I mean, that sultan just sat on his ass all day and let his people starve, you know?" She caught Auzed's blank stare and grumbled, "Right. Right. You have no idea what I'm talking about. I'm gonna have to work on that. Probably half of everything I say is a movie reference."

"A Swadaeth knows when their *sway* has been broken. How did you fool Relli?" Auzed stepped in front of her as she rooted through another cabinet, demanding her full attention.

"Can we eat this?" she asked, holding up a large fuzzy yellow oval.

Like lightning, Auzed snatched it from her hand and stared at her hard.

"You men! You're all the same no matter the planet. None of you ever really pay attention to the women in a room, do you? While you and Officer Douchebag were having a glare-off, Relli figured out I'd broken out of my trance. Everything on her face said so; you guys just didn't notice." At Auzed's confused expression, Alex clarified, "She figured it out and helped us. She knows I lied."

Understanding dawned, his eyes widening. Then he dragged a large hand through his light-blond hair. "That's not good. Another person knows. A demskiv knows."

"Yeah, what is a demskiv anyway?" Alex asked, sniffing at a bottle of thick brown liquid. Spice and acidity burned her nostrils, and she quickly stuffed the cork back in.

Auzed paced around the room, scrubbing his hand against his chin in thought. "Uh, it's a female who's chosen not to choose a new husband. She just keeps extending her contract with one male."

"And that's a bad thing?" What the hell was he talking about? He'd told her about temporary marriages very briefly, but now he was making it seem like being in a permanent relationship would be looked down on here. Her mother would be rolling over in her grave at the very idea.

"Yes. By remaining with one male she's not mated to, she's deprived all of the other husbands she may have had. At the very least, she's made it so there are even more males who will never have the opportunity to prove themselves as excellent husbands and fathers."

"You've succeeded in confusing me."

His eyes strayed toward her as though he just remembered she was there. He scanned her one more time, then sighed. "Go bathe. I'll make us some food while you do. Then I'll try to explain everything."

"Can't we eat first?" Alex just held back the desperate whine in her voice. "I'm starving…like, literally, in case you hadn't noticed."

Using those powerful thighs, he crossed to the kitchen and started rummaging through the cabinets again. He tossed her a vine with berries tumbling off the sides. "Here, eat this while you bathe. You may have gotten used to your smell, but I haven't."

Her palms clenched in embarrassment, and she accidentally smashed a small berry in her hand. God, she must smell. Out in the woods for weeks? She was surprised he'd gone *this* long without mentioning it.

Nipping the pea-sized, sweet berries off the vine, she scanned the room. There wasn't a door, room, or toilet to be seen. "I'm gonna need a little assistance with the bathing thing. Should I use the sink?"

Auzed glanced over his shoulder at her and swung his own eyes around the room. Seeming to gather his patience, he crossed to an empty area of the room and motioned for her to join him. Now that she looked closely, the floor where they were standing was not a round wooden inlay like she'd thought but a segment of floor.

With a forceful "Up!" from Auzed, the portion of floor floated upward and through a now-empty circle of ceiling above them until they were in the hallway of another floor, one door on the right and one on the left.

He walked ahead, peering into both rooms, while Alex discreetly gobbled the rest of the berries. They sat like grains of rice in the gaping chasm that was her empty stomach.

"Through here. This is your room," Auzed said, motioning through one door.

Alex glanced at the other as she passed and saw a small-yet-comfortable bedroom.

This other room was also a bedroom, except this one was huge in comparison. And lavishly decorated with feathers and furs. He'd given her the better room. She quelled a smile at the thought.

A deviant voice in her head mourned the fact that they wouldn't be forced to share a bed. She moved past him and saw his eyes lingering on the over-large mattress floating a few feet off the ground. Was he thinking the same thing?

"Do I need to show you how to use the foam shower?"

The berries instantly soured in her stomach. She peered to the ground, trying to play off her next words as if they were nothing. It wouldn't do to dwell. "No, they had one in the…uh, the bunker."

All at once, Auzed's stiff posture stiffened even more. His lips going thin and his feet spreading ever so slightly as if bracing for an earthquake. His Adam's apple bobbed with his swallow, but all he said was, "Makes sense."

She lifted a brow at him. More confused than annoyed by his uncaring tone. It was clear he felt something but liked to keep everything to himself. *You're a hard nut to crack, Auzzy.*

She backed into the bedroom through the door, openly analyzing him until he finally glanced around the hall as though uncomfortable with her studious gaze, and walked away.

7

∾

Within minutes Zed had used the foam shower in his room's bathroom to clean off, then returned to the lower level of the nest home and began preparing a meal with ingredients from the modestly stocked cabinets. His preparation was clumsy, sloppy even, and he felt a rush of annoyance that he hadn't occasionally practiced the skills he'd learned during his husbandry school cooking classes. He never cooked for himself at home, preferring the efficiency of ready-made meal bars. And as the head guard for the Pearl Temple, he was exempt from marriage, so practicing the skill had always seemed pointless.

What would happen now? Would he have to abandon his high-ranking position? *No,* he thought with a flicker of irritation. Alejandra had made it clear she wouldn't be marrying him for real. It was just an act. Once they were back in Tremanta, he'd bring her to the Temple and resume life as normal, leaving this blunder in the past and praying he never had to visit Sauven again.

As he roughly chopped a handful of thematun leaves, he considered his current predicament. The little female had fooled a room of well-trained males, including him. Her jab at his obliviousness to Relli's assistance had been…enlightening. Auzed didn't miss things.

Normally he didn't miss things. But normally he didn't have an intriguing human running about telling lies and threatening everything he'd worked so hard to achieve in his life. Like it or not, he was now tied to Alejandra, responsible for both her and her impulsive reactions.

Auzed's knife scored the wood surface underneath as he sliced the meat with a bit too much ferocity. Running away from the rest of the females at the facility…impulsive. Lying to a Sauvenian official…impulsive. His mind wandered back to the brief kiss she'd given him, and his movements stilled. That kiss had been impulsive too. For a moment, his mind and body battled with each other, trying to decide whether or not he should lump that kiss in with the other things he wished she hadn't done, but he couldn't seem to be as upset about the brief brush of her lips to his as he should've been.

Collecting his ingredients, he moved to the cooking table and activated it. He then sat and waited for the surface to heat up. Gnawing on a raw thematun leaf, he thought through his options and grimaced. There was nothing he could do at the moment. Not until the regents made up their minds as to what they would do. If he was very lucky, they might decide he and Alejandra were cleared of charges and send them on their way. But that was the best-case scenario. Worst case? He didn't want to think about it. All there was was to wait.

"Down," he heard Alejandra call from the floor above. When the through-level platform didn't respond, she said, "Down!" more clearly.

Zed stared up at the ceiling and smirked. Under his breath, he muttered, "It doesn't respond to your language yet."

"Auzed!"

Leaning back in his chair, he crossed his arms over his chest and stretched his legs out in front of him. He chewed on another bittersweet leaf. "Have you tried commanding the platform to go down?" he called. His grin widened as she let a string of foreign curses loose.

"Down! Down! Down!"

Suddenly, the tuey she called Wilson barreled inside. It clambered up a post and stared at the spot on the ceiling where Alejandra was currently stomping. The creature leveled Zed with a glare and glided over to him. She squeaked and trumpeted, rolling around his chair and bopping his shin with her small trunk until he rose with a grumble.

Zed walked within the command area and said, "Down."

It was childish—and not at all in line with his usual behavior—but the look of sour annoyance shining in Alejandra's narrowed eyes as she lowered to the ground almost helped to make up for the rotten position in which he currently found himself. Wilson, satisfied her favorite human was no longer in distress, rolled to a low-cushioned chair and relaxed onto it.

81

He took in Alejandra's newly revealed appearance and clenched his teeth. *Fuck. She's gorgeous.* Her large brown eyes were deep-set and framed by thick lashes. Her lips, a lighter shade of brown than her skin with just a touch of pink near the center, were full and seemed far too soft.

Thick, dark-brown hair fell over one bare shoulder, curling into waves. She'd wrapped herself in some kind of large piece of fabric. A blanket or other form of bedding, likely. The odd ensemble left the silken skin of her shoulders bare.

He felt the urge to stand up straighter and give her a practiced litany of compliments as he would to a Clecanian female he found attractive. Instead, he coolly asked, "What are you wearing?"

The slightest hint of rusty red darkened her cheeks. "It was the only clean piece of fabric up there. I think it's a sheet. Or maybe a towel. I really don't know. I found it in the bathroom."

Her gaze darted toward the cooking table, where pieces of meat sizzled happily on the shared surface. As though pulled by an unknown force, she floated over to the table and sat down, eyes riveted to the meat.

"Can I eat it?"

"Give it more time." Zed dropped into the seat across from her.

Alejandra swiped her tongue over her bottom lip, then leaned back. Zed shifted in his seat, suddenly uncomfortable. He was around females often, no question. But it was rare he was ever alone with a female who openly touched him and who'd claimed she'd be marrying him. Even though it'd been a lie, the uttered words had still done something to him, no matter how much he denied it. Now, sitting across from that female, alone, in a house, feeding her…it wasn't something he was used to, and it felt altogether too intimate.

"I don't even know what I should be asking about, so can you just explain what you think I should know?" she asked, barely tearing her gaze away from the cooking meat.

Her attention caught on his shirt and crossed arms before fixing on his biceps. He'd removed his top shirt, now wearing the thin protective barrier most guards and soldiers wore as a base layer. The strong, silky fabric wouldn't stop a Yulo blast or a knife, but it would slow down the momentum enough where he might not die from the injury.

Her gaze remained caught on his upper arms. On instinct he tensed, flexing the muscle for a more impressive display. Heat rose on his neck at the immature response. But then a different kind of hunger briefly lit in her eyes, and his embarrassment vanished.

"Let's start with you," he said, turning the conversation back toward her and the decisions she'd made to put them in this position. "Why did you run into the forest in the first place?"

Unperturbed, she tilted her head and continued to study his body appreciatively. He shifted in his seat. "What else should I have done? The only aliens we'd met had either snatched us from Earth or locked us in cages. Why would we wait around for more? How were we to know good ones existed at all?"

A frustratingly logical response if he'd ever heard one. "And how did you survive?" He used a small wooden spear to poke one of the pieces of meat and held it out to her.

She snatched the spear from him and shoved the morsel into her mouth. The too-hot piece of meat made her breathe in and out through an open mouth for a few moments.

Markedly too late, he drawled, "Be careful. It's hot."

Covering her open mouth with her hand, she lifted a sardonic brow at him and chuckled. When she was finally able to swallow, she sighed. "Yup. I never wait long enough. Been a problem since I was little. Uh, anyway..." She held the next piece of meat out a bit longer, learning from her mistake. "The girl I was with, Lily—who I need to talk to, by the way—was a crazy survivalist woman. She found us food and shelter and made fire. Just a magnificent example of a she-ro. But my dumb ass got us into trouble, of course. We fell into the river and got separated."

It suddenly occurred to Zed that he hadn't yet seen her ass, but if it fit with the rest of her body, it would be far from dumb.

She swallowed another bite and pointed her eating spear at him. "Okay, now you. Why was I brought here? What did those guys want with us? Why did they lock us up? What is this whole marriage thing about? Why is everyone so intense about me and where I should live? *Et cetera, et cetera, et cetera.*"

She said the last in that way she did when she was quoting the things she called movies.

"Just keep talking so I can eat and listen. That doc found a whole host of bad juju in my gut from the water I drank. Luckily, he fixed it all, but I'm somehow even more starving than I was when I was literally starving."

Zed recited the explanation he'd heard the Queen give to the confused and unsure females who'd arrived at the Temple. "Clecania is a planet that, along with many others, belongs to The Intergalactic Alliance. This alliance has laws prohibiting communication with underdeveloped Class 4 planets. Earth is considered a Class 4 planet. As such, there is no possibility that humans can be returned home. The law requires you to stay on Clecania for a period of one year, after which you may leave and visit any Class 3 or higher planet."

"We aren't allowed to go home?" Alejandra said through a mouthful of the grilled thematun leaves. Her eyes were round and entirely focused on him, an unspoken plea for him to deny the fact clear in their depths.

"I'm afraid not," was all he could think to say.

This was always the sticking point. Not just with humans but with the few other Class 4 beings he'd encountered. And shouldn't it be? The poor individuals had not only been thrust into a universe they'd never known existed but they also now had to grapple with the idea that they'd never return home. Never see their loved ones again.

The Traxian side of Auzed surged with a roar. The Insurgents—or PRIC, as they were known—deserved to be ripped limb from limb, even if they had somehow managed to find their people's salvation.

He wished he could explain to her that the cretin who'd taken her had been slaughtered or remained in prison, but as a female, he assumed she wouldn't like hearing it. So, as she slowly lowered the piece of meat dangling on her spear, he continued with his professional explanation.

"Our planet has a disproportionate number of females to males, and our fertility has steadily declined since a virus wiped out most of our female population centuries ago and also damaged our ability to recognize a mate. All the cities across the planet have developed their own way of dealing with the issue. Most have decided that the burden of repopulation falls to the females; therefore, most straight females capable of carrying children are encouraged to marry various worthy males and try for offspring. To give the overabundance of males an opportunity for a wife and for children, marriages are usually short, and we are urged not to become too attached to any wife or husband. Only the most accomplished of males are chosen.

"Unknown to the leaders of Clecania, or so we believe, an underground group of Clecanians known as the Insurgents began abducting and experimenting with species from other planets, hoping to find a cure to our fertility issues. They found that cure in humans. Humans can call forth mating marks on our people and can also successfully give birth to Clecanian offspring." Auzed stopped there, although there was so much more to explain, more than he could even imagine.

Her dark brows drew together, and she studied him while

she thought. "Shouldn't you be happy about them thinking we're engaged, then?"

"Of all the…" Zed stopped the shout rising in his throat. "That's your first thought after all that?"

She shrugged again, a little more sharply than before, and adjusted the knot near her shoulder holding her ensemble together. "No. Obviously that was not my first thought, Auzzy. But I'm trying to keep it together and figure out what I need to know in order to get back to the other city, since you said I'd have more freedom there. My *first* thought was, *What in the holy shit balls have I been dropped into?* but that didn't seem like a helpful thought to bring up."

Auzed narrowed his eyes on her, but before he could think of a retort, she spoke again.

"I *asked* because if it's an honor to be picked, as you've implied, then why would you be walking around looking at me like I just stole your favorite teddy bear? If this is gonna work, you're going to need to act appropriately, and I'm just trying to figure out what 'appropriate' is on this planet. How would a man just picked for marriage act toward his future wife?"

Her flippant tone and the logic to her words grated. "I wouldn't have to act at all if you hadn't lied. You don't even understand the position you've put me in or what's at stake for me."

Throwing down her utensil, she rose; the usual mask of nonchalance she'd worn throughout this endeavor faded, and he could see anger, fear, and pain all playing across her features. "No. I don't know what's at stake for you. But let me ask you this—have you been torn away from your friends and family and everything you've ever known? Are you in danger of being forcibly married off to some stranger and never seeing anyone you care about ever again? Because those are the stakes for me—"

A chime from the ceiling told them they had a visitor.

"What's that?" she asked, studying the ceiling.

He was still fuming. Just because she was right didn't make him any less upset. "Someone's here. Maybe the regents. Maybe someone delivering clothing for you. I don't know."

Alejandra raised her brow pointedly. "So, what it'll be, Auzzy? You gonna tell me how to act, or should I go on guessing?"

His body tensed as he thought, but she was correct. If they were going to do this, they needed to do it right. The chime rang again. "Fine," he said with a growl, "you need to be more aloof. You don't compliment me; I should be complimenting you, trying to win your favor. Don't smile at other males. Don't smile at me. Don't be too friendly with other males either—it'll suggest you're not entirely happy with our arrangement."

He moved to the door of the home as he spoke. Alejandra's brows were scrunched in confusion, yet she nodded along.

Auzed clasped the handle of the door and took a deep breath. *Here we go.*

8

The small bit of hope that Relli was the one visiting sputtered out as an unfamiliar man walked into the house. Alex tried to think through what Auzed had told her and donned the bland-yet-polite expression she used whenever her boss's assistant, George, tried to micromanage as if *he* were her boss. *Don't be nice. Don't smile.*

She settled herself next to Wilson on a large chair by the window and peered out, trying to seem uninterested as Auzed greeted the man. Her ears perked when she heard the guy say, "I was instructed to let you use this communicator."

Attempting to reel in her enthusiasm as much as she could, she all but ran over to the pair. "Could you connect me with Lily?"

The Sauvenian man grinned and shifted fractionally closer, an eagerness to interact with her clear in his eyes. His tail swayed behind him as he said, "Hello, human. My name is Noito. Who is Lily? I'd be happy to assist you."

Her voice faltered as she took in the intensity of his stare. He was searching her face, a small wrinkle between his brows as if he were waiting for something other than her response. When he tilted his head toward her and sniffed, Auzed stepped closer; a low rumble pulsed in his throat. The man's smile twitched.

"Uh, she's—" Alex broke off when Auzed placed his large palm on her lower back.

"I will assist my future wife, Noito. You may wait outside."

Noito frowned at Auzed, his polite smile gone. "I was directed to monitor the call. The regents have asked that you contact them first. I'll wait here with…" He swept his charming smile back to Alex and held a narrow black rectangle out to Auzed.

"You may wait here alone," Auzed snapped before she could answer. "And I'll call my Queen first and then the regents." He swiped the object she assumed was the alien version of a phone from the man's hand and pressed against her back until she turned and followed him a few steps away.

The man kept his eyes glued to Alex while he dropped the large sack he'd been carrying. She tilted her head as he tore his gaze away to examine the front and back of his hands. Appearing to not find what he was looking for, he lowered them back to his sides.

"He's being really intense," she whispered while Auzed fiddled with the device.

He eyed the man. "He's trying to recognize you as his mate. Hoping that if he sticks close enough, his marks will come out."

Alex was about to list off the many questions she now had, but he held the small device up to his ear, and she slammed her mouth shut. *Mate?* This wasn't the first time he'd said that.

"This is Head Guard Auzed," he said into the device.

Alex kept her eyes on a spot in the kitchen and tried to ignore the sensation of Noito's stare on her. She didn't mind being checked out, but this guy wasn't ogling her ass or chest. He was looking at her like this because she was human and different and he wanted her to be his in a way that seemed very permanent, though they'd only just met. He didn't even know her name. It was unsettling.

Seeming to sense her unease, Auzed stepped between her and Noito, turning his impressively wide back to the man and blocking his view. "Hello, my Queen. Have you been apprised of the situation here?" His words were slow and careful, and she could tell he was trying to communicate without really communicating.

Alex studied him as he carried on his conversation, answering with single yesses and nos.

He was standing firmly again. Not stiff, as if he were angry or tense, but strong, unbending, solid. Like there wasn't a power on this planet that could move him unless he allowed it. Control radiated from every corded muscle. Alex couldn't decide how she felt about it.

On the one hand, he made her feel safe. He'd directed his considerable strength toward protecting her, after all. But she wondered whether he was solid and stony through and through. What would it take to get him to crack? To smile or laugh?

His mossy-green eyes fell on hers, and she had the feeling the Queen was talking about her on the other end. He searched her face as he listened, then his gaze lingered on her mouth. A fleeting hint of warmth lit his eyes.

Her stomach did a little flip, and a wave of heat prickled up her neck. Peering over to where Wilson sat curled up and darting glares between the two men, she noticed Noito had moved. He'd inched far enough to his left so that he could see her again.

Be aloof? I wonder if direct would work too.

Without waiting for permission, she drew herself up fully, looked directly into Noito's eyes, and said, "Your staring is making me uncomfortable. Stop."

Her abrupt matter-of-fact tone registered like a slap, and he lowered his gaze; dark green tinged his cheeks and forehead.

When she looked back to Auzed, he was peering down at her, his mouth twisted into something that seemed like approval. Not exactly a smile or a frown, but still, he seemed to like that she'd taken charge.

After a couple more yesses and nos along with a "Lily, ma'am" and an "I'll do my best," he paused. Whatever the Queen said next had his stare turning furious. He shot another glance at her and then stomped away. "But isn't there a way... No, she... I understand." He lowered the communicator and stood staring at the wall for a moment.

Whatever he'd just been told had not been good. She could practically see the livid heat rising off his body. Without turning or saying a word, he slid his fingers across the communicator and held it back up to his ear. "This is Auzed. I was told you requested I call."

There was a wince threatening to form on her face at the restrained anger in his voice as he carried on another conversation. She tried to follow, but he was so tight-lipped that it became impossible.

Her attention drifted to Noito. He'd been staring at her again but quickly dropped his gaze when he saw her looking. Should she ask him questions? Would he know anything about what the regents had decided?

She jumped when she turned back to find Auzed only a few feet away, glaring at the ground and holding the communicator out to her. Tentatively she took it. "He-hello?"

"This is Queen Dasa. King Bet and I have come to a decision concerning you and Auzed. He has already agreed to our terms. I just need you to agree as well."

Alex's stomach felt overfull all of a sudden. "Okay."

"We will raise no charges against Auzed for entering our territory or killing the sefa, but in return, we'd like you and him to stay in Sauven for a week. In that time, you'll be allowed to move around freely. After the week is out, you may return to Tremanta."

"Okay." She said it slower this time, holding her breath against the inevitable *but*.

There was a moment of silence before the queen spoke

again. "I'm sure you can see the position we're in. There's no real way for us to corroborate your story, but there's no way to disprove it either. We ask that since you are not mated to Auzed, you allow the people of our city to speak with you while you're here."

"To just speak with me?" There had to be something she was missing.

"Well...if you're recognized, we would, of course, expect you to remain here with your mate. We feel it is our obligation to give our people the opportunity to at least attempt to recognize you before you leave. Tremanta has so many humans already, after all." She could hear the tinge of disdain in Queen Dasa's voice as she said this.

"And what if I refuse?"

It was the king who spoke next. "Then Auzed will be considered a convict, and although we will not be pushing to detain him, he will be stripped of his title and deemed unfit for any future marriages or children."

"Ah." She chanced a glance at Auzed and found him glaring at Noito as if the poor guy had had anything to do with this. How could she deny the simple and seemingly reasonable requests of the regents if Auzed's whole future was on the line? "I guess I accept, then."

"Wonderful. We'll send a messenger tomorrow with details."

"Could... Hello?" Alex lowered the communicator and grumbled, "I guess goodbye isn't a thing here." She stared at Auzed's unmoving frame. Both she and Noito seemed to grasp how furious Auzed was and remained lost for words. "Uh," she finally mumbled, "do you think I could call Lily now?"

Like a shot, Auzed was crossing to her. She took an instinctive step back, but he only snatched the communicator away and then stalked toward Noito who, to his credit, remained still. "The Queen explained to me that Lily is not available at the moment. She will be alerted that you wish to speak to her and will contact you at her earliest convenience," he explained as he gestured toward the door, making it clear he wanted Noito gone.

The man stepped backward while pointing to the bag. "These are clothes and other things. Please let me know if you need something else or if the clothing isn't to your liking. I'd be honored to—"

"She will tell *me* if she needs anything else. Don't make me say it again." Auzed crowded Noito. His words, filled with authority, boomed in the small space. He'd said he was a guard, but he sounded more like a soldier.

Noito shot her one last look before leaving. Auzed watched him go with his feet spread and his large hands on his hips.

The deafening silence fell again. Alex was beyond uncomfortable. Every move of her body felt shaky and awkward the way it did whenever she was about to ride the Goliath at Magic Mountain. "Jeez, Auzzy, no need to scare the poor boy." As he spun toward her, she instantly knew her default of humor was not winning her any favors at the

95

moment.

"Au-zed. And yes, there was. You as good as told him you had no interest, and he persisted...in front of me. It's an insult to both of us, yet he pushed again. He's lucky I didn't pummel him."

She made her way toward the kitchen and pulled out a few bottles she'd seen before. "I don't know about you, but I could use a drink." She sniffed at the contents of a few as he stood silently brooding across the room. "Which one of these is sweet, and which one will get me drunk?" she asked, pointing to the bottles strewn across the counter.

He clenched and unclenched his fists, staring at her for a few moments. "Aren't you going to ask me what the Queen said?"

"I thought maybe I'd give you some time to cool down first." She gave him a tentative smile she was sure looked awkward as hell. "But I can guess—stick to the lie and try not to get caught?"

Auzed's brows drew together, and his gaze briefly darted around and then back as though he couldn't make heads or tails of her. "Yes. How did you know?"

Alex shrugged. "'Cause we're still here and you're still upset."

"I might lose my job. They know we're lying but can't prove it. They're bitter toward her for giving the humans shelter, and they'll use me to make their disapproval known. My Queen believes they're going to try to circumvent the laws so they can *sway* me. I can't shake it off like you. Do you know what will happen if they *sway* me?"

She couldn't think about that. It was too much. This was all too much for her right now. Sensing her agitation, Wilson followed her into the kitchen.

"Even if they end up not questioning me, they'll check every detail of my story. Investigate as much as they can. There are loose ends, Alejandra. Witnesses who know I wasn't in that area of the forest." He stepped toward her and boomed, "Why don't you care?"

Her heart was pulsing in her ears now. She barely managed to catch a bottle as it slipped out of her sweaty palms. "I do care, but… 'a lo hecho, pecho.'" Alex shrugged it off, but merely uttering the saying out loud made a spike of pain stab through her heart. She'd never go home. Never listen to her abuela rattle off the phrase again.

Auzed stared at her, his eyes a little wild. "What?"

She could tell he was holding his temper at bay…just. If she were smart, she'd get serious, sit down, and hash this out so he could get it off his chest and they could commiserate over their shitty circumstances, but fuck it. She was angry too. And scared. And sad. And a million other things, and the way she needed to deal with *her* emotions right now was to pretend like they didn't exist. Panic was swelling inside her already, along with bitter guilt and helplessness. She'd lied to save him.

Didn't he see that? If they'd told the truth, he would've been punished all the same, wouldn't he? And she'd be hitching her wagon to some random alien. He was just upset, rightfully so, but she didn't want to go in circles arguing with him right now. It wasn't like there was anything they could do about it anyway.

He closed his eyes and tilted his head toward the ceiling. When he regained his composure, he looked back at her. "What about a chest?"

She paused sniffing at the contents of each bottle. Had he understood her? "¿Hablas español?"

Auzed blinked at her. "If you're speaking another language, I can't tell. My translator translates all Earth languages the same."

"Oh! That makes sense. To be honest, I don't speak much Spanish myself. My abuela does, but my parents..." she rambled, feigning interest in a dark-pink bottle, and swallowed the lump forming in her throat. "Um, my parents were second-generation Mexican American and spoke mostly English at home."

Alex nodded and took a sip of the liquid, then made a face as the bitter substance similar to vinegar hit her throat. She closed her eyes and thumped her palm on her chest a few times.

He remained silent, so she continued, "The saying doesn't really translate, I think. My mom and abuela always said it when my brother and I did something we weren't supposed to and got caught. It just means, what's done is done. Gotta deal with the consequences now."

Alex tried another bottle, desperate for a distraction. What she wouldn't give to be alone right now. Auzed growled, and before she knew what had happened, he'd stepped behind her and turned her around to face him. Wilson trumpeted a screech from the top of a cabinet above Auzed's head.

"It's okay, Wilson," she assured in a tremulous voice. The little creature scampered to a corner, where it glared at Auzed from afar.

Alex leaned against the counter behind her and stared up at him. *Keep it together. Keep it together.* She was acting juvenile, and she knew it. He'd helped her so much, and he had every right to be pissed off. But this was her MO. She liked to avoid problems when possible. At least initially. She'd slink into her own mind and work through the situation alone, and then eventually, when *she* was ready, she'd address it. It drove her family crazy and was the reason she hadn't worked up the nerve to officially dump Ray yet.

"We need to talk about this. We broke the law. You have to take it seriously. What happens if we do leave in a week and they find out we never married? Because they know the Queen is lying to help us, they won't accept us not marrying well. They'll see it as a slap in the face."

"What would've happened if I hadn't lied?" she asked without accusation. "Wouldn't you have been in a similar situation? You'd have lost your job and all that for breaking the law and killing the sefa. And I'd be stuck here."

The light green of his eyes darkened as he thought through her question. "Maybe. But that wasn't your choice to make." He was less than a foot away, hands gripping the counter on either side of her.

Her eyes stung. "What can I do, then? Should I make the

lie real? I'll do it. I'll marry you." Her vision grew glassy as she tried to hold his stare.

His brows drew together, and he scanned her face. She didn't think he realized it, but he moved closer to her. "You'd marry me?"

"Is that what you want?" she asked, her voice thick. "Then it won't really be a lie, and you won't get caught." Maybe that *was* the easiest solution.

"Really?" he rumbled. His gaze slid down her body, lingering at her bare upper chest. She shivered. Anger thinned his lips. "I don't like being toyed with, Alejandra. If I married you, it wouldn't be to get out of a lie. And it wouldn't be because you pity me or feel indebted or because you're desperate. Don't offer it again." He grabbed a light-green bottle near her elbow and pushed it into her chest. "When you're ready to actually deal with this, let me know."

He stalked toward the lift that went to the upper floor and was gone.

9

That female! How was he supposed to make it through a week with her? He scanned his bedroom, looking for something to break. The wooden chairs in the corner would shatter nicely. He hissed out a calming breath—no. Destruction of a Sauven home they'd been kind enough to offer up would not help anything.

Auzed paced back and forth in the room, wishing he weren't hundreds of feet from the forest floor. What he wouldn't give for a run right now. Or a gym. Or a lake. Anything to get out some of this aggression. The conversation he'd had with the Queen rang through his mind again. She'd begun by reassuring him she'd revealed nothing to the regents when they'd contacted her. She'd also explained she was solidifying his alibi even now. Contacting the two soldiers he'd been searching with earlier that day and apprising them of the situation.

A bellow built in his throat at the shame of it. She would

have to reveal he'd gotten himself in trouble, and she would have to urge them to lie for him if necessary. Their superior! What an embarrassment.

He dropped to the ground and began a round of vigorous push-ups, his teeth grinding together. He focused on his breathing and attempted to see things from Alejandra's side, even though his mind was screaming she was the cause of all his problems at the moment.

She'd asked him what would've happened if she hadn't lied. Truthfully, he couldn't be sure, but in his heart, he knew what the sentence would've been, and it grated against his nerves to know she'd assumed right yet again. The Sauvenians took their laws and their borders very seriously. In the aid of a female or not, their judgment would've been harsh.

Her lie might very well have been the one thing that could keep him out of trouble. But only if they could make it through this. And only if his Queen could make sure he wasn't *swayed*.

His arms shook as he pushed his body harder and harder. If he really sought to blame someone, he should be blaming the Queen. She'd asked him to enter Sauven illegally, after all.

Auzed was a bit concerned with how willing his Queen was to lie. A part of him wanted to believe her actions were selfless. But another part of him, a part that'd learned strategy during his time as an intergalactic soldier, wondered if doing whatever she could to gather the humans and feed into their requests wasn't more of a power play than anything else. Who would be more powerful in a world slowly dying of infertility than the leader who housed and protected the humans?

He shook off the thought. Even if she were gathering power, she was still allowing the humans to live more freely than they would in other cities, so he supposed her actions could still be considered honorable.

Turning and lowering to his back, he shut his eyes and practiced some breathing control. Alejandra had offered to marry him. The muscles of his body, now cooling down, shot tight in an instant. Despite everything he stood for, he'd wanted to take her up on her proposition. Even knowing she was only offering out of guilt. Even knowing she didn't fully understand what their marriages were. And even knowing she had a male of her own back on Earth.

Her personality irked. She was unpredictable and emotional and couldn't take anything seriously enough, but...she sparked something in him. And his baser side whispered that he should take advantage.

The regents had given them a proposition, though. They wanted to expose her to their people in the hopes she'd be recognized and any outrage at letting a human slip through their fingers would be quelled. He'd need to watch from the sidelines as all manner of Clecanians attempted to charm her away. What if someone *did* recognize her as their mate?

The regents would be so overjoyed that they'd likely forget all about him and he'd be free to go back home. She'd remain here, of course, but with a mate. A flare of jealousy lit in his chest, but he brushed it away, sure it was just his want of a mate and not of Alejandra in particular.

Yes, bringing her out to socialize with everyone was his best bet. With any luck, she'd meet her mate and he could go back to his well-ordered life. But he'd need to act like he cared. Any male would if others were blatantly flirting with their future wife, a human at that. He'd need to act as if the attention she received angered him. Thinking back to the furtive looks Noito had given her had his hands fisting. He might not have to fake it at all.

A part of him *did* want her. The lie they were in together had him feeling more protective than usual. He just had to make sure he didn't let himself get too attached. She wasn't really his in any way. She was a human under his care, the same as the others at the Pearl Temple. Nothing more.

He thought about her quietly getting drunk on the floor below him and groaned. No way to care for her if she stumbled drunkenly off the side of the house. Rising, he headed downstairs and promised himself his now-cooled and controlled temper would remain so. For the next week, a level head would be paramount.

When he reached the main floor, he scanned the room. His stomach clenched when he didn't see her. He searched all the corners she might have crawled into, then walked outside, praying she hadn't fallen into the net below. Although the regents had claimed they were free to move about Sauven, they hadn't provided them with any travel platforms. He'd have no way to retrieve her if she'd fallen.

It was only after he spotted her sitting on the edge of the round porch that circled the house that he realized how hard his heart had been beating in his chest.

She'd changed into silky white shorts and a matching shirt. She must not have realized how formal the attire was. The shimmering top was asymmetrical. Cut long in the back to cover a Sauvenian's tail and angled up to a high hem in the front. If she lifted her arms, the bottoms of her breasts would peek out. Blood pulsed to his shaft at the thought.

Her dark hair fell in soft waves over her shoulders, and healthy warmth seemed to light her skin from the inside while the lights of Sauven twinkled in the distance behind her. Fuck, she was beautiful. Something in his chest expanded, and he took a few quick breaths to calm himself before walking toward her.

If she noticed him, she didn't show it. She just sat there with her legs dangling off the side of the porch, sipping from the bottle and humming a soft tune. When he reached her, she silently held the bottle up to him.

With a sigh, he sank beside her and took a small swig.

"Is it day or night?" She tilted her head toward the treetops. The movement made her hair drape down her back and exposed the curve of her neck.

He quickly looked away. "Early evening, I'd say."

"How can you tell? Because of those lights inside?"

She observed so much. It continued to surprise him. While she quipped and bounced around, seemingly uncaring of the world around her, she was actually taking in and processing everything. "Yes."

Scuffling from above had him leaping to the ready, but he

slumped back down when he spotted Wilson settled on the sloped roof above them.

A small grin played at her lips, but she said nothing.

"Your tuey doesn't seem to like me much," he grumbled.

She grinned and peered at him sidelong. "That's 'cause you always look like you're preparing to go into battle. Maybe if you relaxed a bit, she wouldn't be so uptight. Just look at this." She gestured to the gently glowing city sprawled all around them.

In direct opposition to her observation, his shoulders tensed. He leaned back on his palms and gazed out at the view in an attempt to relax, but he couldn't understand it. How did people sit and stare like this? It was a waste of time. If he were home right now, he could be accomplishing so much. His legs itched to rise and patrol the porch, but he forced himself to remain still.

"A for effort," she mumbled, her lips twitching.

He only grunted and took another small sip of the alcohol. He couldn't tell exactly what flavor the liquid was, but he decided that would be his last taste.

"What is this whole thing about mates? You mentioned it before, and you said Noito was trying to 'recognize' me, and the regents said something about it too." She continued to gaze into the distance, but he could tell by the tightness around her eyes that she was far from relaxed. "What does it mean?"

"Historically, our people have had the ability to recognize a mate. Someone who you'll bond with and spend your life with. Sort of like Wilson there"—he nodded toward the tuey sleeping on the roof—"but in a romantic way. There's a reaction that occurs. A mated pair are linked to each other inextricably. Mating all but died out when the plague hit, though. There hadn't been a report of mating marks appearing on a Clecanian's hands in centuries. Not until the humans arrived."

"That's why he was checking his hands," Alex said softly. Her eyes were unfocused, like she was dazed, having this conversation while also listening in from afar.

Auzed leaned forward, his brows creased in concern. "Are you alright?"

She took a deep breath and peered at him with a weak smile. "No."

The sadness in her eyes jabbed at his insides. What was he supposed to say to that? Of course she wasn't alright.

At length, she cleared her throat and spoke. "If those are the CliffsNotes, then what's the real meaning? Everyone is tense. Everyone looks at me like I'm something sparkly they want to take home—except for you, that is. Don't just tell me the facts, tell me the reality of my situation…please." She studied him, her piercing dark-brown eyes searching his face for the truth.

Auzed clenched his jaw, trying to decide whether to soften his words or not. "That may be because on some level you are. For hundreds of years, every person on this planet has grieved the loss of matehood. We've worked so hard to get to a place of peace, to a system that works, but it doesn't mean it's perfect or that most of our people are happy. You…humans…are the key to fixing that. Males could finally be judged for more than their ability to please a female. Females could finally let down the walls they've built. Clecanians, like Relli, wouldn't be shunned and mocked for their choice to remain with the one they loved. So, are you something sparkly they all want? Yes and no. They don't want *you*—they want what you can do, what you represent."

A smile suddenly broke out over her face, and she let out a derisive hoot of laughter.

"What?" This female made no sense. On the verge of tears one minute and laughing the next.

"I'm just…I'm livid. Beyond angry that some fuckers took me and who knows how many other women from Earth just 'cause they could. For a damn experiment." She looked at him and shook her head, still smiling. "But if everything you've told me about this place is true? If that's what this world is like? I mean…" Her brows rose. "I get it. I hate it. But I get it."

"You get it?"

She chuckled under her breath and swung her legs back and forth over the ledge. "Yeah. I get it. This place sucks. What's happening to you guys sucks. And even though they're bastards and should be stampeded Jumanji style, I understand *why* they did it. Desperation. And the worst part of all?" she practically shouted before laughing again. "They succeeded. It doesn't make it right, but they found what they were looking for. Wow, Auzzy. What a fucking nightmare for humans, and what a fucking blessing for you lot."

Auzed clenched his jaw as her nickname for him skittered over his shoulders. He wished she'd stop using it. The familiarity of it made his insides heat, but he wasn't sure if it was in irritation or...something else. He suspected that even if he gave her leave to use his common nickname, Zed, she'd still refuse to use it.

"They broke intergalactic law and imprisoned hundreds of races before they ever found humans. They don't deserve any understanding," he shot back.

"I mean, that's how *I* feel, but I can understand someone from here not feeling that way. They've basically saved your people, haven't they? It seems to me that if they hadn't done what they did, you'd continue to slowly go extinct. And as you said, it wouldn't even be a good ride out."

Auzed shifted in his seat, growing uncomfortable. He enjoyed black and white. Gray areas were too complicated. He held out the bottle to her, hoping the alcohol would interrupt her musings.

She chuckled again and took a swig. Luckily for him, the questions that followed fell within safer territory. They talked seriously for hours, just as he'd wanted. He explained everything he could think to explain. The reasons she wasn't allowed to return to Earth. The ceremony in Tremanta, husbandry schools, The Intergalactic Alliance and their function among the planets belonging to the alliance. The roles of Clecanians males, females, and all who fell between and outside.

As she lay on her back staring up at the dark undersides of leaves, he recounted the history of their planet and the planet they'd inhabited before. He could've stopped there, but something about the way she gazed at him, the softness and interest in her eyes, pushed him to find more to say.

He thought of everything he could, no matter how innocuous, just to linger on the dim porch, inhaling her scent and watching her lids start to grow heavy. When the only thing left he could think of was information about himself, he stopped.

She turned her head, the alcohol making her movements sluggish. He ground his teeth against the urge to ask her about herself. What her planet was like, what her life was like. Where she'd gotten that gold ring she kept twirling around her finger.

Most Clecanian females wouldn't answer such questions when asked, and he knew why. It formed an attachment. A bond that hurt to cut. He couldn't allow himself to form that bond with Alejandra. He already felt too drawn to her as it was. Better to keep things need-to-know.

She raised an arm to cover her yawn, and her shirt lifted slightly.

His gaze lingered on the smooth skin covering her ribcage just a little too long before he tore it away. "We should get some sleep."

"What about Wilson?" She remained lying and scrunched her forehead upside down until she spotted the tuey.

"She'll come in if she wants. Wilson may be bonded to you, but she's still lived the majority of her life as a wild creature." Standing, he held out a hand to help her up. When her soft palm slid into his, electricity crackled under his skin.

They silently walked into the house, then stood together on the lift.

With an abrupt "Good night," he turned to his room, but she gripped his forearm, halting him.

She stared up at him and swallowed. "Look, I know I haven't said it, but...I *am* sorry. You're right. I didn't know what I was doing. I just made a snap decision. It was naïve of me to think I knew better."

Auzed shifted from side to side. Females didn't apologize like this. He didn't know how to react. Any anger he still had with her fizzled out, but flashing warnings blared in their place. He needed more distance and for her to act more like a Clecanian female.

He pulled his arm out of her reach and straightened his shoulders. "Thank you. I'll see you tomorrow, and I'll make sure to load your language into the home so you can control the lift."

Her brows knit together, but then she nodded, as if the brisk tone he'd used was understandable. "Alright. Good night, Auzzy—sorry, Auzed." She gave him a brief, apologetic smile, then disappeared into her room.

The grimace pulling his mouth tight remained in place far too long. Why did he suddenly dislike the sound of his proper name?

10

Alex pulled a pillow over her head to block out the bright light shining from the ceiling. Although she hadn't drunk much last night, the lack of food in her system had ensured a mild hangover this morning. Her head pulsed, and her mouth was thick and dry.

Wilson, who'd somehow managed to find her way to the second floor and into Alex's room last night, squirmed until her face was smooshed under the pillow as well. She blinked at Alex with her wide, intelligent eyes and gave a short little purr. The tuey rolled over and over in a circle, her large ears flapping around her head until she stopped upside down and trumpeted quietly at Alex.

Despite herself, Alex grinned. "Is this your way of telling me it's time to get up?"

With a groan, she rose. As she used the bathroom and readied to face whatever the day threatened to bring, she thought about Auzed.

Last night, she'd thrummed all over as his deep rumbling voice lulled her. She'd forced herself to listen to what he'd actually been saying as well, but it'd felt so good to just be next to him and hear him talk.

After they'd returned inside, he'd become a little distant, and although it was unfortunate, she understood. He likely still held a bit of a grudge against her but was trying to be professional. For someone as uptight as him, this whole situation must be torture.

She planted her bare feet on the lift, Wilson by her side, and commanded it to go down. To her surprise, it responded. A muted conversation floated to her when she reached the first floor. She spotted the corner of Auzed's large shoulder, just out of sight through the open front doors.

Before she could convince Wilson to play it cool so she could eavesdrop, the tuey had skittered outside and caught his attention. His eyes met hers, then scanned her body. Was it her imagination wanting it to be true, or did his perusals always take a beat too long?

"There's food waiting for you in there." He motioned to a small grass-green compartment on the kitchen wall, then turned back to whomever he was talking to.

Alex crossed to the compartment and then quickly tried to smooth the cowlick that always popped up on the crown of her head. She found that the inside of the compartment was warm and a plate of food lay waiting inside. Had he cooked this too? 'Cause he'd already been up, or specifically for her? Either way, she quelled a small smile. It wasn't every day a sexy guy made her breakfast, after all. Ray never had. He'd always been more of the "can't you just Postmates it?" type.

Sniffing at the hunk of lumpy pink…bread, maybe?…she took a small bite. It wasn't the worst thing she'd ever tried, but not the best either. Like a stale, crumbly English muffin. Still, it was better than the smashed bugs she'd been surviving on the past few days.

She studied Auzed as he said goodbye to the visitor, who was still out of sight, and stepped back inside. He wore simple clothing. Comfortable and so different than the tactile pieces he'd sported when they'd first met. A berry vest—the same cut as the soldiers from yesterday but in a softer, more relaxed fabric—covered his broad, naked chest devoid of that odd undershirt from yesterday. His pants were a bit tight as well.

Although she appreciated the amount of smooth skin and rigid muscle displayed by the outfit, she felt bad about how out of place he looked in it. She wondered if the clothing choices for men here were meant to be revealing. Was it a cultural norm as the opposite was for women on Earth?

He made his way over to her, and her gaze kept straying to his wide shoulders and those curling, shimmering markings as they disappeared beneath his top. She focused on her food instead.

"The regents would like us to visit the market tree today."

She glanced up at him and saw that restrained look on his face again. "Th—" The large bite of crumbly bread she'd taken threatened to fly out with her words, so she covered her mouth and finished chewing. "Thanks for the food."

A muscle ticked in his jaw. "Sorry the quality isn't better. I...don't cook often."

"Well, I don't cook at all, so I love it. No work, and I get food. It's a dream come true." She thought she saw the corner of his mouth twitch and wondered again what he would look like if he smiled.

"Would you like me to make you more? You seem to be very hungry."

Heat rose on her cheeks, and she followed his gaze down to her almost-cleared plate. "Aren't you supposed to say you love a girl with a big appetite?"

He shifted from foot to foot again and tilted his head. "Why would your appetite affect my affection for you?"

Because that's what guys in romantic movies say. Unsure how to respond, she shrugged. As she licked her lips to make sure the crumbs were gone, his gaze focused on the movement.

His voice was a bit raspy when he said, "Is it because human males like to watch your mouth as you eat?"

Heat bloomed low in her belly at his fixed stare and the dark tone of his voice. A squeaky "no" was all she could manage.

She had to bite back her tongue to keep it from running over her lips again. Her body seemed to have a mind of its own where Auzed was concerned.

He focused back on her eyes and made a low, thoughtful sound as if he didn't agree.

"Do *you* like to watch my mouth?" Alex had no idea where that had come from, and she felt her face immediately flamed.

She wasn't a shy woman when it came to flirting or men. In fact, she was usually pretty brazen, but she wasn't sure he wanted her attention in that way. And if he was trying to keep things platonic between them, she should try to do the same. No need to make either of their lives any harder.

But to her surprise, rather than stiffening and hastily changing the conversation, he rumbled, "Unfortunately, I do."

A little thrill raced up her spine, and in a moment of delight she wondered if he wasn't so closed off to her as she'd thought. But then his expression grew tight again.

"I should pick out your outfit today."

So much for that. "Oh yeah? Is it makeover montage time?"

He shot her a perplexed look as he hunched over and rummaged through the bag of clothing Noito had left with them the day before. She licked the last crumbs of her breakfast off her index finger and ogled his thick thighs and firm ass. *Don't sigh, don't sigh.*

"Just making sure you don't walk around in evening wear." He gave the white outfit she still wore from the night before a pointed look. "Like you are now."

"This old thing?" She laughed, twirling in place. "It's so comfy, though. What was I supposed to sleep in, if not this?"

"I don't believe most Sauvenians sleep in clothing." He held her gaze as he handed her a few folded items. "I think it tangles with their tails."

Did that mean he'd slept naked last night too? "You don't strike me as the commando type, Auzzy."

116

She was about to correct herself, knowing he didn't like the nickname, but his mouth softened and tipped into the faintest smile before falling again. Maybe he did like it after all. "Sorry, *Auzed*." She grinned as she spoke, seeing what his reaction would be.

A muscle twitched in his jaw, and she had her answer. He wouldn't admit it, but she was certain he did, in fact, like the name.

"Get changed, and we'll leave. You can pick out any clothes you'd like while we're out."

"Oh yeah? On whose dime? By the way, did they pack makeup in there?"

After hearing about how women-obsessed the guys on this planet were, she expected Auzed to act a certain way. Immediately tell her she didn't need any makeup and was beautiful. Her confidence faltered when instead he easily answered, "No. You can get that while we're out too." He started to walk away.

"Uh, well, do you think I need any? Do I look alright without it, I mean?" Back home, Alex had worn makeup every day of her life since she'd turned fifteen, the age her mother had finally allowed it. She didn't always wear a ton of it, mostly mascara and some lip color, but it was now hitting her that she'd been makeup-free for weeks. Here was a hot guy seeing her mussed, blemished, puffy-eyed morning look, and she hadn't thought anything of it. Not until just now.

His brows drew together as he studied her again. "You seem very concerned with my assessment of your appearance all of a sudden. Are your males particularly picky?" His shoulders tensed a fraction. "Does your *boyfriend* prefer you with makeup?"

"Ray? Yeah, he does…did…does? He's not really my boyfriend anymore." She unfolded the clothes and half studied them as the urge to blatantly announce her availability shot through her. "I mean, besides the fact that I don't do long distance." She chuckled at her own joke, but Auzed only watched her. "Uh, well, I was going to break up with him anyway."

Auzed crossed his arms over his chest. "Why?" As soon as he'd asked, he appeared upset with himself. "No, never mind. I don't need to know—just go change."

"Okay," she chirped, hiding her disappointment as he stalked through the front door.

Muttering to herself, she headed to her room. *What the hell am I doing anyway? Even if I did get him to flirt with me, what then?* Alex didn't know what she wanted to happen with Auzed. She was attracted to him for sure. She liked his hard outer shell and wanted to dig deeper. But did she want that because she actually liked him? Or because it was a challenge and she was curious? All of this, from her abduction to her harrowing adventure through the forest, felt just like a movie. And Auzed was the broody male lead you couldn't help but be intrigued by.

After changing into the multicolored shirt and pants, she pouted at her reflection in the mirror. "I look like MC Hammer." With a sigh, she joined Auzed by the front door.

He tipped his chin as he quickly took in her appearance but said nothing. "Who picked this stuff out for me?"

"Don't like it?" The question was innocent, but his lips twitched.

"If I were a foot taller and had a tail and a skin tone that didn't clash with these particular colors, then sure." The hole in the back of the underwear provided to her had been enough to indicate these pieces were not made for a tailless wearer. She fiddled with the flap opening near her rear, making sure it was closed.

He leaned toward her, drawing her attention back to him. Damn, he smelled good.

"If it makes you feel any better, I don't particularly like my outfit either."

"Yeah, but you look sexy!" she said in exasperation. "I look like…"

Auzed flinched like she'd insulted him. He stood frozen for a moment, still leaning toward her before stretching and clearing his throat. She could see his Adam's apple bob up and down as he shuffled in place. "You need to remember what we talked about. About how we should act together."

Forgetting her own ridiculous appearance, she smirked. "Oh, I forgot. You compliment me, I don't compliment you, right?"

He muttered a sound of agreement but still seemed perturbed.

She stretched her arms wide to show off her outfit. "Well, Auzzy, maybe you should practice before we go out in the real world. I could use an ego boost too, 'cause I feel like someone just tossed me into a bin of fabric and sent me on my way."

"Very well. You…" He looked her up and down with scrunched brows. "No. Ah, your…" He gestured to the shoes she'd slipped into that were a size and a half too big, then shook his head.

Alex wanted to laugh at how flustered he'd become. "Nothing good about my outfit?"

He took a deep breath and smirked, seeming to alight on something. "Well, if you fall off our transport platform, at least you'll float down to the net."

Alex's chin dropped in stunned humor. "Was that a joke, Auzzy?"

His eyes widened at her broad grin. He frowned and turned on his heel.

"Not just a joke but a sick burn too. Oh man. Auzed is *funny*." She trailed after him, badgering his retreating form.

With the patience of a saint, he guided her to a new floating platform and waited for her to step on and grip the handlebar before joining her.

Turning within the circle of his arms, she peered over his shoulder and searched for Wilson. "Should we wait for Wilson to come with us?"

"No. Tueys have lived in this forest forever and are excellent gliders and climbers. She can find you if she needs to." To illustrate his point, he guided the platform away from the hanging house with a lurch.

Facing the wrong way, her hands shot out to steady herself on his firm arms. He let out a grunt. And pulled the board to a stop so she could spin toward the bar.

Incrementally she rotated her body, gripping his right bicep to steady herself. As she turned, she ran her hands down his thick forearm until she faced forward again. He let out a low growl from behind her then steered the platform forward again.

"I know. No touching, sorry." He'd outlined again last night how odd it was for Clecanians to touch one another out in the open. Even when they were alone together, it was uncommon for a woman to touch her husband unless she was seeking sex.

"Maybe I could show you how to operate one of these on your own." His voice was husky when he spoke. He may not *want* her to touch him out in the open, but he liked it.

She peered at him from over her shoulder. "Why are we following all these rules, though, anyway? Everyone knows I'm not Clecanian. Won't they assume I'm going to act differently? *Humans* touch their partners. I'm not going to start sucking on your neck at the mall or anything. I don't like that much PDA, but surely me touching your arm isn't going to be the end of the world."

He growled and abruptly steered their platform out of sight behind a low-hanging branch laden with leaves the size of hula hoops. She was about to ask what he was doing when he moved behind her. Stepping close, he placed his right hand on her stomach and pulled her back against him.

Alex's breath caught in her throat, and her sex clenched. She could feel something large and hard pressing into her back.

"This is why," he breathed into her hair. "Touching may be normal for you, but it isn't for me."

Alex's breaths picked up speed, and her grip on the handlebar grew slick. God, she hoped he wouldn't move away now that he'd proven his point. She held back a whimper when he replaced his hand on her belly with his forearm and plastered her more tightly against him.

He took a step to the side, bracing his feet apart, and let go of the handle altogether. He swept her hair off her neck and dipped his head. His warm breath brushed over her ear as he rumbled, "How do you expect me to concentrate when you talk about sucking on my neck?"

"I… It was an example…" Her words died in her throat as his nose brushed the curve of her shoulder and he inhaled deeply. She felt her core growing hot and slick.

He ran his large palm down her arm, and she shivered. "When a Clecanian female touches someone like this and calls them sexy, it means she's looking to be pleasured. Is that what you want?"

Fuckin' A, right now it is! Pride and a little fear of floating high in the air kept her from shouting her agreement. At the brush of his lips against her ear, she moaned aloud.

The sound seemed to rouse him, however, and she immediately clamped her mouth shut.

He pressed his nose into her hair and let out a frustrated

growl. "Give me a moment."

Alex held the handle tightly as Auzed leapt onto the nearby branch and paced. God, she wanted to help him with his *problem*. Instead, she took the time alone to calm herself down as well. Slow breaths in through her nose and out through her mouth helped, but she knew herself, and without any relief, she'd be hot and bothered for a while.

She bit her lip and daydreamed about how good he probably was in bed. *Husbandry school.* He'd explained it last night and she'd let it go without too many questions, but now she burned to know what kind of grades her big, grumpy, fake fiancé had gotten.

11

This was going to be harder than he'd thought. Why couldn't this female just do as he asked and behave the way a Clecanian would? Why did she have to push him until his sense fled? Auzed ushered her through the crowded market tree and glared at anyone who gawked.

He'd never been to the market in Sauven before, but he would bet his bhadsit suit—which hadn't been returned to him yet—that the market had never been this crowded before. Shoppers stood together under the glowing storefront signs or on platforms transporting them to one shop façade or another, whispering as Alejandra passed. The more polite of the bunch at least feigned interest in the plethora of products being hocked, while the brave stared openly.

"This place is incredible," she whispered, gazing up at a window snack bar with customers a couple floors above. The Sauven market consisted of thousands of establishments all stacked on one another against the side of the great market tree. The layers and layers of stores formed a vertical wall of options for market goers. The snack bar she was still studying had diners seated on cushioned stools that were floating over nothing as they faced into the small restaurant.

The shops on the floor level were the oldest and most valuable pieces of real estate, as they were the most easily accessible. Above each building on the first level were floors of ramshackle boutiques, showrooms, and stands, each growing newer and newer as they climbed their way up the side of the tree. The same way one could read the age and prosperity of a tree by its rings, one could tell the age and prosperity of Sauven by studying the layers of the market wall.

Out of sight far above, the signage for the higher-level stores—and thus the newest stores—were more ostentatious and eye catching, while the floor-level shops were regal and relaxed, if not a bit squashed.

The scents of roasting meats, syrupy-sweet pastries, and tart citrus fruit hung in the air below the many snack bar restaurants and mixed with the earthy smell of the damp wood walkways beneath their feet. The day was a bit cooler than it had been yet no less humid. Though he felt ridiculous in his tight clothing, he enjoyed the relief the thin material provided from the heat.

"Would you like something to eat?" He motioned toward the snack shop she'd been eyeing, then to the platform station to the left.

She watched the market goers zooming about above her head on the platforms and bit her lip. "Uh, maybe in a few. I think I need to get more used to the idea first."

He nodded, and they continued on, stopping every so often so she could press her nose up to the amber, cured-sap windows of the floor-level stores and marvel at the items for sale. They'd both decided to work their way through the ground level once as the regents had suggested, but at this pace, they'd be here all day.

He pressed closer to Alejandra when he noticed her bunched shoulders and fidgety hands. She was twirling that ring around her finger again the way she did when she was truly uncomfortable. When she gave him a small but grateful smile, his heart pinched. He cursed inwardly.

This was exactly why he'd wanted there to be no touching between them. No personal conversations. And certainly none of whatever had happened on their way here. He could still smell her on his clothing, and it was ratcheting his baser instincts to a new height.

And now, after smelling her arousal—her arousal for him, no less—he was supposed to just let other interested Clecanians speak with her? The Traxian in him was raging that he hadn't pushed for more on that platform. She'd wanted him, he knew it, and if he'd worked her up, used his mouth on her neck, he felt she would've let him take her right there.

An older Sauvenian male—handsome and well off, by the look of his clothing—stepped up to Alex and greeted her with a graceful swipe of his tail. His pointed ears were larger than most, and Auzed wondered if he'd had them altered—large, pointed tips being particularly attractive to the Sauvenians. "Hello, beautiful. You are the human Alejandra?" He framed it as a question, though it hadn't sounded like one.

"Yes." Her voice was tight, and she looked away as though only half listening.

Good.

"I would love to visit with you sometime." The male stepped closer to her, and his nostrils flared. Auzed held back a growl.

The male was being more relaxed about it than Noito had been, but he was attempting the same thing. It was common knowledge that smell was often the catalyst to recognition. Clearly he was trying to urge his marks forth by smelling her.

Auzed wanted to bellow with satisfaction when she stepped back toward him, seeking his comfort and showing everyone watching whom she wanted near her.

For the first time, the male acknowledged Zed. He gave a quick tip of his chin and backed away.

As they continued on their way, it happened more and more. Clecanians of all genders waited to speak with Alejandra. She acted exactly as he'd asked her to. Remaining aloof yet polite and waiting for each person to linger for a moment before moving on.

It cut at his insides to see the weary tightness around her eyes when she thought no one was looking. None of the people attempting to speak with her actually cared to hear what she had to say; they only wanted to get close enough to induce recognition. They were treating her as she'd said they would. Like an object.

"Alejandra!" a female voice called from behind them.

She turned, and a smile lit her features as she watched Relli push her way through the crowd. "I'm so happy to see you!" she cried.

A few passersby shot dirty looks toward Relli, but they vanished into the crowd with a single deadly glare from Auzed.

Relli peered around her and grimaced. "This is…a bit much."

Alex exchanged a wide-eyed glance with Auzed, then muttered, "Ya think?"

"Come with me." She guided Zed and Alex to a small storefront a short distance away and motioned for them to wait outside. As they did, three more males approached Alejandra. At this point, Auzed's teeth must be no more than dust.

Relli popped her head out and waved them through, then closed and locked the door behind her.

Inside, they found a small clothing café. Bright gold-and-navy fabrics draped the walls and ceiling, making the room cozy and muffled against the outside bustle.

"I told Fenut here that if he closed his shop for us, Alejandra would meet with him and his sons."

An older male stood behind a rack of sample fabrics and grinned over to them. He raised his tail and nodded toward Alejandra first but then, to Auzed's surprise, did the same to both him and Relli. At least this gawker was respectful.

"What do you think, Auzz—Auzed?" She'd just stopped herself from calling him Auzzy and made him wish he hadn't discouraged her from using it. Although uncommon, the use of the nickname would show anyone within earshot whom this female preferred and whom she would be leaving with.

"I'm enjoying the silence, and if you're comfortable meeting this male and his sons, I'd be happy to stay."

She let out a long, pent-up breath. "Oh, good! I need a break."

Realizing he was about to get an opportunity very few ever would, the male bustled over. "Hello, incredible human! I'm Fenut. It's so wonderous to meet you—please have a seat. I'll retrieve a viewer for you at once if you'll provide me with your measurements."

"My measurements?" Alex looked to Auzed in confusion, and he cursed himself for not realizing he'd need her sizing if he were to buy her clothing. He was so out of practice with husbandry etiquette, it was laughable.

"To make you clothing. They need to know your size."

Understanding lit her eyes.

Relli chimed in, "I can help if you have a scanner and a privacy room."

Fenut nodded, clearly relieved, and returned in an instant with a small measurement scanner. "Through the black curtain in the back." He motioned toward a narrow hallway and, with a fleeting glanced toward Auzed, she followed Relli.

The café owner watched her retreat with rapt curiosity, his tail twitching while curling and uncurling around his leg.

When she was finally out of sight, he seemed to remember Auzed existed. "Oh! And will you be ordering any clothing?"

He hated the clothing he'd been provided. It was too tight and didn't cover nearly enough skin, but Alejandra's compliment echoed in his mind and kept him stalled, unable to decide between comfort and vanity. Finally, he grumbled, "Yes."

Fenut rushed away after writing down his measurements, happy to be away from Zed. When he returned with the viewer and a food menu for the table, Auzed scrolled through the clothing choices, only half paying attention, as his gaze kept drifting to the curtain Alejandra had disappeared through.

Maybe he could purchase a few traditional vests...to honor the culture, of course.

***

"You have no idea how happy I am to see you!" Alex breathed when she and Relli were alone.

Relli's brows lifted in surprise, and a tremulous smile crept over her mouth. "Really?"

"Yes, really." Alex laughed; her brows scrunched. Why was Relli so surprised by that? Alex now knew that as a demskiv, Relli's life was hard. Harder than it should've been, but surely she didn't think everyone disliked her...did she?

A true smile transformed Relli's appearance, and she let out a breath. "It's very nice to see you again as well, Alejandra."

"You can call me Alex if you want," she said as she turned

130

and examined the room. It looked like a typical fitting room, although the large floating bench was new.

"The news that you'd be staying for a few days spread so fast. Everyone has been talking about it," Relli whispered. With a glance toward the curtained door, she added, "Fierad is still upset. He's working day and night to prove Auzed's lying."

"That *Auzed's* lying? What about me?"

Relli shrugged. "Well, he now believes you've been coerced into this whole situation…" She shot Alex a sudden concerned look, her light-teal brows creased, and she leaned forward, dropping her voice even more. "You haven't, right? Is that male forcing you to claim him?"

Alex muffled a bout of laughter with her palm before whispering, "If it were up to him, I'm sure he'd love nothing more than to drop me into a room with the other humans and never speak of this again."

"Oh." She let out a relieved breath but then raised her brows in question. "Good?"

Alex sighed. Was it good that Auzed wanted to be rid of her? "I guess. He's starting to grow on me, but I'm not sure how well we'd work, you know? He's so uptight, and I'm…not. And also, marriage here is weird, and if things worked out, I'd probably end up doing what you do and become a demskiv, and I'm not certain I could handle being treated the way people treat you—which is just terrible, by the way. I'm so sorry you have to deal with all these chismosas. It's your business, not theirs."

"I appreciate that," Relli breathed, and Alex could see in her shining eyes that that was an understatement. "I did the right thing my whole life, you know. I was married"—she looked to the ceiling in thought—"seven times before I met Jut, and I was never able to bless any of my husbands with a child. But with him, it was different. He didn't care about that. He just wanted to be around me, and he…saw me. When it was time to leave him, I couldn't. It's hard, the way we're treated, but it's worth it to us."

"I'd love to meet him sometime. Could we all have dinner together, maybe?"

The dreamy grin that had spread over Relli's face as she talked about her husband grew even wider. "Yes! That would be wonderful! I have so many questions about humans. Is it true you ride massive insects around your home planet instead of transport boards?"

Alex chuckled. "No, and I can't even begin to guess how that rumor was started."

"Oh." Relli's mouth curled in disappointment. She lifted the scanner she was carrying and directed Alex to strip down so she could take her measurements.

After a long, thoughtful pause, while Alex got undressed, Relli said, "My husband's sister told him her friend met a human from Tremanta, and they told her the earthling children can kill with their cry like a sefa." She raised her brows curiously.

"False again." Alex laughed while spinning in place for the scanner. "Either your husband's sister's friend has never met a human, or the human they met was playing a joke on them."

Tilting her head, Relli peered at the floor. "So, it must not be true that you press mouths together with those you find attractive."

"Press mouths…you mean kiss? Yeah, we kiss. You guys don't do that here?"

"That's true? How odd. But it would be so wet!" She chuckled and wiggled her shoulders as if she'd just touched something particularly slimy. She lowered the scanner and said, "You can get dressed again."

Alejandra froze and recalled the odd look Auzed had given her when she'd kissed him. She groaned in embarrassment while she got dressed. Had she done something considered to be incredibly odd and maybe even kinky before even learning his name? No wonder he thought she was so weird.

Relli chatted happily to Alex as they walked back to the table. When she spotted Auzed looking devastating and powerful while sipping from a large wooden mug, heat rose on her cheeks.

Was that why he always stared at her mouth with that unreadable expression?

12

As Relli guided her through making purchases using the incredibly cool shopping hologram, Alex's gaze continued to drift toward Auzed. Half of her concentration began straying to why he kept sneaking odd glances toward Relli.

Jealousy lit a fire in her stomach before she studied the glances more carefully. They didn't appear to be looks of interest, yet what did she know? Maybe subtlety was the preferred way to flirt.

"Are you sure you don't want anything else?" Relli asked again as she stowed the small cube that had projected an image of Alex's body clad in different clothing.

"No," Alex replied with pursed lips. Immediately she checked herself. This wasn't Earth, and the odd glances Auzed was shooting toward Relli didn't necessarily mean anything. And even if they did, she had no right to be sour. "This is a nice place." She pushed out a smile and took a sip of the sweet warm liquid Fenut had served her. "Do you come here often?"

Relli settled into a more comfortable position on the backless bench and grinned. "Yes, we do. Fenut's wife, when she was alive, was also a demskiv, so he and his two boys have always been very kind to us."

Across from Relli, Auzed covertly shot his gaze downward and took another sip of his drink. Regretfully, Relli noticed. Her tail, draped over the edge of the bench, flicked back and forth, and her shoulders slumped ever so slightly. Fenut, who was on his way over to their table, seemed to be focused on Auzed's reaction as well.

Alex wanted to smack Auzed in the back of the head. Why was he being like this? It wasn't attraction, she now knew. He had a bias toward demskivs. She could see it written plainly now that the brief cloud of jealousy had dissipated.

Well, fake fiancé or not, they would be having a long talk about it as soon as she was sure Relli was out of earshot.

"I've left messages for my sons. I hope they get them in time to come meet you before you leave," Fenut said, joining them at the table with fresh drinks.

Alex didn't know how to respond appropriately so she just gave a short nod of agreement. Though Auzed had told her smiling wasn't done often, she couldn't help but notice both Relli and Fenut smiled. Was it because they were in a more relaxed and intimate setting?

Fenut's features softened, indicating her nonverbal answer was enough. But then he shot a veiled grimace at Auzed.

"Have you ever met a demskiv, Auzed?"

Both Auzed and Relli stiffened. Or maybe the talk would happen now. Would an open dialogue help or hurt?

He took a longer-than-necessary gulp of his beverage while holding Fenut's stare. Finally, he answered, "A few."

"And what are your thoughts on the matter?"

Alex tried to feign mild curiosity so as not to appear judgmental even though her mind pleaded for him not to reveal himself to be an ass. She glanced to Relli and saw her friend was just as uncomfortable as Auzed, if not more.

"I have mixed feelings," Auzed answered slowly as he aimed a stony stare at Fenut, who returned it.

Auzed's frame was still and imposing, his firm mouth turned down into a frown, but she got the impression he wasn't as upset by the idea of demskivs themselves as the forward manner in which he was being urged to voice his opinions.

It didn't surprise her at all to find that Auzed was a private person. Thinking back, he hadn't revealed anything about himself to her at all, even though he'd spoken a fair amount.

Fenut interlaced his fingers and raised a brow to Auzed, waiting for him to elaborate. The tension in the air surrounding the table grew.

Lowering her hands to her lap, Alex began twirling her gold band around her finger. Auzed's gaze shifted to her movements, and a small line appeared between his brows.

He released a forfeiting breath. Choosing his words carefully, he spoke. "With the state of our planet being what it is, I have to agree with some that refusing to give other males the opportunity to have a family is...unfortunate."

Alex, Relli, and Fenut shifted in their seats as one at his statement.

"But," he continued, "my mother herself was a demskiv. An off-worlder, but still...she chose to remain with one male. I saw how they acted with one another. And I saw how much happiness could come from such a union."

Alex stared at Auzed as he spoke, refusing to meet her gaze. Greed had her body going still. That little nugget of information drew her to him like Indiana Jones to a precious artifact. She wanted to know more about him. What his life had been like with not only a demskiv mother but an alien mother. He kept telling her she didn't act like a Clecanian and that he wanted her to. Was that because he'd worked his whole life to be more like a Clecanian? To remove his ties to all that was unacceptable in this society?

"So, you must understand, then? How could you look down on either of us for wanting the same?" Fenut all but pleaded, leaning toward Auzed with confusion wrinkling his brow.

Auzed thought for a moment before answering. "Because of the males I oversee and the many males I've fought alongside. They work so hard to be chosen, and they're honorable males." He shook his head, and she saw a true glint of sad turmoil in his eyes. "My father loved my mother so much, but there was always guilt. They had six children between them. Six. When most will never have one. If she had conformed and married other males, she could've given a measure of happiness to so many. Not as much as she and my father had together, but some. Yet then I look to my sister, and I can see the ache she carries inside. She let herself become too close to her first husband, and it hurt her deeply to leave him. I often wonder whether we're depriving females of happiness as well."

Fenut stared at the wall above Auzed in thought.

"I see both sides, and I believe I'll always be torn on the issue," Auzed finished. He caught Relli's attention and, in a soft tone, said, "I understand it's a difficult choice either way. I'm sure you didn't plan for it. I don't look down on you."

Fenut and Relli must've both seen the sincerity in his eyes as much as Alex did because they each gave small nods.

Auzed resumed sipping his drink. Though he'd only revealed a small tidbit of his personal life, his body remained stiff and a muscle ticked in his jaw. To look at him, one would think he'd just laid himself bare. Although she loved that he'd explained his opinions and had at least tried to make Relli feel better, she wondered why he'd answered at all. It'd obviously made him uncomfortable, and nothing would've happened if he hadn't spoken.

Yet another curiosity in the tightly locked safe that was Auzed.

After many uncomfortable moments, Fenut brightened. "But that's why the discovery of humans is so amazing!" He gestured to Alex and studied her as if she were a rare object behind glass.

"Yes, it is." There was an air of authority in Auzed's voice as he spoke. "But please keep in mind, Alejandra is only one human, and though she's been gracious in accepting us, I doubt the whole of the human race will be the same way. Some of the humans back in Tremanta have had trouble adjusting, and that's putting it mildly."

Alex would have to question that comment more when they were alone. How was it for the women in Tremanta? Images of the women she'd escaped the bunker with flashed through her mind. He'd explained they'd been doing well, but he'd also explained they were relatively isolated, living in a place called the Pearl Temple, which he oversaw.

Everyone who'd approached her today, with the exception of Relli, had acted the same way Fenut did. She understood why. Like Auzed had explained, it made sense they were all curious about her. Not because she was particularly special on her own but because she was human, and humans equaled a kind of salvation.

Exploring this astonishing place with its impressive vertical mall, numerous alien races, and odd but incredibly interesting customs was one of the most amazing experiences she'd ever had. But she was tired. This must've been what celebrities felt like whenever they left their fortresses. No wonder they rarely did. The realization that she was still waiting to meet Fenut's two sons drained her even more.

They chatted for a while longer, Fenut and Relli asking her questions about Earth while Auzed remained quiet and thoughtful. It was interesting how harshly they judged certain aspects of Western culture. When she'd explained social media and how odd she felt not having her phone with her or easy access to Google, they'd balked, calling the practice old-fashioned and comparing "earthlings" to Runcula—a species who very rarely, if ever, saw one another outside of their high-tech homes in the sky. Alex smothered the odd instinct to defend her planet and instead decided that if she were a Runcula living in a floating home above a turbulent, monster-infested sea, she'd stay home too.

Fenut's smile faltered a bit in disappointment as he glanced to a communicator for the umpteenth time. "Well, I suppose they will have to meet you another time. I can't keep you here all day."

Relief and guilt warred in Alex. He'd closed down his shop to give them some privacy and space from the crowds for a few hours all for his sons, and though she was ready to get back to the nest for some quiet time, she felt bad leaving without holding up her half of the bargain.

"You could join us for dinner?" Relli spoke to Fenut but peered at Alex with raised brows, silently making sure she was onboard.

"Yes!" Alex exclaimed in relief. "A nice, quiet dinner would be great. Tomorrow? Or the next day?"

Warmth flooded Fenut's face. "Wonderful! The night after tomorrow would be fine. The games start the next day. It'll be a good way to celebrate."

"The games?" Alex lifted a brow toward Auzed.

Relli clapped her hands together. "The marriage games!

Aren't you going?"

Again, she peered at Auzed.

He nodded without a lick of enthusiasm. "Yes, the regents requested we make an appearance."

"What happens in the games?" Alex asked, propping her chin in her palm. "Is this like a Spock battles Kirk in the kal-if-fee situation? Like, two men fight over lady?" she said, using her best *Tarzan want woman* voice.

Relli giggled. "I don't think so."

"It's easier to explain as you watch than to try now." Auzed smirked and rose. "We should be getting back to the nest. Fenut, will the clothing be ready soon?"

Fenut stood and pressed his tail to his forehead. "Most assuredly. I'll deliver it myself no later than tomorrow."

As they said their goodbyes, Alex rifled through all the new information she'd learned and held in a sigh of frustration. The briefest glimpse into Auzed's life had only made her hungry for more.

They silently made their way back through the market, which had gotten surprisingly less crowded in the few hours they'd been gone. No longer able to keep it in, she whispered, "Why do you hate talking about yourself so much?"

His shoulders stiffened, and he ground out, "I don't."

"Could've fooled me," she grumbled. A group of men passed, holding large leaf cones filled with bright-blue bubbles the size of golf balls. One of the men, who was much shorter and burlier than the rest, reminded her of Gimli from *Lord of the Rings*. He shoved a bubble into his mouth, his cheeks bowing out cartoonishly, then popped it.

"Just because I don't enjoy telling strangers the intimate details of my childhood doesn't mean I don't talk about myself. Do you want one of those?" He pointed toward the man, who'd seemed to realize he was under scrutiny and was shuffling away.

"One of what? The muscly ginger dude, or his food?" She held in a laugh at the frustrated exhale behind her before turning to nudge him in the ribs. "Just joking, Auzzy. No, I'm good."

They made it toward the loading section of the market tree, where transport platforms waited, and stopped. Both staring at a floating board, something unspoken sizzled between them. Maybe she *should* learn to ride her own because at the moment, she was liking the idea of having him close a little too much.

He peered at her warily as she stepped onto the board, and she raised her hands in surrender.

"No touching, promise."

They'd almost made it back to their nest home without incident when Fierad intercepted them. "Hello, Alejandra." The smoothness that had vanished from his voice upon her declaration that she was engaged to Auzed yesterday was back. And so was the interest in his stare.

She recalled what Relli had told her about his new theory that Auzed was forcing her into her current position and just stopped herself from curling into Auzed's chest. She nodded her hello.

"I just came from your nest. I dropped off the belongings we found at the scene yesterday." He shifted his inscrutable gaze toward Auzed. "Odd amount of food to still have on you after encountering a starving female. The first aid items seem to have been unused as well."

"Was there a question in there?" Auzed all but growled.

A faint smirk lit Fierad's features. "No."

Small dings from Auzed's pocket interrupted the tense exchange. Behind her, she felt him retrieve the communicator and waited an awkward silent moment for him to check it. "It's Lily, I believe."

Alex forgot herself and spun on the board before snatching the object from Auzed, then looked up at him pleadingly because she had no idea how to use it.

He paused his glaring at Fierad for a second and answered it for her, but Fierad didn't leave. The man stayed in place with a hand up, indicating they shouldn't move. He watched Alex intently. Waiting for her to say something she shouldn't, no doubt.

God, she was tired of this cabron. "Hey there, Lilypad!" she said brightly, holding eye contact with Fierad in challenge. Her focus shifted all at once as she heard Lily begin to sob. "Oh, hey, don't cry. I'm good."

"What happened to you?" Lily squeaked.

She was acutely aware of Fierad and Auzed's eyes on her. Whatever she said in this moment would be important, and she only hoped they could get away soon so she could actually talk to Lily. She whistled low and tried to organize her thoughts. "Oh, dude, so much. You really need to get over here, or I need to get over there. I'm in Sauven right now, but I'm supposed to go to some other city pretty soon. Trema...Tremeada...I can't remember what it's called. I don't even know where to start. I woke up on the shore of that river with a major headache. Pretty sure I had a concussion, and I spent I don't know how many days just vomiting and sleeping. But that's not the craziest thing that's happened."

Auzed shifted behind her and whispered a harsh "We'll be returning home now" to Fierad.

"Lilypad..." Alex paused dramatically, needing Fierad to hear her tell her lie to someone else. "I'm freaking getting married!"

There was a long pause on the line before Lily finally asked, "Wait, are you being forced into a marriage?"

"Well..." They were pulling away from a scowling Fierad now. Just a bit farther, and she could spill the beans.

"Tell. Me. Everything."

13

A uzed paced around the nest. For the last hour, he'd been straightening furniture and wiping down the already spotless surfaces as Alex chatted happily to Lily on the porch. Wilson, who'd dashed to her side when they'd arrived, was hanging from the ceiling watching him again.

"What?" he snapped at the creature and its penetrating stare.

For a moment, he felt silly. Why was he snapping at an animal? But then Wilson narrowed her eyes and scrambled over to the long bench near the window. Before exiting, she jostled the bench, leaving it crooked. They exchanged a final glare as Wilson disappeared through the window.

Stomping over, he straightened the bench. "Damn tuey. Doesn't have any reason to dislike me, but why should that matter? I only saved her bonded human—"

"Are you talking to yourself?"

Auzed shot up and spun. Alex stood in the doorway,

grinning from ear to ear. An odd flush crept over his neck. That smile turned her features from distracting to downright unfair. Two small freckles dotted the right side of her mouth tantalizingly close to her lips. The more he looked at her, the more details he noticed…and liked. So, he looked away.

"Judging by the ceiling light, it must be…almost evening?"

Auzed stared at the wall he was now facing and felt his skin heat. This was ridiculous; he had to look at her. He nodded. "About. Unless you have a preference, I'm going to *retrieve* dinner for us tonight. My cooking isn't what it should be."

She shrugged and grinned at him again while walking a ring around the room. "I'm not picky." Opening a couple of cabinets, she stopped. "You said you have five siblings?"

Auzed grunted. This was exactly what he didn't want. Revealing personal information to Relli and Fenut had seemed harmless enough in the moment and had helped to illustrate his point. But as soon as he'd opened up a little and seen the flash of interest light Alex's expression, he'd somehow known she'd ask for more.

"Four brothers and one sister." Maybe if he kept his answers short, she'd take the hint. In no way did he enjoy that she was so interested in him. Not even a bit. Because with any luck, in a few days he'd find her a mate, and then she'd be out of his life.

"Wow, big house. And your parents are still together?" Alex asked as though the conversation were only mildly interesting, but he could tell it was an act. Her gaze flicked to him in that assessing way, and it seemed as though she truly wanted to know more about him.

"Did you enjoy the market?" he asked instead.

Her lips pursed. "How many toothpicks do you think a tree this size could produce?"

"What?" he asked in confusion.

She shrugged and widened her eyes. "Oh, I thought we were ignoring each other's questions. No?"

His lips quirked, but he managed to hold his smile back. "They're no longer together. My mother died when I was young, and my father died about five years ago."

The sarcastic glint in her eyes faded at once. "I'm sorry." She walked closer and draped her arm around the large trunk that acted as a beam in the nest. "My parents both died too. In a car wreck two years ago."

This isn't good, Auzed thought as he kept his feet from taking a step toward her. The vulnerability on her face pulled at him. "It's the order of things," he said, his voice tight.

Her lips twitched downward. "Doesn't make it any easier," she grumbled in a flat tone that clearly conveyed her disappointment in his response.

He wanted to say something better. Somehow win and keep her respect without lowering his guard. The task seemed impossible, though. "*Car* is translating as *transport.*"

She sighed, and her lips thinned as though she were trying to keep a frown at bay. "Yeah. It's this big metal piece of transportation with a motor and wheels. Humans drive them on roads to get around. There was this dangerous stretch of road by my house called Blood Alley. It's very curvy, and a lot of accidents happen there for some reason. My parents had this tradition on their anniversary of going to this fruit stand along the 126 by our house and then having a picnic at Castaic Lake, but…well, Blood Alley did what it does, I guess. They were hit head on by another car."

Her voice had become softer and softer as she spoke, and a faraway look made her face appear haunted. Her eyes were dry, but Auzed expected it wasn't due to a lack of sadness. If anything, it felt like she'd already cried all the tears she had and her body simply couldn't find any way to express the heart-wrenching ache that resided in her. He knew that look. His brother, Theo, had worn it for years after he'd witnessed their mother's death.

"Do you have any other family?" he croaked, not knowing what else to say. No kind words had ever helped his brother anyway.

Eyes still glued to him, she sauntered over to a long couch and sank into it. "Yeah, lots, but…apart from my tía Vero and my brother, I haven't spoken to them in a while."

Why not? Auzed groaned inwardly. He had no choice. Gingerly settling himself into a chair that was both a safe distance away from her and uncomfortable as hell, he readied to speak to her. The curiosity was just too strong. "Why not?"

"It's painful." She shrugged, glancing away and fidgeting with that ring. "My parents and I always went to family gatherings together." A grin tugged at her lips, and her gaze grew distant as if she were thinking of them even now. "My mom always made such a big deal of me saying hello to everyone. And I mean *everyone*. People I couldn't remember ever meeting before." Her grin softened. "I went to my nephew's birthday a few months after they died, and it just wasn't the same. You're supposed to find comfort with your family after something like that, you know? But everyone was laughing and having a good time, and all I could think was, *How?* How could they be laughing and celebrating, knowing my parents would never come to another party? I couldn't bear being around everyone without them, so I just kind of cut myself off for a while." She let out a sad chuckle. "Rather, I cut myself off as much as someone from a family that doesn't recognize personal space can."

Auzed's heart clenched. He knew how she felt. He'd been lost after his mother had died as well. Always trying to figure out how he fit into his family.

She sniffed and gave a small smile, brushing away the emotion rising again. "I figured I just needed time to heal and then we'd go back to normal. I regret it now, believe me. All that time I wasted feeling sorry for myself in my dark apartment. Making excuses why I couldn't visit with everyone." She shook her head. "And now..."

Now she'll never see them again, Auzed finished for her.

"My brother was being such a dick about it recently. Easter—" at his blank look she clarified, "a holiday on my planet. It's coming up, and he was nagging me to go." She suddenly laughed, but the sound rang with miserable disbelief. Her chest rose and fell rapidly. Panic tightened her features.

"I suppose you have an excuse not to go now," he murmured, attempting to lift her mood.

She shook her head. "I was dreading going and being around everyone. Now…" Her gaze grew wide and wild, skipping around the room as tears glistened on her lashes. "Now I don't know if there's anything I wouldn't give to be sitting in our stuffy church on Sunday. To see Mateo's new baby. Oh my God!"

Zed rushed over to her as tears started to stream down her face. She sucked in a large gulp of air and covered her mouth with her hand, staring in horror at the floor.

"My brother," she said, looking up at him. "He has a baby on the way. I'm never going to meet her, am I? My niece."

It only took one more shaky inhale, and Zed was on his knees in front of her. His hands clenched at his side. The need to reach out and pull her into his arms pulsed through him, but he wasn't altogether sure how humans liked to be consoled. Should he leave? Let her try to compose her emotions by herself, as a Clecanian female would want? "What can I do?" he rasped, feeling each of her tears like a punch to the gut.

"It's hitting me all of a sudden. I mean, I knew logically before and I was upset, but…I'm never going to see my family again." With that, her head dropped into her hands and she cried. All the pent-up emotion she'd been holding back filled her sobs and deepened them until Zed's chest was tight and throbbing as if he could feel her pain too. His body was stiff with the effort to restrain himself.

One of her hands reached toward him, and he snapped. Pulling her off the couch and into his arms, he gripped her body. She curled into him almost instantly, causing an out-of-place surge of warmth to ripple through his chest. He should've felt guilty for enjoying this so much, even as he ached for her. But he felt like this was helping somehow. Inexplicably. His mind grew drunk with satisfaction as her cries softened until she only sniffed and gripped him. Did all humans get this much fulfillment from comforting their partners?

With a jolt, he realized his eyes had slid closed and his cheek rested on her head. *She's not my partner, though.* The thought sobered him and made his gut bubble. Although it felt wrong, he gently pushed her away. At first, she gripped him tighter, but then she allowed herself to be moved.

They stared at each other, both in a tangle of limbs on the floor, and unsaid understanding passed between them. "Thank you for the hug. I know it must've been weird for you, but I needed it."

A screeching Wilson barreled through the window at full speed. She saw Alex and rolled around Auzed in an angry blur, clearly believing he'd done something to upset her. Alex gave the tuey a sad smile and pulled her into her lap, then shifted back onto her seat.

"I'll go get us something to eat," Auzed said, ignoring the electric glares shooting from Wilson. "Are you going to be okay on your own?"

Alex gave him a watery smile and nodded. "It's just going to take some getting used to."

He stood and hovered for a moment longer, not wanting to leave her despite how hard his logical mind argued that it was for the best. At length, he did leave.

The blessed silence and solitude that greeted him when he boarded a transport platform didn't bring him as much joy as it usually did. Rather, a bitter hollowness niggled at his senses. For the first time since he'd been a child, he felt lonely.

Only away from her for less than five minutes, and I feel lonely? Shit.

Food would make her smile again. She loved to eat, so he'd get her some of his favorites to try and hope that sampling it all would at least distract her from her grief for a time.

When he returned to the nest, hauling a larger-than-necessary meal complete with the kinyberry jellies she'd eyed earlier in the day, he found her sound asleep in her bed. He left the food by her bedside in case she woke up. Retreating to his room, he ignored the disappointed part of him that had greedily anticipated more time with her before he was forced to be alone again.

***

The next few days passed slowly. Alex and Auzed exchanged morning pleasantries, but neither mentioned her mini breakdown a few nights before. She wasn't embarrassed about it. Realistically, she should've been a messy puddle of tears for the past two weeks, so she felt the couple hours of crying were actually impressive, considering. But she didn't know whether it had made Auzed uncomfortable or not.

He'd been acting like a skittish animal around her. Or as skittish as an enormous, elite guard alien could act. Meaning he spent most of his time giving her stiff nods, straightening the home, and randomly breaking into workouts on the porch.

That night, after she'd crawled into her bed and cried herself to sleep, she'd awoken to a tower of food piled on a low table like an offering. As she'd attempted and failed to eat one of the odd gushing blue balls, she couldn't keep the smile from her face. She'd never needed a man to take care of her that way, but she sure as hell liked when Auzed did it.

Yesterday and today, they'd traveled to the market again, meeting and greeting people from all over Clecania who'd come to Sauven to watch the marriage games. During these exchanges, Auzed remained as inscrutable as ever.

Though he urged her to speak to the interested males who approached and even some of the females, he always looked upset about it. One minute introducing her to a flirtatious suitor and the next using some lame excuse to guide her away. Was he trying to weed them out? Logically that made sense.

Now back at the nest, Alex sat on the couch and went through the large container of clothing Fenut had delivered. She inspected each piece, examining the interesting stitching and fabric. It was the only thing to do at the moment. Although she would've thought it impossible on an alien planet, she was bored.

Back on Earth, her DIY padded, dark living room acted as her home theater. She'd never been bored there.

She glanced over and saw Auzed was feeling the effects of their forced vacation as well. It was almost impossible for him to sit still. Even now, when he'd cleaned, exercised, cooked, and offered to put away her clothing for her, he still paced, looking for something to do.

Alex frowned. The answer was right there in front of him, though he refused to cooperate. They could have fun together, talking, playing a game, doing other things. But every time she tried to start a conversation with him, he made an excuse and left or answered her with single words.

She held in a chuckle as he sank into a chair and glared out the window. Maybe he was finally antsy enough to give up looking for something to do. With a huff, he rose and moved to the kitchen.

"Do you know how to relax?" she chided as he emptied the cabinets, organized the contents, then refilled them.

He gave a comically confused glance toward the cabinets as if he *was* doing something relaxing.

"It's odd to me that there's no kind of entertainment here. No TV, movies, music, plays? What do people do for fun?"

"What are movies, and why do you talk about them so much?" he asked, handing her a glass of juice made from the sap of the massive trees.

Her mood brightened at once. She leaned forward, and he tensed, still standing. "Oh, they're awesome! They're like stories, but you watch them."

He tilted his chin up and studied her.

"Huh. Hard to explain to someone who doesn't have

154

them. Do you have plays here?"

"Yes."

"Well, they're like if you recorded a play and watched it later."

Auzed lowered himself into a chair in that controlled way and thought. "How do you experience it if it isn't live?"

"I…" Alex came up short. "I don't know what you mean."

"How do you feel the play while watching it at home? Do you have playhouse hookups in your recorded theaters? How can you tell how good the actor is if you experience a recorded performance?"

Alex blinked at him. "I'm really lost, Auzzy. Hookups? Feel the play?"

He sat back, looking just as perplexed as she felt. "Maybe the easiest solution would be to take you to a playhouse."

Her brain quickly latched on to the idea of going to a play with Auzed, but she forced herself to remember it would be platonic and not a date. "I'd like that."

"I believe the playhouses are closed in Sauven now because of the marriage games, but I'll arrange for you to attend one once we return to Tremanta."

She deflated. Working very hard to keep her face from showing her annoyance, she tried for a grateful smile. "Thanks."

Auzed inclined his head, then silence hung in the air. He looked from side to side, then back to her and drummed his fingers on the arms of the chair. Did he hate talking—or just hate talking to her?

"My whole job back home was movies, you know," she blurted as he made to rise.

Squatting in a hover over the chair, he stilled, then sat back down. "Oh?"

"Yeah, I was a movie reviewer for the *Santa Paula Chronicle*. It's a small newspaper."

"You must've enjoyed your job, if the amount of time you reference them is any indication."

"Yeah, I did. Mind you, I don't know how much longer I could've kept it for. I'm surprised our tiny paper has clung on for as long as it has. They'd already cut my review column from the physical paper and relegated me to online content only, but still, I got to talk all day about what I love. Back on Earth, I was thinking about starting my own social media series reviewing films, but I don't think I could do it."

Auzed lifted a sardonic brow. "I find it difficult to believe there are many things you can't do."

She preened at the compliment. "Thank you. I guess I meant I wouldn't like doing it as much, not that I *couldn't* do it."

Ridiculous excitement swept through her when Auzed fully relaxed into his seat, resigned to have a conversation with her. "Why wouldn't you like it?"

"Well, I love movies. Like, even the bad ones are worth watching to me, but I've noticed that famous reviewers of things are often famous for their ability to seriously critique work, which often means tearing it apart. I prefer to gush over everything. I've tried and tried to change in order to make myself and my work more marketable, but my critical pieces always lacked something. I was never happy with them. Then my hometown paper offered me the position after my predecessor retired, knowing I'd work for peanuts. And they didn't care how fluffy my reviews were. Win-win."

For the first time, Auzed actually looked calm and content. He watched her as she spoke, the ghost of a grin playing at his mouth. "I assume 'work for peanuts' is an expression and you weren't really working for food."

"Ha. Yup. What about you, Auzzy? Have you always been a Temple guard?"

He hooked an ankle over his knee. "I was a soldier for a very long time before I became a guard. The Queen promoted me to the position three years ago."

So that was why he always looked so stiff and controlled. He'd actually *been* a soldier. For an alien army, no less. "Why did you choose to become a soldier? No offense," she added quickly. "It's an honorable profession, but from what you've told me so far, it seems like Clecania is pretty peaceful."

"Our forces mostly defend against interplanetary hostility. Races from non-alliance planets are known to attack regularly, and we often send aid to planets within the alliance that request it."

"Huh. That's so interesting. I'm straight-up terrestrial because I didn't even think about other races on different planets being an issue. It really is *War of the Worlds*." She giggled and gave him and exaggerated wink, even knowing he didn't understand the joke.

"It is," he replied seriously. "My father was a soldier and my father's mother was a soldier, so when I had to decide what my path would be during husbandry school, it made sense to me."

His jaw tightened, and he stared at her as though deciding whether or not to say something. She attempted her best impression of a sloth, not moving or breathing in the hope he wouldn't get scared away from speaking. *Don't move! He can't see us if we don't move,* Sam Neill's voice echoed through her mind.

His gaze grew distant, and a crease appeared in his brow. "My mother was a casualty of a war on her home planet. My brother was with her at the time and was severely injured. I always wished I could've helped them somehow. I was too young to go with them by mere years. If I'd been there, maybe…" Coming out of his trance, he shrugged. "There was nothing I could've done, obviously."

All Alex wanted at the moment was to hug him. She imagined him scared at home after receiving the news his mother had died and his brother had been hurt. No wonder he'd dedicated his life to protecting others and forgetting about his own happiness. The man she saw before her suddenly made so much sense.

"I'm so sorry. That's terrible. Did your brother recover?"

"He lived"—he sighed—"but he was horribly scarred. Made fun of all the time, and I don't think he ever recovered from the ordeal mentally." A corner of Auzed's mouth lifted in a smile. "Before the accident, he was so happy. A young handsome male who loved to interact with everyone. He was always playing jokes on people. Then everything happened and…well, it was like I lost two family members that day."

The poor thing! Alex's heart cracked more and more the longer he went on. "You must've been close with your dad."

He gifted her with a real smile, and her heart just about dropped into her stomach. He was devastating when he smiled. "I was. Once we were old enough to be on our own, he resumed his post. He was in my unit until the day he died. Loved being a soldier. He always said how lucky he felt to be the one to personally protect his children."

"I'm sure he'd be proud that you're now head guard." She grinned but immediately realized her mistake.

His smile transformed into a thoughtful frown. "Maybe before, but now? I'm not so sure. I may not be head guard for much longer."

"You mean if we get caught?" Guilt wormed its way deep into the marrow of her bones, and she actively tried to keep the cringe from showing on her face.

A hint of anger lit his eyes again, though he didn't direct it at her. "Even if we make it back to Tremanta without incident, Sauven may still call for my resignation as a sort of punishment." He locked eyes with her. "You see, the head guard isn't allowed to be considered for marriage. They could claim that if we were planning on getting married, I would've already begun my search for a replacement. They know the Queen chose me for the post as well, and they may seek to punish her by punishing me."

Oh shit. Alex let out a long groan. "So that's what you meant about what you might lose." She couldn't stand to look at him anymore. Not after hearing about how his whole life had been building to this prestigious position, only to be destroyed by her effort to help. She felt tears building behind her lowered lids, but she pushed them back. If he saw them, he'd probably comfort her, and that wouldn't be fair. "I am so sorry, Auzed."

"It's not your fault. Like you said, I would've been in trouble either way. The real mistake was crossing their territory in the first place."

Alex jerked as the sting of that statement settled over her. If he hadn't, she'd be dead right now.

In a low rumble, he added, "I don't regret it, though. Whatever happens now, I don't blame you for any of it."

His sincerity soothed her injured feelings, and she nodded. The thought that had wormed its way into her mind on their first day together came back to her. Maybe the way she could truly make things up to him *would be* to marry him. She could make sure she was a good consolation prize if he lost his job. It didn't hurt at all that she actually liked him. She wouldn't be trying to have children, of course. He probably wouldn't want her to marry him if he knew that.

Changing the subject, she held up a sleek sunset-orange dress. "How's this for tonight?"

His jaw clenched as he ran his gaze over the dress. "Any Clecanian attracted to females will have a difficult time thinking if you wear that."

Auzed's heated stare made a shiver run down her spine. Did that mean he'd have a difficult time thinking too? "I can find something else," she ventured.

"No." Auzed frowned, his good mood disappearing. "You should wear it."

Alex could only stare at him as his words settled over her. Her initial response was a shuddering *Yes, sir!* but his unhappy stare didn't match the sexy comment. Knowing Auzed was a complicated creature she may never fully understand, she shrugged it off and floated to her room to get dressed, Wilson hot on her heels. Once her new clothing and accessories were neatly stowed, she studied them. Finally, Auzed was coming around.

He'd revealed such personal information to her today, and it had only made her like him more. Concerns about the future, what her life might look like in Tremanta, and his own reticence to even speak with her hung around the edge of her thoughts like a dark, foggy border, but she petulantly ignored them.

Glancing at Wilson now perched on her shoulder, she whispered, "How good do you think I should look tonight? I can go casual good or make-him-forget-his-own-name good. Thoughts, my little Wilson Phillips?" she scratched Wilson's large floppy ears, then set her down on the bed and got to work.

14

Zed stood with his feet spread, looking out into the distance of Sauven, and contemplated the call he was about to make. He didn't know exactly what type of advice he was after, but he needed *something*. Staying in this house with Alex, not knowing what would happen and being helpless to alter his situation, was going to drive him mad.

Not to mention the impossible task of introducing her to the interested Clecanians who all so plainly aimed to steal her away. Well…they weren't *actually* going to get married, though, so it wasn't *actually* stealing. But they didn't know that, dammit!

Whenever she directed a smile toward someone else, his veins sparked with electricity. And when other gazes lingered too long on her body, it took a considerable amount of his control to not physically shield her from view.

It must've been their extended proximity making him feel this way. Every other female he'd been with had ensured their encounters were brief and goal oriented. He'd never before had to smell the scent of a female clinging to the furniture or hear the comforting sounds of her off-key humming as she floated around their shared home.

Even her brief touches, clearly innocent and normal from her point of view, were like kindling to the flame burning in him. But it was because they were always together, wasn't it? He'd feel this way about any female if he were around her this often and in such an intimate place.

Yes, all he needed to clear his mind was space and routine. Neither of which he'd have for another few days at least. Never in his life had he had so little to do. Alex's quips at his restlessness had been sarcastic, but she was right. He now realized he didn't know how to relax. Aside from the activities he did every day as part of his job, he had no hobbies. No close friends. No interests. And for the first time, he wondered if that was a problem.

Even his father had enjoyed various things in his off-hours. He'd made time to bond with his children and had liked going to plays and exploring the Histanuth Mountains to the east of Tremanta. He'd also loved to drink and laugh with his friends back home. It had Zed questioning how satisfying his life really was if it could be destabilized this much by a week away.

Unsettled, he'd thought through every possible way he could to get out of here sooner and return to normal life, but when he came up empty, Maxu's name popped into his mind. Out of sheer desperation, he decided Maxu might be able to brainstorm some less-than-legal approaches that he wouldn't have considered on his own. He wanted to speak to someone who skirted the line of the law, after all. Out of his siblings, Maxu fit that bill.

Not only was his younger brother a successful ex-mercenary but he despised the temporary marriages forced upon their people and would no doubt sympathize with Auzed's current predicament.

Each and every time Maxu had become eligible for participation in the ceremony, he'd carefully broken the law. Only enough to be deemed unfit for marriage, but still, Maxu had a way of working around a problem that Auzed found both distasteful and impressive. Resigned to the idea that his brother might actually have some good advice for him, Zed lifted the communicator and waited for the call to connect.

"Brother?" Maxu's deep voice questioned. He sounded surprised—and for good reason too. They hadn't spoken much recently.

"Are you busy?" Auzed asked without preamble.

A loud shout of pain echoed from the line and then was suddenly gone, as if whoever had made it was now unconscious…that's what Zed chose to believe anyway.

"I'm free for…let's say ten to fifteen minutes," Maxu rumbled.

Zed let out a deep breath, not sure whether to be relieved or more worried. Deciding not to question Maxu about whatever he was up to, he quickly explained all that had happened in the past few days.

As reserved as always, Maxu grunted in response.

"I've never found myself in a position like this before, and I wondered if you had any thoughts on what I might be able to do to get out of it."

"None that are legal."

Auzed scrubbed a hand over his chin and frowned into the empty room. "If I needed advice on what legal options I had, I would've called Asivva."

"Oh my. Zed, are you finally giving me the appreciation I deserve?" He could hear the grin in Maxu's voice.

"Do you have any ideas or not?" he snapped.

"Say that you recognized her. Your eyes changed but your marks haven't appeared," Maxu said, in a bored tone.

Zed sucked in a breath. "That's reprehensible. Who would lie about something like that?"

"You wanted ideas; I'm giving you ideas."

"I haven't sunk so far as to lie about feeling a mating bond," Zed growled. Lying about recognition was equivalent to lying about a fatal disease or the death of a loved one. It wasn't inherently illegal, but it was so abhorrent, he almost lost a bit of respect for Maxu for even suggesting it.

"Fine. Let me think." After a long pause, Maxu probed, "What are your thoughts on threats and/or violence?"

"This was a mistake." Zed shook his head. "Never mind."

It always stunned him to see how different Maxu was than the rest of his siblings. Since they'd been young, Zed and his brothers, along with Asivva, had battled their Traxian sides, always considering them to be the temperamental barbaric parts of their personalities that needed to be tamed in order to fit into the world around them. Maxu, on the other hand, had embraced that half of himself. Never wanting to fit in, he often allowed his temper to flare wild and free.

Now as an adult, Maxu might on occasion do things that would be unthinkable to most Clecanians, but he was also more in control than any of them. It was as though letting his Traxian side guide him had helped him to become one with it. His brother knew himself. Accepted every facet of his personality and railed against the rules that directly opposed it.

"I'll keep thinking on it, but it seems all you can do at this point is ride it out," Maxu said, uncaring that Zed had scoffed at his completely unrealistic suggestions. "Why don't you just enjoy the time off? The female must be interested in you to lie like that. Is she attractive?"

Stunning. Glorious. Wipes every thought from my mind with a smile. "Attractive enough."

"Perfect. You two can enjoy each other until you get out of there. Learning the ins and outs of a human female's form should keep you busy and out of trouble."

Zed growled out a sound of frustration. "I thought of all people you would understand. I don't want to marry her. I have a duty to the Temple. I can't just give up my post for a few months of marriage. I'd have to accept an inferior position somewhere else, possibly off-planet once it was over."

"Whoa. I wasn't suggesting you throw your life away. I just

meant while you two are locked up together, might as well have some fun. For once in your life," Maxu added in a grumble.

His body tensed, not because of Maxu's crass words but because his mind hissed the same thing in his ear every time he looked at Alex. Hell, every time he even smelled her.

"Oh, let me guess. It would be *reprehensible*, right?" Maxu taunted.

Zed grunted in agreement, even as his gaze was drawn to the ceiling where Alex's room was. "I'm attempting to find her a mate. I can't do that while also bedding her."

"Why not? She doesn't have a mate *yet*. If her mate is in Sauven, they'll recognize her whether or not she fucks you in the meantime."

"Goodbye," Zed snarled and disconnected the communicator.

He stalked around the perimeter of the nest. Why had he thought calling Maxu would be a good idea? His brother cared about societal conventions and traditions about as much as a sefa did. Not at all.

He rounded the house, returning to the entrance, and stilled.

"I'm ready," Alex said in a low, sultry voice. She stood on the porch clad in the soft orange dress he'd insisted she wear. Inexplicably, it somehow looked better on her than he'd imagined, which was saying something, since he'd seen it on a holographic replica with her exact measurements in the clothing café.

Her beautiful brown skin set off the subtle fiery-orange of the dress, like the colors of a sunset. Vibrant, yet soothing at the same time. She'd piled her curling hair on top of her head. The result was all at once messy and deliberate. Small locks clung to her long neck and brushed her shoulders.

She spread her arms out and raised a knowing brow. "How do I look?"

Auzed gulped. She'd also used the makeup they'd purchased to enhance her features. Muted burgundy highlighted the rich brown of her eyes. A similar color on her mouth directed his attention to how lovely the delicate bow of her lips was.

He didn't think she was any more beautiful than before. It was still her. But she was certainly more dangerous this way. She wasn't the type to focus on how she looked at any given moment. Her willingness to wear ill-fitting clothing to the market told him so. But now…now she knew exactly how delicious she looked, and that kind of confidence on a female like Alejandra could bring a male to his knees.

"Hard to think? Good. Mission accomplished." She gave him a tight smile, but fire danced in her casual gaze.

Maxu's words played through his mind. *Why not keep her to myself for a time?* He pushed the thought away and guided her to a transport platform before the urge to ask her to change her outfit overcame him.

Zed placed so much distance between them on the board that his heels hung off the edge as he guided them to the nest Relli had indicated.

"How can I act with these new people?" she questioned.

"What do you mean?" The dark tone in his voice that so matched his thoughts did not go unnoticed.

She glanced over her shoulder at him, and in doing so, her pinky brushed against his hand, tightly gripping the handle. "Well, I noticed that when we were at Fenut's store, Relli smiled at both of you and Fenut did too. It felt more relaxed than what you told me is common for Clecanians. Is it because we were alone? Or because Fenut isn't looking for a wife, or something? I'd love it if I could just be myself and not have to worry about not smiling or not being nice or anything, but I don't want to offend anyone or act incorrectly and lead Fenut's sons on."

"Those guidelines are in place when interacting with strangers, especially male strangers, since they're often searching for opportunities to interact with available females. Remain distant toward Fenut's sons for a while during dinner and make it clear that you intend to marry me. Relli and I will let you know when it's appropriate to relax your mannerisms."

Zed ground his teeth together. It was like a blow to the gut to think she might act toward Fenut's sons the same way she acted with him. He had no idea why, but he'd felt as if he was special to her in some way. The idea she might look at all males the way she looked at him had never occurred to him. True, she'd been instructed *by* him to act a certain way in public. Did that mean when he gave her the cue to relax her guard, she would smile at Fenut's sons and reveal intimate details about her life and let them touch her?

Had he been fooling himself to think she treated him differently? That she'd been vulnerable with him alone? And why should he let himself care this much? The goal was still to find her a mate, wasn't it?

He tried to ignore the dread and bitter jealousy that had suddenly worked its way into his stomach. *Idiot.* This was exactly why he'd worked so hard to keep her at a distance. Despite his best efforts, he now felt a bond with her that, in all likelihood, was something he'd completely manufactured.

On the trip over, Zed weighed the pros and cons of pushing her to remain distant the whole evening, though it would end up being very odd for her to do so, especially when everyone around her wouldn't be. They arrived at the nest to an overeager welcoming party. Zed's glare immediately landed on the two unfamiliar handsome males and their wide-eyed gazes as they scanned Alex up and down.

Alex averted her gaze from the eager males as she boarded the porch of the home and instead made her way over to greet Relli. Her lips appeared pinched, and Auzed was sure she was forcing herself not to smile.

"Alejandra," Relli greeted warmly with a grin the way any close friends might. She gestured to a male next to her who had overlarge ears and an open, curious expression. "This is Jut."

"It's so nice to meet you. Relli has so many nice things about you." Alex nodded at the male, her face unnaturally blank, and reached out a hand.

Jut glanced at her outstretched hand, and his brows knit.

Alex gasped and snatched her hand back. "I'm so sorry. We shake hands on Earth when we meet new people, and I just offered it out of instinct." She peered at Relli, her eyes worried. "I didn't mean to touch him or anything. Damn, I was trying to be so careful."

Relli chuckled.

Zed walked up behind Alex and placed a palm on her shoulder. He wanted the gesture to be reassuring, but part of him itched for any excuse to touch her.

"We understand." Relli smiled toward Jut.

He returned her warm grin and nodded. "If you're comfortable, we'd love to learn an Earth greeting. It'd be helpful in case we ever meet any other humans."

"As would we." One of Fenut's sons inched closer.

Zed's hand on Alex shoulder tightened. He didn't like how eager the good-looking male appeared.

Alex glanced toward them and stood silent for a moment as if she were working through something. "Okay. I'll show you first with my future husband." She stared directly at Fenut's sons and emphasized her words just enough so they heard her unspoken message loud and clear. Zed was impressed. She'd made it known that she had no interest while remaining polite.

She turned to face him and held out her right hand the way she'd done with Jut. He felt like an idiot not knowing what this greeting was, but he mimicked her, holding out his left hand in the same way. She gave him a small grin and gently lowered his hand to his side, then directed him to lift his right hand so it mirrored hers. A flush stole up his neck.

Would these males assume they'd never touched since he didn't know this human greeting?

She clasped his hand with hers, squeezing, and raised it up and down before releasing it. The gesture was odd yet formal and brief enough that his bunched shoulders relaxed a fraction.

"There you have it," she said, then turned to Relli and extended her hand.

Zed had to force himself to remain relaxed as she taught everyone how to shake hands in greeting. Though the two unattached males only gripped her hand for a respectful amount of time, Zed still found himself wanting to rip off their male fingers.

Walking a few steps away, he breathed in and out, gathering his temper. No matter how hard he'd fought against it, he'd bonded to Alex, and now his possessive side would not shut the fuck up.

***

"Wow, I love your nest." Alex stared at the ceiling, where a soft melding of oranges and pinks could be seen. Just like a real sunset. "It's so cool that it looks like the sky."

"Thanks. I installed it, oh…" Jut glanced to Relli for confirmation, "three years ago."

"Yes. I'm half Swadaeth. I need more sun than a typical Sauvenian."

Relli gestured for everyone to sit at a large table set up in the middle of the main floor. This nest was set up the same way her and Auzed's was except the vining plants, cluttered corners, and savory scent of cooking food gave the place a warm, lived-in feel. Her heart pinched. Relli and Jut had built a life here and filled their home with what could only be described as love. Despite the disconcerting feeling of being watched by everyone in the room, Alex relaxed.

She peered at Auzed as they approached the table, and he directed her to a seat beside him—one of the only two with a back, she noticed. She was sure Relli would sit on her other side, but then one of Fenut's sons—Calep, she recalled—plopped down instead. Unable to stop herself, she shot a confused glance toward Relli and Jut, who were standing by the table as if waiting.

"In a Sauven house, the guests choose their seats first," Auzed whispered, giving Calep an annoyed grimace.

The man appeared unfazed by Auzed's glare. Both of Fenut's sons were large with green skin, thick black hair, and gorgeous purple eyes. Calep, the man next to her, grinned at Alex in such an infectious way that she had to bite her cheek to keep from grinning back. It was unfair that she, as a woman, was supposed to appear so emotionless, but she shrugged off the feeling. She wasn't in California anymore, and continuing to be sour about the customs here would only turn her into an unhappy person.

"Do you come from a forest on Earth?" he asked, leaning his elbows on the table and giving her a full view of his large biceps. Was he flexing?

"Contain yourself." Gosten, his brother, whacked Calep on the arm and forced him to lean back in his seat. "You aren't even eligible for marriage."

"Neither are you," Fenut all but scolded, relaxing into a chair across from her.

As soon as Fenut was seated, Relli and Jut joined them at the table in the last two unoccupied seats next to each other.

"That's right!" Relli grinned toward Gosten, and Alex found herself once again confused. Then she recalled that Relli knew Gosten, probably had for quite a while.

"Gosten is competing for a bride this year," Jut explained, grabbing a pitcher from behind him.

Calep, Fenut, and Relli turned over the wooden cup placed facedown in front of them.

"If you'd like a drink, flip your cup over," Auzed instructed, turning his own over, to Alex's surprise. The tight lines of his features told her he wasn't completely thrilled to be here.

She flipped her cup, and Jut filled it with thick golden liquid.

"No yubskani for Gosten!" Fenut said, slapping his son on the back with a proud grin. "He needs to be prepared for opening day tomorrow."

Gosten accepted a glass of water from Relli with a clenched jaw. He peered down at the table with a far-away expression and gulped.

Alex melted a little at the slight worry she saw in his eyes. "Are you excited?"

He turned toward her and lifted his chin, hardening his expression. "I am."

"I competed about five years ago now," Calep added with another broad grin, this time directed toward his brother. "I'm sure you'll do better than I did."

Gosten gave Calep a small smile of thanks and let out a long breath, allowing some tension to leave his body.

The unexpected sting of tears started behind her eyes, and Alex took a drink from her cup while trying to get them under control. It hurt more than she'd thought it would to see Calep and Gosten together. Her own brother, Mateo, had always been supportive of her too.

She caught Relli's concerned gaze, and the damn goddess of a woman seemed to understand exactly what she needed. She spoke, distracting the curious gazes being sent Alex's way. "And Calep is ineligible because he has just finished with a marriage. A successful one, from what I hear."

Calep's smile grew even brighter, consuming any lingering sadness in Alex. "Yes! Mageba is with child. She chose to finish her pregnancy at the Moisa Tree with other females, but she has kept me informed."

"Congratulations," Auzed said.

"Thank you. I wish she would've let me care for her at my home, but…" He shrugged, his grin dimming a bit.

"Most females in Tremanta prefer to finish off their pregnancies around other females as well." Auzed nodded. "I've seen a few at the Temple over the years."

Alex drank again, realizing that if she ever chose to get

pregnant someday, her choices would be to either let her temporary husband help her while pregnant or go and live with her friends. Neither of those options included her family back home. The recognition that any child she may have would be raised without them made her doubt she'd ever choose to have children.

"Would you tell us more about Earth, Alejandra?" Jut asked, refilling her cup. She distantly wondered whether he'd continue to refill it as long as it was turned over.

"Sure, and thanks," she said, lifting the cup. What should she tell them about Earth? She didn't want to talk about her family as she was a bit too raw at the moment, so she shoved those feelings down and described what she knew about Earth as a planet. Seven continents, five oceans, billions of people. The information was boring in her opinion, but they all seemed interested just the same.

After a while, Relli and Jut rose to retrieve dinner.

"Could I help?" Alex asked, hoping to get a break from being the human representative teacher for a little while.

Jut gave her a funny look. "Guests don't help."

Leaning back in her chair, she took in Calep and Gosten's eager expressions. It was clear they wanted to know more.

"What did you enjoy doing on Earth?" Gosten asked.

What did *she* like doing? Now there was something she could talk about.

15

"I still don't understand." Calep laughed. "How could a person who's been dead for thousands of years and had all their organs removed return to life?"

Alex fell back in her seat and clutched at her sides, sore from laughing so hard. Who knew describing one of her favorite movies would be this difficult and this hilarious? They'd asked ridiculous question after ridiculous question. Things that'd never crossed her mind before.

"You have to just accept the premise," Relli wheezed from across the thin table.

"I refuse!" Gosten boomed in a falsely outraged tone. "It makes no sense. Even if I believed that a male long buried could be brought back to life by a simple phrase, the whole reason he *could* be brought back makes no sense!"

Jut snorted as he refilled Auzed's and Alex's empty glasses yet again. She sipped the sweet golden yubskani, alcohol made from the sap of the trees here, and grinned wide. "Please enlighten me." She chuckled toward Gosten.

He gave her a dazzling smile as he leaned toward her, ready to argue his point. "So, you said they buried him alive to punish him for killing their king and put a curse on him that allowed him to live forever?"

"Pharoah, yeah," she corrected, taking a sip of her drink.

"Okay." He lifted his brows as if about to make a killer closing statement. "Then why would they write a book with words to allow him to awaken again, knowing he would be all-powerful?"

Calep approvingly clapped his hands together next to her at his brother's point.

Alex tried to answer through her giggling, but suddenly Auzed, who'd been silent for most of the night, beat her to it.

"They were ensuring he would suffer endlessly and never be set free. I assume they didn't imagine anyone would be dumb enough to wake him."

She gave him a small grin. "Exactly! He's a cursed mummy. They took that seriously."

"Fine. Fine." Gosten sighed. "You win for now, but I'm still left with questions."

"I'll explain the rest another time."

"I'd like that very much," Calep chimed in from her right.

She chanced a glance at Auzed again and found him staring daggers at Calep's elbow only a few inches away from hers. She wasn't attempting to make Auzed jealous, but a wicked part of her brain reveled in his disgruntled expression. After an hour or so of getting to know everyone, Auzed had pulled her aside and assured her she'd passed the social line, invisible to her, that divided "strangers" from "friendly acquaintances."

When she'd returned to the table, she begun to allow herself to smile at everyone. Her mood had been bolstered from that point on. Holding back from the emotion that came so naturally to her was exhausting; she could also admit the many yubskanis she'd drunk helped as well.

Throughout the night she'd checked in with Auzed to make sure he was enjoying himself too. When he'd continued to answer her in grunts and short nods, she'd given up and instead tried to get to know everyone else. Jut was a calm, caring man who radiated warmth. She would often look over only to find him grinning toward his unsuspecting wife as if they were newlyweds. Alex had also learned he ran a snack bar in the highest section of the market tree, a level she hadn't yet explored.

She enjoyed getting to know Calep and Gosten better without the fear that she was leading them on. Calep was a bit younger than Gosten and built like a tank with a tail. He was one of those burly men who had a rounded stomach and love handles but could also probably lift a car off you if needed. His wide, infectious grin added to his charm. She had no trouble understanding why a woman had picked him for marriage when so few men were ever picked.

Gosten was a bit more reserved but no less charming. He turned out to have a quick wit and sly humor that caught her by surprise.

For a long while, Auzed had remained an indomitable statue in the room, but he eventually settled and even appeared to have a good time. He drank the drinks that were served to him and listened to the conversation with a restrained interest. Whenever she moved around the nest or went to the bathroom, she'd made sure to give him a brief touch. She knew he'd claimed soon-to-be-married couples didn't do it, but she also knew his bunched shoulders and tense jaw consistently relaxed when she brushed her hand over his arm while walking past. The knowledge that her presence comforted him in any way made her almost giddy.

The night was turning out to be wonderful. She was pleasantly buzzed. She was having a great time chatting the night away with a new group of friends. And she suspected Auzed liked her. Really liked her. Puffed-his-chest-out-with-a-sort-of-satisfied-pride-every-time-she-referred-to-him-as-her-future-husband type of liked her.

"We should be leaving." Fenut sighed as he rose from his seat. "Will you join us tomorrow for the opening ceremony?" He pounded his palm on Gosten's shoulder and added, "We'll be the ones cheering the loudest."

"I'm not sure if we have somewhere we need to be, but I'd love to if we can." She turned to Auzed and found him staring at her.

At length, he replied, "The regents have asked us to lap the arena before the games start, and they've assigned an area for us to sit. Apologies."

Fenut's sons both stood and joined their father without a

word of argument. "Maybe we'll see you after?" Fenut asked, lifting his tail to his forehead in farewell.

"Yeah, maybe!" Alex replied, though she had no idea if it was possible.

Calep shot her a crooked grin. "Do humans shake hands when parting as well, or do they kiss?"

"Calep!" Relli squeaked.

A chuckle burst from Alex's lips in surprise. "What?"

The scrape of a bench behind her told her Auzed had risen to his feet.

"I heard it is a common human custom." Calep looked between her and Auzed, the realization that he'd been wrong turning his smile nervous.

"It is not," Auzed growled ominously.

She got to her feet and stepped between them, hoping to cool some of the rising tension. "I imagine the kind you heard about isn't something I'd do with someone I just met. It's an intimate act humans do with their partners. There are other kinds too…uh, it's hard to explain."

Calep tilted his head as he digested that. "If I somehow find a human of my own, will she want to save kissing for marriage? Have you two kissed yet?"

At the same time Alex shook her head and said no, Auzed very firmly said yes.

"No?" he boomed, affronted. "We did. You kissed me."

Alex felt her cheeks flaming. "We… Not really… I mean, I guess it was a kiss." The way he was looking at her as if the mere idea the brief peck they'd shared wasn't a kiss made her squirm.

Turning back to the rest of the room, she saw they were all staring. There wasn't a hint of shame at enjoying the overheard conversation to be seen of any of their eager, amused faces.

"He's right. We've kissed," she said quickly, wanting this conversation to be done with.

Relli and Jut hid their grins by clearing the table. Calep didn't bother to hide his.

Changing the subject, she addressed Jut. "Thank you for dinner. It was so good." He'd lovingly prepared a feast, not knowing what foods she liked. Big surprise, she'd liked them all.

"It was our honor." Jut beamed at Relli and twined his tail around hers.

"It's time for us to return to the nest as well," Auzed said from behind her. The cool indifference was back in his voice, but his movements were rigid as he helped Jut clear off the table, blatantly ignoring Relli's hands shooing him away.

As they said their goodbyes and left, she could feel Auzed's intense stare on her. How had they managed to end the night with him mad at her?

When he remained touchy and silent after they'd boarded a platform and made it out of earshot, she rolled her eyes and asked, "Are you going to tell me what's wrong now?"

He shifted his weight from one foot to the other and tightened his hands around the bar in front of them.

"Why did..." He let out a low breath and a short grumble.

"Are you interested in either of Fenut's sons?"

"What?" She turned on the board to face him, holding the bar behind her back. "No. Maybe in another life. They were nice and all, but not my type." They were totally her type, but these days, it seemed that if a man wasn't blond, sullen, and statuesque, she had no interest.

His gaze narrowed on her, and his lips twitched. She imagined he'd just stopped himself from asking what her type *was*. Pushing his shoulders back a bit more, he stared ahead of him. "Why else would you have lied about us kissing?"

"Is that why you're upset? I'm sorry." She grinned up at him. "But I wasn't lying. I mean, that little peck I gave you wasn't *really* a kiss, you know."

He blinked ahead of him, still focused on the open air he was guiding them through while digesting that bit of information. "But you pressed your mouth to mine."

Alex shrugged and leaned back against her hands. "Sure, but it was only for a second, and you didn't kiss back or anything. Tight, dry, closed-lip mouth contact is not my definition of kissing. Unless you're giving a friendly peck to your relative or buddy or something."

He finally looked at her, and then his gaze heated and slid down her body. His attention lingered on her chest pushed out in front of her to accommodate her hands behind her back. Alex shivered.

"Why did you do it?" he rumbled.

"Kiss you?" She shrugged, then laughed. "Oddly enough, a quote from that movie we were discussing comes to mind.

You were about to be mauled by a sefa. 'Seemed like a good idea at the time.'"

Alex jumped as he suddenly vaulted off the board. Her heart leapt into her throat for a moment before she realized they were back at the nest and he'd jumped onto the porch around the hanging home.

"You thought I was going to die, so you kissed me the same way you would a friend?" He shouted his words as if he were repeating them to himself, not asking her a question.

A bit more carefully than *he* had, she stepped onto the porch and trailed after him. "Well, we didn't exactly have time for a make-out session or anything. Why are you so mad about this?"

"I thought..." Auzed spun and tapped on the center of his chest with his fingers. "I don't know what I thought, but I assumed you'd kissed me because... It doesn't matter." He waved his hand dismissively and stomped into the house.

Wilson, who'd appeared bleary-eyed on the roof, glanced down at them in annoyance.

While following Auzed into the house, she waved Wilson away and whispered, "It's fine, go back to bed."

She heard Wilson's annoyed little trumpet as the creature relaxed into her nest.

"I could show you how it really goes if you want?" She sent him a sultry grin to go along with her suggestion. She almost giggled at his sharp double-take.

He scratched his temple and tipped his head at her, confused. "I don't understand you, female."

Before she could think better of it, she hiked her dress up to her thighs, charged toward him, and leapt. Without any hesitation, he caught her. Slithering her arms behind his neck and wrapping her legs around his waist, she leaned in close. "It's better that way," she whispered, playfully nuzzling his nose with her own. "Gotta keep you on your toes, Auzzy."

He held perfectly still, but his hands twitched where they gripped her thighs, and his chest rose and fell quickly. Gaze locking onto her mouth, he let out a low, rumbling growl that sent an electric current right to her core.

One of his large hands shot up her back and clutched her nape while the other curled around her ass. The last of his control cracking, he used his grip on her neck to pull her mouth down to his.

Alex's stomach flipped, and she let out a victorious moan. Aching to kiss him for real, she ran her tongue over the seam of his lips until they parted and then kissed him slowly and sensually, hoping to give him time to learn what she was doing. His arms encircling her tightened even more, and he met her motions with a ferocity of his own. Strong lips sliding over hers had her mind melting into a sizzling puddle.

With no idea how it'd happened or when, she found herself pulled tight to him, her back crushed against one of the large tree trunks running through the room. And he'd taken control. Barely letting her get a breath in as he explored her mouth with his hot, greedy tongue.

His cock, which she hadn't noticed before, had grown large and rigid between her legs. Slanting his head to deepen the kiss, he rocked his hips, making her release a low moan into his mouth. With an answering growl he did it again and again and again, until she was wet and throbbing.

Breaking away, he found her neck. "Hold on to me," he commanded in a guttural voice between sharp bites and soothing kisses along the column of her neck. He stepped away from the tree, and she clung tightly to his shoulders. Both his hands flew off her. She was about to put up a fight and demand he return them, but then he fisted the back of her dress and, with a vicious wrench, tore it in half down her back. Any argument she'd been ready to have was swallowed by her low moan.

Snapping the two thin straps holding her dress on her shoulders, he reached between them and pulled the bunched fabric away, letting it fall in a ragged heap on the floor. His arms drew around her waist and squeezed while his mouth latched back onto hers with a groan as though she were the best tasting thing he'd ever had on his tongue.

She arched her back, pushing her chest against his, but his damn shirt was still in the way. Grabbing a handful of fabric at his back, she pulled it up, showing him without words she wanted it gone. He let her slide down his body, craning his neck to continue their kiss until she was finally on her feet. Then he gripped the shirt and pulled it over his head. As he did, Alex worked to unlace the intricate knots of his pants.

Once his shirt was gone, he didn't help her. She glanced up to find him staring at her hands fumbling at the opening of his pants. The pure lust burning in his gaze had her breasts aching. He wanted her to undress him, and he wanted to watch her do it.

She slowed her movements, letting him savor the sight. His wide chest rose and fell before her eyes, the defined muscles of his torso expanding, then bunching together with each controlled breath. One of his shimmering white markings curved around his chiseled V-cut and disappeared below his waistline.

While untying the last knot keeping his pants up, she leaned forward and ran her tongue over the dip between his large pecs. He let out a low, rumbling groan that vibrated through his chest. Trousers coming loose, he grasped her shoulders, intending to pull her away, but when she slid her hand between them and gripped his large shaft, he stopped.

Wrapping her palm around his girth, she pumped her fist slowly up and down. With a low growl, he jabbed his fingers through the hair at her nape and pulled her mouth away from the slow kisses she was planting on his chest. He brought her face up to his and kissed her deeply while she glided her hand over his heated length.

In slow, restrained steps he backed her up until her calves hit the long couch at the back of the house. He turned them both, then sat and pulled her down to straddle him. Trailing scorching kisses along her jaw and down her throat, he clutched her waist and lifted her higher onto his body, putting his mouth in line with her hard nipples.

Alex tried to keep her mind on the task she'd been focusing on, but their sudden shift had made it impossible for her to stroke him. Never in her life had she felt the need to pleasure a man this viscerally. She wanted to watch his hard stomach tighten and relax as he came. Hear that deep, rumbling voice groan or roar or snarl. Just thinking about how he might sound when he broke apart made her whimper.

She attempted to pull away, but his strong hands kept her in place. He sucked and kissed her breasts more intensely. Sliding his hand under the thick band of her underwear, he flattened his palm on the center of her low spine just above her ass and roughly pressed forward, forcing her to arch into his mouth even further.

Alex's mind went dizzy at the sensation, and she rocked her dripping core against his shaft in time with the pulsing swipes of his tongue. This man was fucking worshipping her body and with a crashing realization she recalled that this was what he'd been taught to do. He ran his teeth over the underside of her breast, and she inhaled a sharp breath. Well, maybe not this specifically. But from what she'd gathered, everything Clecanian men worried about focused on ensuring a woman's comfort. That had to have parallels in what they learned about sex with a woman too.

She pulled away more forcefully, and he allowed it. Chest heaving in ragged breaths and eyes gone dark, he kept his gaze locked on hers as she stepped away from him, then sank to her knees. A low growl broke from his chest as she lowered her head to his lap.

For the first time, she looked down at his shaft and couldn't contain the moan that built in her throat. He was glorious. A slick, wide crown leading to a thick shaft with pulsing veins. She grinned up at him and felt a surge of confidence when he hungrily licked his lips.

She ran her palms up his thighs, tracing the progress of his pale markings. A portion of his markings high on his left quad were different. They were thicker and black, but they felt the same as the other markings as she ran her fingers over them and then let her palms rest by his hips. She lowered her lips and breathed hot air onto the head of his shaft, making him curse.

In an almost unrecognizable voice, he rumbled, "Alejandra, this isn't done."

She grinned and took the tip of him into her mouth

16

Zed gripped the back of the couch he was sitting on with all his strength to keep from clutching at her hair as she slipped her mouth over his cock. Her hot tongue licking and sucking at his shaft felt indescribable, and it took much more focus than he had to give to keep from bucking farther into her throat.

When she wrapped her palm around the base of his shaft and began pumping in time with her mouth, he could no longer keep his groans of pleasure in. He needed to pull her away before he came, but he didn't trust his hands at the moment. "Alex, move away."

Instead, she moaned around him and increased her devastating rhythm. His head fell back, and his body began to shake. This female was going to be the death of him. She ran one hand up his stomach and chest, then back down, scraping her nails against his oversensitive skin as she did.

No longer able to help himself, he shot his hand down and

buried it in her hair, which had come free at some point while they'd been kissing. He tugged gently, forcing her to meet his eyes. Although her mouth on him was pure bliss, he needed to see that she was okay.

When she locked gazes with him and he saw her lids heavy with lust, he broke. He roared to the ceiling as he came, and to his shock, she didn't move away. She worked his cock with her mouth, sucking him until there was nothing left.

As soon as she released him, he tugged her up and spun her around, then pulled her down so she was sitting on his lap, her back to his front. Wrenching her legs apart so they draped on either side of his thighs, he delved his hand beneath the thick underwear shielding her scent from him. Even through the material, he'd scented her arousal as soon as they'd started kissing.

Sweet and potent, it had drugged him instantly. As he slid a finger over the folds at her entrance, learning how she felt, she squirmed on top of him and rested her head back on his shoulder. He slipped his middle finger into her drenched sex and grew hard again at her choked moans.

He pumped inside as far as he could go and curled his finger, hoping to locate the pleasure center every Clecanian female had buried deep. Her hips rocked gently against his hand and she panted out sighs, but he couldn't find the bundle of nerves inside that he needed to stroke. "Where is your pleasure center?" he rumbled into her ear as he brought his other hand up to cup her breast.

"My what?" she breathed, covering his hand with her own.

He wiggled his finger deep inside to illustrate his point. She gave a small hoot of surprise. "The knots of nerves that will make you come," he growled as he nipped her lobe and teased her nipple with his thumb.

"Oh, it's farther down, but the main one's on the outside."

On the outside? She ground her pelvis against the heel of his hand, focusing on one particular area at the top of her lips. Could it be so simple?

He experimented, pumping his finger in and out of her core while rocking his palm against the small nub outside until she was shaking with need. The scent of her arousal built, and he nuzzled his head into the crook of her neck, inhaling every bit of her he could and promising that next time they did this, his face would be buried between her soft thighs. He peered down her writhing body, drinking in the sight of her small, round breasts and dark, rosy, brown nipples. A soft area of her low belly trembled as her hips twitched in time with his movements. He pressed her mouth to his ear, needing to hear her cries more loudly.

Her body grew taut and still, her breathing stopped altogether. Even her tight core around his finger clenched. And then she was coming, her loud moans echoed in Zed's ears, and he couldn't get enough. He didn't want this to stop. Didn't want her to go back to her room and leave him alone again. He kept the pressure of his hand firm and still until her cries faded into soft pants against his ear.

Removing his hand from her soaked underwear, his clouded mind raced to think of anything that might get her to linger here with his arms wrapped around her, her body plastered to his. She squirmed in his grip, and he tightened it. Dipping his head to her shoulder, he inhaled a final time, then forced his arms to open.

But she didn't leave. Heat spread through his hammering chest as she turned in place and straddled him again. He was sure he looked as confused as he felt from her grin and raised brow. Placing a soft palm on either side of his face, she pressed a soft kiss to his cheek, then his forehead, then his lips. Zed's lids went heavy. When she peered back at him, she asked, "So how do you like *real* kissing?"

A wide smile spread over his face, and he barked out a loud laugh. Her eyes caught on his smile, and her own grin widened in answer. "Well, you're really smiling for the first time, so I assume you liked it."

Liked it? It was the most wonderful thing he'd ever experienced. Being face-to-face like that. Mouth-to-mouth. It was so intimate and so raw. "I did."

She crossed her wrists behind his neck and leveled a sarcastic look on him. "You are a man of many words, aren't you?"

Auzed wished he had something more to say, but he couldn't think clearly. Contentment radiated through him to just be holding her close like this. As if his soul recognized he was lost for words, a purr suddenly rumbled through his chest.

He stilled and studied her bewildered reaction. Slowly she slid a hand down to his chest and flattened her palm over his heart. A smile curled her lips as she felt the vibration on her hand. She gave him a tentative grin. "Is that a happy sound?"

He nodded, but a spike of unease tempered his mood. Zed couldn't remember the last time he'd purred. And he certainly couldn't remember it ever happening with a female.

"Uh-oh." She let out a sigh and scratched her nails through the hair at his nape. "You're getting all stiff again."

Zed's lips twitched, and he looked pointedly into his lap, where he was indeed hard.

With a gentle laugh, she tossed her hair back. "Yeah, that too. But I meant your demeanor." Her warm gaze grew serious as she ran her palms over his shoulders. "I'm not telling you to become a different person or anything, but just for a few days, can you try to relax? Go with the flow?"

The arguments rising in his throat deflated when she pressed another soft kiss to his lips.

"We could do that more," she urged through her grin.

Fingers sinking into the flesh of her hips, he tried to think. But she was right. Holding her and talking to her and kissing her felt incredible. Much better than the frustrating distance he'd been trying and failing to keep. So far, he'd been helpless against her charm. What was the point in continuing to fight?

He trailed his finger up her naked spine and almost groaned at the flush that suddenly darkened her chest and cheeks. Relaxing his guard around her until they went back to Tremanta might mean he'd need to go lock himself up in a dungeon underground for a few weeks until he could purge her from his system, but if their last hour together was any

194

indication, it'd be worth it.

Alex stared at him, her eyes assessing and waiting for his response. In lieu of voicing his assent, he pulled her down for another kiss. His scalp tingled with awareness as she sighed and melted against him, draping her arms over his shoulders.

The only frustration that lingered in his dazed, contented mind was that he had to wait for her to recover before pleasuring her again.

***

Alex stretched her arms overhead while lying in bed. The soft illumination from the ceiling lighting told her it was morning. Legs itching to leap out of bed and find Auzed, she forced herself to remain put.

He was still a bit skittish, even after their amazing night, and she didn't want to push him. Although she'd been ready to go all the way with him last night after their chat, he'd kept his caresses soft and more or less innocent, never touching her breasts or slipping his hands back under her panties.

And then when he'd decided it was time for bed, he'd bid her good night with a toe-curling kiss and left her on her own. She'd quickly ignored her initial instinct of hurt. Just because he didn't want to cuddle up in bed didn't mean he was blowing her off.

She replayed their night together in her mind and had to bite her lip. Ooh, that man knew how to touch and kiss and lick. It still shocked her that although not *inexperienced*, he'd never been with a human. Never kissed and hadn't even known what a clit was, and yet…damn, he'd picked up on what to do quick.

How good would he be in bed if that was his pregame performance? She shivered under the covers. Without any of the normal morning dawdling, she sped to the bathroom, readied for the day, and dashed to the lift. Smoothing her hair, she commanded the lift to lower and marveled at how hard her heart was thrumming in her chest.

Her focus immediately zeroed in on Auzed's large form in the kitchen. To her surprise, Wilson was there too. She sat on the counter in front of Auzed, whose back was turned. Alex quieted her steps as she heard him carrying on a one-sided conversation with Wilson.

"Like I said, a civil understanding is all I ask."

Wilson let out a shrill squeaky honk and zoomed in a circle before settling. Her little trunk spewed toots and trumpets as if she were arguing back.

Auzed's shoulders slumped, and he released a frustrated breath. Before he could speak again, Wilson noticed Alex approaching and glided over to greet her.

"She's your bonded human, I understand, but that doesn't make me an enemy..." His words trailed off as he spun, intending on facing Wilson but finding Alex instead.

"Heeeyyy," Alex sung with a sly grin. "Whatcha talkin' 'bout?"

A pale flush stole over Auzed's face, and he straightened. "Wilson and I were just having a conversation about boundaries after I found her tearing up one of my new shirts for her nest today."

Alex winced and shot an accusatory glance at Wilson. The tuey looked back at her with wide, innocent eyes, and Alex folded, scratching her behind the ears. Lowering Wilson to the floor, she approached Auzed's turned back and wondered if his openness to her touching him had carried through from yesterday.

Tentatively, she ran her hand up the smooth fabric of his shirt and felt the firm muscles of his back bounce under her touch. Gone still, he let out a low hum.

"Personally, I wouldn't think it the worst thing in the world if you had all your shirts destroyed."

He turned in place, half his mouth lifted in a grin. "Is that right?"

Tilting her head up at him, she tugged at his pale-green, form-fitting shirt. "This one is atrocious." She wrapped a palm around his neck and pulled him down for a brief kiss, breaking to say, "You should definitely give it to Wilson."

When she kissed him again, he remained stiff for only a few seconds before groaning and returning her kiss but then stepped away. "As much as I'd love to, we have to leave for the opening ceremony soon." He handed her another piece of pink bread, and she huffed out a disappointed breath.

"Mmm. This is getting better," she said through a mouthful after trying a bite.

He looked pleased by her compliment but said nothing, only sipped on his beverage and eyed her with an odd intensity.

"This is, like, a game, right? But also an important

tradition. So what should I be wearing? Fancy? Casual?"

"Somewhere in the middle, I'd say. I can help you choose something after you eat."

Should I bring it up? I shouldn't bring it up. I'm gonna bring it up. "Oh, are you okay going into my room, then?" He raised a brow at her, clearly not understanding her subtlety. "I thought maybe Clecanians didn't go into other people's rooms, since you didn't join me last night and all."

His brows drew together, and he studied her while taking a long drink.

"I mean, it's probably for the best that you didn't. Might've led to…more, and I need to see that doc before we go any further."

Auzed's confusion morphed into concern in an instant. "Are you unwell?"

She stifled a grin. "No, I just would need to get birth control. Fingers crossed it works faster than the stuff on Earth." She let out an awkward chuckle.

Like a shot, his gaze grew heated. In a low rumble, he asked, "You wanted me in your bed last night?"

"I was thinking a good cuddle, but…" She shivered at his tone, and heat pooled in her belly. "I wouldn't have kicked you out."

"You needn't see the doctor. I'm dormant." The briefest growl broke from his lips before he could stop it, as if he'd just realized something infuriating. "That is, unless you'd like to be dormant in case you meet someone else."

Would I like to be dormant? Eyes widening, she blurted, "Do you mean you're on birth control? For men?"

He rested his fists on the table between them. "Yes. I told you, I cannot marry while holding my current position, so I ensure I'm dormant."

Alex threw up her hands and laughed. "Then why didn't we do more last night?" His jaw was still angrily tensed. It took her a second to understand why. "And no. I don't need to be dormant as long as you are."

As soon as the words had left her lips, he let out a large breath he'd been holding.

"So why didn't you come into my room?" she tried a little more insistently. A brief flare of uncertainty flickered to life. What if he regretted fooling around with her? Or what if he'd gotten all he needed and didn't want to cuddle?

As if he couldn't figure out how else to put it, he hiked his shoulders and said, "It's not what's done."

Alex rolled her eyes. "This again. Apparently blow jobs aren't done either, but you seemed to like that. And kissing."

"Blow job?"

She clicked her tongue and dropped her gaze pointedly in the direction of his lap.

"Ah. I can learn to live with *that*."

She almost missed the smirk as he hid his lips behind his glass. "I'll bet you can." She laughed. "So, what isn't done exactly? Sex in a bed, or cuddling in a bed?"

"Cuddling," he said matter-of-factly. "We wouldn't share a room with our partners for long after pleasing them. It never occurred to me you'd want me to stay. Especially since you hadn't had enough time to recover yet."

Alex tipped her head. "No offense, you were really good and all, solid A-plus from me, but…you didn't exactly *break* me. What did I have to recover from?"

"From the penetration and orgasm," he said, as if it were obvious. "I know it'd be only a short while compared to the recovery time you'd need after sex, but you still came." A sudden look of worry passed over his features. "You did, didn't you?"

"Yeah. Yeah, I did," she confirmed quickly. "But I don't need any recovery time from having an orgasm." Alex made a face, the mere thought of it unpleasant. She wondered if all Clecanians required time between orgasms or just the women. They were kind of like human men in that regard. Only able to orgasm once, then needing to recuperate. "Do you need recovery time?"

"No." Auzed tightened his fists even more as he stared at her, except this time, he definitely wasn't upset.

Feeling daring, she rose. "Oh well, Auzzy." She pouted and shrugged while sauntering to the lift. "Guess you missed your chance, huh? Gotta get ready for the games."

Wide eyes narrowing, his lips curled into a wicked grin and his gaze darkened. As the lift levitated toward the ceiling, she gave him a flirtatious little wave.

17

A uzed scanned their section of the arena a final time
before settling. While most of the stadium was near
bursting with all manner of Clecanians, the area in which
they'd been seated only had a few occupants.

"I didn't realize this many people even existed in this city!"
Alex commented while staring around the jam-packed arena.
She looked lovely in the pale-purple ensemble he'd helped her
select. The fabric shifted and flowed in time with her
movements.

Unsurprisingly, their lap around the walkway circling the
arena had been exhausting. The regents hadn't pushed
Alejandra to be out for long the past two days, content with
a few hours here and there at the market tree, and now he
understood why. It seemed as though every single Sauvenian
and hordes of other Clecanians from different cities were at
the games today. If Alex were to be recognized by someone,
the regents had a pretty good shot of it happening here.

Alex took it in stride, politely greeting everyone who introduced themselves to her before moving on. But now things were different. He was different, and they were different. Even though their tryst was not meant to last, all the possessive instincts raging through him since the day they'd met now felt justified.

She had given herself to him, and if her sly hints were any indication, she would continue to seek him out for companionship and pleasure. She was his, for whatever time they had together. And his insides fumed at the looks the Sauvenians kept directing toward her.

Whereas before, he'd encouraged minimal touching in order to mimic a typical couple, he now found himself sliding his hand across her lower back whenever he got the opportunity. Her quick intakes of breath both encouraged him and calmed him. She liked his touch. The smiles she gave *him* were genuine. That was something he could hold on to when it felt like the itch to grab her and leave was too much.

They settled into their assigned area, and Auzed relaxed a bit. At least the regents had been kind enough to give them deluxe seats. In this section of the ring, spectators were placed much farther apart. Far enough that he wouldn't be concerned about curious onlookers ruining Alex's enjoyment of the game.

"What are these?" Alex asked, pointing down to the control pads hooked to the tables in front of them.

"It's so you can control what you watch." He activated her viewer and showed her how to navigate between the many cameras hovering around the playing area. "The contestants all compete at the same time. You can either watch from here, or you can scroll through different views. Often the cameras will focus on favored players." With a few more flicks of his fingers, he brought up a different screen. "And this allows you to order any food or drink. Shall I pick something for us?"

Alex grinned and brushed her fingers over his knuckles. "You know me so well."

Activity from behind them drew her attention, and she removed her hand. Auzed flexed his knuckles, the loss of her touch oddly distressing.

Under her breath, she mumbled, "Oh great."

He turned and found the regents floating down the steps toward them. They were being followed by a hovering camera. The reason they'd been seated in such a nice area was now clear. A murmur swept through the crowd like a wave, then the frenzied chatter began. Alex was being filmed. Broadcast to the audience at large as if she were also part of the opening day festivities.

She must've realized the same, for she brushed a hand over her hair, smoothing it, and her warm expression hardened.

"Hello, Alejandra." After a long moment, Queen Dasa added, "And Head Guard Auzed. How are you on this fine day?"

Since Auzed remained still, saying nothing, Alex spoke. "Great. Thanks for inviting us."

The queen of Sauven was wrapped in an intricately

knotted ivory gown today. It cinched against her body and created rolls of gauzy pale fabric. The knots grew more ornate as the fabric traveled down her tail.

The king's outfit was drab in comparison. He'd chosen a loose-fitting cream tunic and sandy-brown pants, though his tail was wrapped and knotted in the same delicate fabric as the queens.

"We've had word that you've been exploring the city a bit. How are you enjoying Sauven so far? Is everyone treating you well?"

Alex's mouth thinned almost imperceptibly. Zed felt a rush of warmth in his chest. Was he the only one who noticed it? Could he see changes in her mood that no one else could? Why did it also ache to think that might be true? It came as no shock when she began twirling that gold ring around her finger. Zed had to distract himself from the urge to force the regents and camera away. He busied himself with ordering food instead.

"Yes. I've really enjoyed exploring the market tree, and I'm excited about whatever is going on here today." Alex gestured to the empty air inside the enormous circle of seats.

"Marvelous," King Bet intoned. "We have another surprise for you that should help elevate your mood even more."

Zed tensed.

With a commanding wave of the king's tail, an attendant near the entrance to their section ushered two females through the doorway. He recognized one of the females instantly. Daunet, a guard under his command. The other was vaguely familiar, but he couldn't quite place her. The female gazed around with wide, sparkling blue eyes as though she'd never seen anything better.

Realization hit. Mm…something. What was her name again? She was human. One of the humans under his care at the Pearl Temple. If he remembered correctly, she was the female who talked incessantly about seeing the rest of Clecania. She was odd too. Not once had she bemoaned the fact that she'd been taken from Earth. Quite the opposite. She was overjoyed.

She'd been rescued from the same facility Jade, his sister-in-law, had been over six months ago. A tenacious little thing, she'd learned to read their language on her own in a matter of months and had combed the archives for information on each and every city, intent to travel this new world as soon as she was allowed.

As far as he knew, this was the first time she'd left Tremanta. But why? And how? Had she requested this visit? Or had the regents brought her here?

"We spoke with the Queen of Tremanta, and she thought you may want to spend some time with another human." Queen Dasa waved the human female—Migs, was it?— through and gave them both a kind smile. The camera hovering overhead zoomed in on the two humans as they greeted each other. "This is Meg."

As Meg and Alex clasped their hands together and moved them up and down, both their eyes continued to stray to the camera hovering nearby.

Auzed still couldn't understand this. They'd allowed the Queen to send a human into the city though they weren't on the best terms at the moment? As the camera hovered closer still, he understood. It made perfect sense. The downsides of doing the Queen of Tremanta a favor like this paled in comparison to the potential. Another unmated human female was now gliding through the trees of Sauven. Another opportunity for one of their citizens to recognize a mate. And another way in which they could legally steal an earthling away from the Queen who they believed to be hoarding humans.

The deep whistle of traditional Sauven woodwinds sounded from all around. He caught Alex's uncomfortable gaze, and they both looked back to the regents, praying to the gods they wouldn't be joining them.

"Enjoy the day one bout. I prefer the complexity of day two myself," Queen Dasa said while taking the arm of the king and lifting her tail in farewell.

As soon as the regents and their camera were gone, Alex and Meg broke into excited chatter. True enthusiasm was visible in both their grinning faces, so Zed decided he'd give them privacy and instead rose to greet Daunet.

She was waiting by the exit and gave him a cursory glance as he approached. Was that judgment shining in her eyes? How much had they told her? Renewed annoyance surged in his gut. He'd allowed himself to forget his current predicament the past few hours, but now, face-to-face with one of his guards…it pushed through the semi-relaxed fog layer in his mind full force.

"Daunet." He nodded, keeping his posture straight and his shoulders back.

"Sir." She tilted her chin down respectfully.

There was an awkward pause before he found words to use that wouldn't be out of place. "How are things running at the Temple? Who has taken up my post in the meantime?"

"Boriq, sir. They're running well enough." Her mouth twitched downward. "He gives the humans much more leeway. It's causing disruption among the guards, in my opinion."

And just like that, a weight was lifted. She was trying to tell him that Boriq, a senior guard he didn't particularly like, was doing a poor job. She'd implied she preferred Zed's leadership even now. Even with the rumors surely floating around the Temple that he'd broken multiple laws in another city.

Why was he continuing to drive himself crazy with guesses as to what rumors were being spread about him, though? "I'd like you to speak freely, Daunet. What are they saying about me back home?"

She shifted from side to side, and the corner of her mouth twitched down again. "Are you sure?"

The mere question was like stone through his veins. He tensed and nodded.

"Well, many—myself included—believe there was simply a misunderstanding, but others…" She took a deep breath. "They say you purposefully went off on your own during the search to find the human so you could claim her for yourself. They say you have a friend here who you colluded with. That's why you were given leave from your duties and are staying with the female. To force more time alone together because supposedly that's the way to make marks come out." Half of Daunet's face lifted in a wince. "They say you are trying to steal a female away as your father did."

Zed, who so often clenched his jaw when angry, now found his chin had dropped. He'd expected outrage over his actual crimes, but never had he thought his own guards would think such things about him. Or his father. That he would intentionally deprive his fellow Tremantians the opportunity to meet a female because of his own selfish interests... How could they think that?

"I don't believe a word of it," Daunet said again, staring seriously into his eyes. "But maybe if you told me what happened, I could try to set the record straight back home."

Controlled breaths in and out were the only thing keeping him from throwing a heavy chair over the railing. Finally, he deflated. "I don't want you troubling yourself. If I haven't proved myself an honorable male throughout all my years of service, both off-world and at the Temple, there is no way you'll convince them with a relayed message. But know that none of what you told me is accurate."

Her expression grew pinched, an argument still brewing in her throat.

"When I return, I'll tell everyone what happened. For now...let them believe what they want."

They continued talking for a while, but Auzed's mind was only half aware of the conversation. Daunet was there to escort Meg around Sauven.

Auzed ambled back toward Alex and Meg, who were leaning close and speaking happily. He paused. Most of his guards had lost respect for him and not even for the reasons he'd assumed. Petty gossip and hearsay had taken the place of actual dishonorable behavior. And his father...

It was common knowledge his mother had pushed to remain with one male in accordance with her Traxian culture. It was a well-known fact. Yet now, in the wake of the last four days, they were doubting his father's honor as well? Had they always believed his family to be duplicitous under their guise of respect? Or were their opinions so fickle they could so easily turn rotten?

If his reputation could be swayed within a matter of days, then why was he holding back at all? He could take what he wanted now and work to win their respect when he arrived home and made it clear he would not be marrying Alejandra. She wasn't his for long, after all, so why not take advantage of her warmth while he could? Why continue to cling to codes of conduct he seemed to be the only one to care about?

He gazed at the soft brown waves falling over Alex's shoulder and recalled how those curls had felt in his fist the night before. Why care? Why try? Especially when the alternative had proved so much more gratifying.

***

"How many of us are there?" Alex whispered.

Meg waved her hand. "Planet-wide? Who knows? But at the Temple, hmm, maybe two dozen or so?"

The woman was pretty in an odd sort of way. Her features were all exaggerated. Almost like she was a cartoon character. Her large lash-framed eyes were a startling shade of steely blue, and her lips were puffy and rosy but not very wide. With her short curly hair and pixie nose, Alex imagined her features would've been the ideal back in the 1920s. Yes. She could easily see her starring alongside Louise Brooks and Clara Bow.

Out of nowhere, she wondered if Auzed found Meg attractive. Chancing a glance over to him, she saw he was still talking with the woman who'd brought Meg. She was beautiful too and a Clecanian. How well did Auzed know that new woman?

When she glanced back, Meg was sweeping her gaze around the treetops. She sighed. "Isn't it amazing here? I mean, Tremanta is incredible, but...wow...just wow."

The look on her face was so peaceful. Like she'd just won the lottery and had not a care in the world. Alex could only hope *she* felt the same way in six months. Out of curiosity, she probed, "How did you get past the shock of it? When did you get over the fact that we can't go home?" Since her emotional realization the other day, Alex had not been able to push the nagging depression to the back of her mind. She'd never see her family again. How could anyone get over something like that? How was she supposed to move on and live a normal life?

Her gaze slid to Auzed, and she bit her lip to keep her small smile at bay. He'd been helping, that was for sure. But she couldn't go on forcing herself not to think about the bad stuff forever. One day soon, she'd need to actually come to terms with what her life would be. Despite her growing attachment to Auzzy, he was temporary. He had a life of his own. Her chest tightened at the idea of not seeing him every day.

Meg's dark brows drew together, and she shrugged. "Honestly, I never had that stage. My life on Earth…well, it wasn't the best. On top of that"—she bit her lip, and her eyes strayed toward the ground—"some things happened, and…"

Meg cleared her throat, and Alex wondered if there weren't other women who might see their abductions as a sort of salvation. She covered Meg's hand with her own and gave her an encouraging smile.

"Let's just say being here and seeing all of this and knowing I'll never have to worry about my past ever again…" Meg's grin returned in full force, illuminating the pink undertones of her skin. "It's a fresh start."

A fresh start, huh? Alex leaned back in her seat and pondered that. Would she ever come to think of it that way? She'd been in a dark place back on Earth. Her parents were both dead, and she'd let her grief overtake her for far too long. Being here on this new planet had done something odd to her. Almost divorcing her from the realities of her life back home. She could imagine her life and her family on Earth, but there was so much distance.

It was like when they rebooted a movie with a new cast. The main character was generally the same. Had the same mannerisms for the most part. The same backstory. But they felt different. She wouldn't call this opportunity a fresh start. But maybe she could think of it like a reboot. The ache she felt at the loss of her family that rang dull and constant in her chest would never go away but instead become part of her character.

For most of her life, Alex had clung to her comfort zone. Her hometown, family, and friends. She'd gone off to college for a few years, sure, but at the first opportunity, she'd jumped at the chance to move back home, where things were warm and safe and consistent. But then, after her parent's death...all of that had changed.

If she wanted to make it here, she needed to change her ways. Glancing back toward Auzed, who was staring at her from a few feet away, she had a sudden tug of fear. Was she turning him into her safety net? Was his strong, unflinching demeanor something she'd gravitated toward because she liked *him*? Or because she wanted to feel protected again? What if something happened to him? What if he was taken away from her too soon?

The rich, sonorous sound of wood instruments echoed around them with more fanfare than they had the first time. The sound of thousands of people excitedly speaking at once built before mellowing.

Across from them, one triangular section of stadium seating rose above the rest, jarring Alex away from her downward spiral.

Can our section rise too? Now that she thought about it, it was obvious the floating seating could move. Why wouldn't it be able to? It wasn't as if it were attached to the trees. She marveled at the realization all the same, and a flicker of the awe that lit Meg's eyes every other moment reverberated through Alex.

Auzed settled into a seat next to her. His warm thigh brushed hers, though he had plenty of space to avoid it. She peered over to him and found his gaze soft and assessing. It seemed he was working through something as well.

"Who do you think that is?" Meg all but squealed while squinting and pointing to the raised section across from them.

Auzed leaned over Alex and used Meg's control to bring up a close-up view. "Those are the regents, obviously," he said, pointing to the king and queen standing and waving. "And this"—he pointed to a gorgeous pale-green woman with rose-colored hair—"is the bride."

Both Meg and Alex shot confused glances toward Auzed.

"The marriage games have three rounds. Today the entrants will battle one another, and the half who remain will move on to tomorrow. The same occurs then. On the final day, the last fifteen or so males will race. The male with the highest score at the end marries the bride."

Alex scrunched her brows toward the beaming woman on the screen. "And she's okay with that?" It was clear the woman wasn't unhappy. Alex couldn't recall ever seeing a Clecanian woman showing that much emotion before, besides Relli when they were in private.

"Yes, she volunteers for it. It's a great honor to win the games, and there are usually many females vying for the position of bride. They compete in games of their own throughout the year. If I remember correctly, the games are ancient and were played before we left our first planet. They've updated them, of course, to apply toward the current state of the world, but Sauvenians love them."

As the woman posed and waved at the cheering crowd, Alex felt a flutter of anticipation herself. On the one hand it felt barbaric to "win a bride," but on the other…why not? She was going to have to pick a guy anyway. Why not have fun with it?

An instrumental bellow deeper than the others sounded, and Alex had to blink at what appeared in the playing area.

"Is that…" Meg waved a hand at Alex, trying to tap her without tearing her gaze away from the sight before them. She missed slapping her in the face by a millimeter.

Alex brushed her away, giggled, and leaned forward.

A stream of maybe a hundred shirtless oiled-up men had flowed into the airfield all on their own transport platforms. The men, with their glistening muscles, hooted and shouted toward the bride, who batted her lashes and made a show of eyeing the men.

"What exactly do they do in this bout?" Alex asked, attempting to pick out Gosten among the sea of bulky Sauven men.

"They fight, trying to knock each other off their boards

and into the netting below. The last half to remain move on."

Meg released a small squeak, then an incredulous chuckle. "They fight like *that*? With their bare hands?"

"Out of all of them, only one will win? 'There can only be one?'" Alex said in her best impression of Sean Connery.

"There are five winners, but only one gets a bride. The rest have points added to their husbandry-school scores. It allows them to stand out and be more desirable during the Sauven marriage ceremony."

A high-pitched flute sounded, and the men began stretching and eyeing each other. Their joyful calls grew silent.

"Look, there's Gosten!" Alex turned to Auzed and pointed down into the crowd.

Her smile faltered when she noticed the fire in Auzed's gaze. He'd caught how enraptured she was by the brutish spectacle about to unfold before them. In a move that left no room for analysis, he placed his large palm possessively over her upper thigh. Her body began to vibrate all over.

Finger still hanging in the air and pointing, she eyed his hand as he reclined and looked on in dark silence. He didn't move his palm or squeeze her thigh, he just left it there. Scalding and heavy.

Clearing her throat, she turned back to the game.

Meg, who missed nothing, leaned over and whispered, "Damn."

Alex mouthed, *I know,* and widened her eyes.

Meg shot a pointed glance toward his hand resting on her leg, then tilted her head and pursed her lips in a look that seemed to say, "I don't hate it, though."

Alex had to agree.

Her attention was torn away when a second flute sound whistled through the stadium, and all hell broke loose. Slamming fists, flashing tails, elbows. It was difficult to make out what was happening, but here and there men let out cries and tumbled from their floating platforms.

She pointed out Gosten to Meg. "We're rooting for him!"

They cheered and clapped, getting into the frenzied excitement of the game and doing their best to pretend like the floating camera nearby wasn't broadcasting them to the whole stadium. Both on the edge of their seats, they watched in awe as one burly man grappled with five others, jumping over tail swipes and landing smoothly back on his board.

They both inhaled sharp gasps when the man crouched, gripped his board, and spun upside-down one hundred eighty degrees, surprising his attacker with a kick to his shins. At some point in the madness, the food Auzed had ordered arrived. He passed around drinks while Alex and Meg booed the men hovering near the sidelines, attempting to squeak through without fighting at all.

Gosten, Alex realized, was a formidable opponent. As she and Meg watched, enraptured, he sped toward a chartreuse man who'd been excelling by playing dirty—sneaking up behind players, hooking his tail around their ankles, and then speeding away. After a few minutes of sparring, Gosten roared, startling the other man momentarily. Before he recovered, Gosten lifted his tree-trunk thigh and kicked the chartreuse man square in the chest, knocking him off his board.

Meg and Alex looked at each other with dropped jaws half curled in exuberant smiles. Without any prompt, they both yelled, "'This is Sparta!'"

Alex actually choked out a sob then. Something about the shared knowledge filled her chest with painful happiness. "You know movies," she croaked in a weak voice.

"Yeah, girl!"

Alex turned to Auzed wordlessly and saw he was heckling one of the players himself, tracking their movements on the screen in front of him. He threw his fist in the air while muttering something about underhanded play. The muscles bulged under his white shirt, and she ogled him.

"I don't know about you," Meg whispered while eying the savage opponent who'd flipped his own board, "but this ridiculousness is making my weakness for himbos flare up real bad." She bit her lip and watched as the man made a show of lifting a struggling guy bodily, raising him over his head, and tossing him away with a bellow.

"Salud!" Alex shouted and raised her glass, letting the light, joyful comradery of watching a sporting event with new friends wash over her. Things were okay. She'd be okay. And no matter what her future held—whether in Sauven or Tremanta or somewhere else, with Auzed or without—there would still be shining moments of levity and happiness. Moments when her future seemed bright.

18

Meg, Alex, and Auzed remained sprawled in their section long after the winners had been announced and most of the spectators had left—no doubt venturing to the plethora of after-parties held throughout Sauven.

The two females recounted highlights of the game while sipping on yubskani, the sweet alcohol made from the fermented syrup of the Sauven trees. Auzed even found himself interjecting here and there with his own thoughts, their exuberant glee contagious.

Daunet had joined them after a while. There was no one left in their section to guard against, after all. As the cleaners made more and more frequent rounds, shooting annoyed glares their way, and the small bots vacuuming the ground insistently bumped their feet, he knew it was time to leave.

"Where are you guys staying?" Alex asked.

Meg glanced over to Daunet uncertainly. "Somewhere by the restaurant district, maybe? Wherever they put us, it's super crowded."

Alex drew her lips inward and raised her brows to Meg with a conspiratorial grin.

"What are you thinking?" Meg asked, leaning forward with a grin of her own.

"Sleepover?"

What the hell was a sleepover? Was it what it sounded like? Did she want Meg to stay with them at the nest? A sudden wave of jealousy that he hadn't planned for roared through him. Did Alex enjoy a female's company as well? Did he now have to compete with everyone? He peered toward Daunet, who he knew also preferred the female sex, but was relieved to see she didn't appear interested in either human.

All day he'd been pondering Alex's words about sleeping in the same bed and how she'd been ready to fuck him last night. He hadn't let his thoughts linger on the idea too long because…well, because he wasn't sure he'd make it through the first day of the games if he did.

Despite all that he'd learned about controlling his possessive instincts, he found his palm had traveled to rest on Alex's thigh once again. He held back a wince, wondering how she'd respond.

Her leg tensed underneath him, and she gave him an odd look. Then she flashed a glance back to Meg and her brows rose. She bit her lip before grinning brilliantly. "A sleepover is a common thing human women do. *Friends* sleep at each other's houses and bond."

Auzed just stopped himself from releasing a relieved

breath.

"Want to?" she asked Daunet.

With a shrug and a barely contained grin, Daunet nodded. "I don't, but don't let me stop you. As long as you don't mind me returning to sleep in the nest."

"Totally." Meg and Alex stared at each other and released sounds dangerously close to squeals.

***

Bonding, as it turned out, included large quantities of alcohol, loud, off-key singing, and the full spectrum of emotion. At present, Auzed was planted on one of the couches while Alex and Meg tried to re-enact one of the movies Alex so frequently talked about. He'd made a show of refusing to be an audience member, but in truth he enjoyed having something to do. On a deeper level he was not ready to acknowledge, he loved Alex's pleas for him to participate.

When he'd refused, she'd urged and beseeched where most Clecanian females would have moved on. She wanted him to mingle. To participate in her life. Not because she needed something from him but because she seemed to simply want him near. His whole life he'd always felt needed. Needed as a soldier, as a brother, as a guard, sometimes as a male, but he couldn't remember ever feeling wanted.

Throughout the evening, she'd made a point of including him in the conversation, explaining unfamiliar human things and making inside jokes that only he understood.

"Auzed, this is one of the best parts!" Meg shouted, rousing him from his thoughts.

Standing on a chair, Alex wobbled, and Auzed readied to catch her in case she toppled over. Her face was flushed and her hair frizzed out around her temples, both from the drink and from the animated acting they'd been doing for the past few hours. This was the most recent of the three movies they'd acted out for him. The first concerned a male exploring ancient landmarks and, for some reason, wielding an animal-skin whip. The second seemed to explore the intricacies and humor of robbing a gambling den, though he hadn't followed all of that storyline.

This one was turning out to be the most confusing yet, since Alex and Meg kept interrupting each other to go off on tangents about the plot or other things altogether, but he'd gleaned that it was a film about animals from Earth and about the lost king of a ruling family returning to save his kingdom.

With a cranky Wilson clasped in her hands, she raised him high in the air. "And then he shows the prince to all the animals below," Alex boomed in a voice meant to invoke awe and wonder.

From behind her, Meg suddenly began singing at the top of her lungs. "Circle of life!"

Meg's voice was so awful that Alex snorted and broke into a fit of silent laughter, slowly lowering to her knees while she tried to take in air. As soon as she was sprawled on the chair clutching her stomach, Wilson took her moment to flee.

To his great surprise, the tuey rolled over to him and settled beside him on the couch. Her wide, glowing eyes flashed toward him and then back to the two females now gripping each other's hands as they laughed.

"Oh no, I'm gonna pee," Meg wheezed, clumsily rising to her feet. She dashed to the lift, bouncing from side to side as it rose to the upper floor.

Still on the ground, Alex breathed out a sigh and propped her elbow onto the chair behind her. "Are you having fun? No. You're bored. You don't have to hang out with us if you don't want to."

"I'm enjoying myself," he said a bit too quickly, earning him another slow grin. She crawled over to him with that smirk still curling her lips. When she reached him, she slid up the couch, sat next to him, and swung one of her legs over his left thigh. With a small yawn, she lifted his arm and draped it over her shoulder, then leaned against his body.

Auzed sat frozen. He didn't know why, but when he spoke, he kept his voice quiet. Something about the moment felt precious and worthy of whispered conversation. "Did you enjoy the game?" He already knew the answer but asked anyway, wanting to hear her voice.

"Yeah. I'm glad Gosten made it through." His lips quirked when she responded in a whisper.

This felt good. Too good. It wasn't sexual or friendly. It was intimate in a way that made his stomach hollow. Something built in his chest. He glanced to the ceiling and saw no sign of lift movement, so he allowed his purr to sound. Alex tipped her face so it was pressed against his chest and smiled. From his other side, Wilson nudged his right leg and rested her head on his thigh. They sat in silence, and after a while, Alex's body melted against him.

"I should go see what happened to Meg," she murmured in a voice already half asleep.

He grunted in response. Not wanting to admit just how unhappy he was with the idea of her leaving this exact spot.

She let out a long, unnecessary groan, then finally rose. Auzed went with her, scooping a sleeping Wilson into his elbow as he did.

When they reached her room, Alex swung the door open and chuckled to see a snoring Meg sprawled on her bed. She turned to him and gave him an unreadable look. "I should probably sleep in here with her, but I could come tuck you in?" She gave him a flirtatious grin and ran her finger down his chest. The scent of her arousal lifted to his nose.

Zed had to ensure he didn't crush Wilson now sleeping in the crook of his elbow. Spotting the issue, Alex carefully lifted the tuey and rushed into her room to set her down. Heat raced through his veins, filling every vessel with need, but now was not the time. Before she could return, Auzed had grunted good night and sped down the hall to his room.

"Hey," she whispered, catching him before he could disappear behind his door. "Wait for me."

He froze in his doorway, back to her, and reeled in all the instincts and emotions telling him a hundred different things to do in that moment. He wanted her. Badly. But the depth of emotion he felt at that moment scared him. If he buried himself in her supple body now, when a torrent of warmth already lingered in his chest…he'd never be able to leave her and return to his job.

He'd decided after speaking with Daunet that he'd enjoy his time with Alex while they remained in Sauven. But he'd also promised himself he'd only allow that enjoyment if he ensured his heart remained caged.

Emotion was kept out of Clecanian relationships for a reason. But it wasn't kept out of Traxian ones, and right now it was taking all of his control to keep the fiery urge to pull her into his room at bay.

***

Alex couldn't understand Auzed's sudden mood shift. The rigid lines of his body were practically radiating with something. Not anger or lust. It was more like he was trying to gain control.

They only had three days before they left for Tremanta and whatever was between them became infinitely more complicated. She wanted to stay in this bubble just a little while longer and take advantage of every second she could. She placed a palm on his bicep to turn him, but he surprised her by rounding on her so fast she took a step back.

"Not tonight," he all but growled.

Tonight was the perfect night! She'd had an amazing day and an even better evening. Hanging out with her new human friend and Auzed. It'd felt easy and right and so, so fun. Now he wanted to ruin it by being upset with her for some unknown reason when she was offering to fool around with him?

Well, fuck that. Fine. If he wanted to be mad, that was his problem. She wouldn't let it mess with her mood. With a bit less grace than she'd hoped, she turned on her heel and started down the hall, intending to leave him alone until he fixed his mood.

Like lightning, his hand shot out, and he wrenched her back to him. Not hard enough to hurt but hard enough to make her breath catch and her sex tighten. Pulling her into his room, he backed her against the door. "Not with her in the nest," he rumbled, green eyes staring down at her with an intensity that made her insides heat. Was that why he'd said not tonight? Embarrassed at someone hearing them? Maybe, but the uncertain glint in his eyes made her think it was more than that.

She grinned. "It's okay. I can be quiet."

The slow, wicked grin that curled his gorgeous mouth had her own smile disappearing in an instant. His deep voice skated over every nerve, sparking them alive. "Not when I'm through with you."

She shivered involuntarily and made a choked sound.

When his nostrils flared and his gaze darkened, she knew he'd smelled how his words affected her. With a low groan, he dipped his head and moved his lips against hers, coaxing them apart. His delicious tongue swept over hers in movements that were gentle yet commanding. In the part of her mind still functioning, she realized he was doing it on purpose. Kissing her like this to make her melt while not losing himself completely.

The control and the utterly dominant way in which he

worked his tongue…this was the kind of man who made sure his woman was all but panting for him before taking his own pleasure, and she couldn't get enough. On a whimper, she moved to lace her hands behind his neck, but he gripped her wrists before she could.

Lowering them back to her sides, he dipped his mouth to her ear. "I'll take care of you tonight." He nipped her lobe, sending an electric pulse straight to her nipples. "But we'll do no more."

Alex balled her hands and tried to control her erratic breaths as his hand fisted the material of her loose shirt around her midriff.

He slipped his fingers below her pants and cupped her sex hard, putting just the right amount of rough pressure on her clit. "When I get you alone, I won't worry about company." Sliding one finger inside her core, he kept his mouth pressed to her ear, his hot cheek firm against the side of her face, forcing her to hear every word he said. "I won't worry about your cries or how far up into the house we get before I bury my head between these gorgeous thighs."

She let out a moan as he began to rock his hand in the way she liked, slipping another digit into her heat. An unexpected cry burst from her lips when he curled his fingers in time with the motion of his palm.

With a snarl, he roughly covered her mouth with his other hand, smothering her moans as the pressure built and coiled in her core. He kept whispering dirty things to her, but she couldn't concentrate. He hadn't fondled her breasts or ran his hands along the curves of her body. He hadn't even kissed her for very long. This was controlled and raw and oh so efficient, just like Auzed. He'd begun breathing deep, hot breaths onto her ear between his rumbled words, his chest rising and falling quickly, and his hand over her mouth tight and unmovable. Her eyes rolled back when he pressed firm open-mouthed kisses to her throat.

The pressure in her sex built and built until she was crying into his palm on every exhale. Needing something anything to grab, she gripped his forearm. Muscles tightening and knees trembling, she struggled to hold herself upright. Her eyes flashed wide as her orgasm hit. Wave after wave of molten pleasure crashing over her.

He stilled his hand as she came and pressed his body close, inhaling deeply against her neck. A soft, buzzing tingle traveled over her scalp. Her cries turned to soft whimpers against his palm, still firmly wrapped around her jaw, but he didn't release her.

His rigid body was strung tight, and his fingers remained inside her now-slick sex. His hold on her tightened even more. She shuddered with oversensitive pleasure as he roughly pumped his fingers inside her twice, making a clipped growl against her neck each time he did. His whole body moved in time with his hand. The action was so intense and precise. She couldn't help but think he was imagining coming inside her, his cock in place of his fingers.

At length, he slid his hand out from between them and lifted his head. White-hot lust raged in the depths of his cool green eyes, but his jaw was set, his expression determined. He pressed his lips to the back of the hand covering her mouth as though not trusting himself to actually kiss her. Then rumbled, "Go to sleep now, Alejandra."

She wanted to argue, to stay and make him feel as good as he had her, but she also felt compelled to do as he said. He'd just made her see stars with nothing but his fingers and a sizzling tongue. He deserved a little compliance for once.

So, against his palm, she nodded. He let out a low hum of approval before stepping away. Not waiting for her to leave, he stalked to his bathroom.

She paused a moment to let the shaking in her legs subside. Once outside his room, she paused again and actually fanned herself. She scanned the hallway, not sure what the hell to do now. How could she just go lie down and fall asleep after that? Dragging her feet, she shuffled through her room and into her bathroom, where she used the foam shower.

She then stared out the window into the dark city of Sauven for a few minutes, mind still clouded with thoughts of her fake fiancé. Would he even want to hang out with her once they got to Tremanta?

Silently, she slipped into bed beside Meg and stared at the ceiling. An ache built in her chest the more she thought about not seeing him every day. *What if… No.* She couldn't think about what-ifs. The thing he treasured above everything else, what he'd worked his whole life to get, was his career. She wouldn't do anything to threaten that.

"Hey," Meg murmured groggily. "I fell asleep."

Alex chuckled and turned onto her side to face the woman. "Yeah, I noticed."

Eyes still closed, Meg waggled her eyebrows. "Did you and Auzed *hang out* after I left?"

"Hell yeah." She couldn't keep the goofy grin from her face.

"That's nice." Meg chuckled weakly. "It's so weird, 'cause at the Temple he was always so…professional. Always bossing everyone around and being all emotionless. Like a robot. I've never seen him smile like that before."

A lump formed in Alex's throat, but she swallowed it. It only now occurred to her how long Meg had known Auzed. She'd been living at the Pearl Temple in Tremanta for months, after all.

Emotionless. Was that how he'd treat her once they got to Tremanta? She supposed it made sense if his job required him to protect and look after everyone. He'd have to detach himself a bit to do that properly. How sad. Though still rare, Alex got a thrill every time he so much as quirked his lips at her.

"Tell me what it's like there," Alex said, shifting the topic away from Auzed. "How are the women getting along? Have they all accepted it?"

Meg creaked her lids open and shifted onto her back. "Mostly. There are a few women who are pits of despair. Naomi for one. She is just so angry all the time. Hannah did nothing but cry for, like, three months, but she finally got over that stage. Now she's in the fighting stage. She and a group of other humans have formed a type of human-rights thing. They're working with the Queen to get laws changed and stuff so they can go back home."

"What?" Alex said, shooting up into a sitting position. The rush of her blood pounded in her ears. *Home? They're trying to go back home?*

"Whoa," Meg breathed, gripping her head. "No fast movements, alright?"

"Do you think they can do it?"

"Eh." She shrugged. "Maybe eventually. From what I've heard, laws take ages to change, especially when it comes to something like this. All the planets within The Intergalactic Alliance would have to convene and agree that they should reveal the larger universe to the humans. Then they'd have to agree on how to do it. Yada yada. It sounded like it could happen, but I didn't pay a ton of attention. I don't want to leave."

There was something in Meg's voice at the end. It wasn't happiness. More like fear. Meg had told her her life on Earth hadn't been the greatest. She now wondered what exactly had happened. "You don't have any family you'd want to see again?"

Her full lips thinned, and her lids slid closed. "I guess that's an upside of being an antisocial orphan. No one to miss." She groaned and raised a hand to her forehead. "The room is spinning."

Alex winced. Poor girl was gonna be in pain tomorrow. "Need a bucket?" She chuckled.

"Do—" Meg shot to her feet and sped to the bathroom before she could finish her sentence.

Alex stared in front of her, unseeing. There were women and a freaking Queen fighting for the right to go back to Earth. Hope that she hadn't allowed herself to feel roared to life in her chest. What if someday, eventually she could go home?

19

No amount of jostling or urging could make Meg extricate herself from the bed the next morning. Alex and Auzed ate, dressed, and prepared for the second round of marriage games while Meg nursed her hangover, and Daunet, who'd shown up ready for day two of the games, lounged in the living room, reading.

Either Alex drank way too often or Meg was a lightweight because after a couple of hours, breakfast, and multiple glasses of water, Alex's mini hangover had all but disappeared. The games wouldn't be nearly as fun without Meg and Daunet, but excitement at having extended alone time with Auzed tempered her disappointment. Even if he looked like he'd spent the night tossing and turning.

"How'd you sleep?" she asked as they boarded a platform and made their way to the arena.

"With difficulty," he grumbled behind her.

Stepping back into his chest, she looked up at him and

gave an exaggerated pout. "Pobrecito," she crooned. "Maybe you should've let me stay, huh?"

His lips twitched, and he let out a low growl. "Careful, female, or I'll have to make you miss the game entirely."

"Maybe I wouldn't hate that." She turned in his arms, feeling more confident in her ability to balance on the transport platform these days.

Auzed raised a brow and gave her a crooked grin. "Hmm. We have to make an appearance, but perhaps we could sneak out early. Day two is not as exciting as one or three anyway."

"Yeah? What happens today?" She ran her hands over his tight sleeveless vest, smoothing the wrinkles that didn't exist as an excuse to touch him.

"Yesterday was a contest of strength and ability; today is intellect. It's never quite the same, but most of the time they're given problems of some kind and have to solve them. People usually have a favorite day of the games. Today is my brother Luka's favorite."

"That's interesting. Which day is your favorite?"

He looked at her funny as if it hadn't been an obvious question. "The third, I suppose. It combines a bit of everything."

"Tell me more about your other siblings?" Alex pried. Auzed always tensed up whenever she tried asking him personal questions. Apart from the few meaningful conversations they'd had about their parents, he consistently steered clear from talking about his personal life.

A clipped "There isn't much to tell" was all he said.

Alex gave him a small smile as she spun back around to hide the jab of pain in her chest. Although her feelings for him continued to grow, it seemed he wasn't allowing their relationship to become anything more than a temporary fling. And she needed to be okay with that.

Swells of people gliding by on platforms told her they were getting close. She turned and spotted Relli floating a few trees over. That initial surge of excitement at unexpectedly seeing someone you knew while out went through her, and she flapped her arms in the air, trying to get Relli's attention.

Alex lowered her arms. She'd see her tomorrow anyway. Relli had invited them to an afterparty at their nest. Though Relli hadn't seen her, she'd unfortunately drawn everyone else's gazes.

The rapt attention didn't lessen as they made their way in a slow circle around the arena. She recognized a few males who'd introduced themselves to her before. Did they think she wouldn't remember? Or were they just trying to introduce themselves again in the hope they'd recognize her?

Finally, her shoulders began to relax as they pushed their way through the crowd and found their sitting area, but what was waiting for them was somehow worse. Fierad reclined in the seat Alex usually took.

Glancing to Auzed, she caught the smoldering anger in his shocked expression a second before it was gone. His impassive countenance slid back in place, and he became immovable, stony Auzed once again. She could throw her shoe at Fierad for ruining Auzzy's good mood.

With a hand on her spine, he urged her forward. "Fierad," Auzed acknowledged politely, but she could just make out the sharp undercurrent to his tone.

"Ah," Fierad exclaimed, rising with a wide, toothy smile. "Wonderful." To her, he raised his tail in greeting. To Auzed, he remained still. *Asshole.* "I wanted to say hello before the games start."

Alex nodded with pursed lips, wary of whatever his true motives were.

He shot her a grin, and though Fierad was not unattractive, she found her insides squirming with unease all the same. There was something about his expression today. Some confidence he hadn't had before that registered in her mind and sent ice down her spine.

"How's the investigation going? Still convinced we're lying?" Alex asked in a monotone. She couldn't help it.

The flash of shock and then irritation on Fierad's face was worth the jab. Auzed placed a large palm on her shoulder, in essence saying, *Down, girl.* She shrugged it off and crossed her arms over her chest.

"We're tying up a few loose ends," he answered cryptically. "Most still have trouble believing you agreed to marry him after only a few days. That is, they have trouble believing you'd do it if you were given all the facts about our world and how it works. How long were you with Auzed before you agreed to marry him again?" Fierad asked, raising his brows and studying her face. He kept looking at her as if she were a confused little puppy who didn't really understand the things

235

that had happened to her.

She frowned. She'd been vague when she'd first lied; now he wanted a timeline.

"Three days," Auzed growled from her right, making her insides uncoil with relief.

"I was asking Alejandra." Fierad's tone scraped against her brain. Her palm itched to slap him, but Auzed only shrugged, unconcerned.

The wind instruments alerting the crowd that the game was starting soon sounded. "How much of our world did he explain to you before you agreed?"

"Enough for me to fully understand what I was agreeing to," she all but spat.

Fierad's brows crinkled in a way that told her he still thought of her as naïve and woefully misguided. "If you knew you'd have your choice of all the available males in the ceremony and that they'd be vying for you, why would you settle with him?"

She'd been peering toward the field, but upon hearing Fierad, her head snapped around so fast she almost cracked her neck. She felt Auzed shift behind her, and her heart constricted. How could a man like Auzed ever be considered anything less than drool-worthy? And how dare this hijo de puta insult him. "Excuse me? Did you mean to phrase it like that?" She cocked her hip out, gave him her most condescending stare, and waited.

"I… No, I—" Fierad stumbled over his words as he tried to decide whether to hold his high-and-mighty ground.

Before he could figure out what to say, she raised three fingers in the air in front of him. "How many fingers am I holding up?"

Fierad straightened. "Three. Why?"

"Oh good, I thought maybe you had trouble seeing." She shifted to the side so Fierad had a clear view of Auzed then gestured to him as if he were a prize on *The Price Is Right*. "Then use your damn eyeballs and answer your own question. Just look at him. Enough said."

No longer caring about what she should and shouldn't do, she reached out and laced her fingers through Auzed's. To her relief, he squeezed her palm and allowed their hands to remain clasped. She chanced a glance toward him and saw a small, smug grin tugging at his lips.

The odd melodious horn blew again, and as before, men streamed onto the field. The difference was this time, there were only ten men as opposed to the hundred from yesterday.

She turned back to Fierad and found his eyes had narrowed, becoming fiery and livid. He'd finally recognized her for what she was. Not a weak, confused alien in need of guidance and protection but a strong, outspoken woman who knew exactly what she wanted—not him.

Fierad tried to say something else to her, but she interrupted. "Have a nice game. My future husband and I would like some privacy."

His nostrils flared, and a look crossed over his face that made her pause. Was she being stupid for poking him and being so disrespectful? Maybe.

A booming voice sounded from all around and described the challenge of the day, but she couldn't concentrate on it.

Though Auzed had been reserved and infuriatingly polite throughout this exchange, he now stepped in front of her, his large body seeming even wider than it had before as he squared off. "She has requested you leave now," he said in a dangerous growl.

She peeked around Auzed's side and found Fierad had locked gazes with him. At length, he shot her a final glare and left.

When they settled into their seats, the men had already started doing whatever they were doing, and her ears were buzzing with anger. God, that guy was such an asshole. If he ruined the wonderful time she was hoping to have with Auzed…well, she had no clue what she'd do. Nothing most likely. But it would really suck.

Without having to ask, Auzed pulled up the screen she now knew was used to order food. Even though Fierad had soured her mood, she couldn't stop her lips from squirming into a grin. If she knew how to read in the odd language or what any foods were, she'd want to do her own ordering. But the fact that Auzed kept taking the initiative with things like this was so freaking sweet.

Deciding she wouldn't let Fierad ruin her day, she leaned forward and kissed Auzed on the cheek.

Over his shoulder, he glanced at her with lifted brows. "What was that for?"

Hefting her shoulders in a shrug, she shot him a wink. "I

have eyes."

Warmth seeped down her scalp when his chest bowed a bit and a confident grin spread over his face.

Focusing on the field again, she saw the ten men had been arranged in a circle, all on their own boards, and were typing into podiums in front of them. Some men were higher up than the others, and every time another man ascended, the crowds cheered. "What's going on here? I missed it because of Detective Douchebag."

"There are five rounds with ten players each. They have to solve riddles and answer questions." He pointed to lines of script on the screen in front of her, and she understood the audience was being shown the riddles too. "Their board ascends every time they get one right and descends if they get a question wrong. The first three to make it to the top will move on and join the males from the four remaining rounds of the day."

"That's exciting. I love riddles!" Alex chirped toward Auzed. "Read me one. Maybe I can solve it."

"Alright. What has six legs and can be seen but not when it is heard, and heard but not when it is seen?"

Alex scrunched her brows and thought for a few minutes while she watched two of the men stomp their feet as their boards lowered. Finally giving up, she said, "I have no idea."

"I believe the answer is a whistle gnat. Two of its antennae are commonly called legs, but they aren't really. It flies so fast that it emits a whistling sound and is invisible to the eye. When it stops flying, it no longer makes that sound and is visible. Clever."

She wrinkled her nose and nodded. "Yeah, I'm not going to be able to answer riddles about things on an alien planet, am I?" She chuckled.

Her body stiffened as one of the cameras that were broadcasting the game came to float by them. Between Fierad, the lack of privacy, and her inability to understand any of the riddles being asked to the players, she was ready to leave. Maybe they could go back to the market instead. She scanned the crowded arena. It was likely nothing was open right now, though.

The hovering camera zoomed toward them a bit. Auzed unlaced his fingers from hers and shifted ever so slightly away from her, his body growing hard the way it did whenever he was with her in public. He must've noticed her body immediately deflate because he leaned toward her and whispered, "How about we leave?"

She shot him a grateful smile, even as her insides twisted. She knew he hadn't meant to hurt her feelings by removing his hand from hers, but it was still a blow. After everything they'd been through together, he continually chose to act the way he thought Clecanians *should* act. It was true he'd been relaxing more and more when they were alone or around friends, but in public he still wanted to act the *right* way.

She hated and loved this trait. He had an internal code he followed, and although annoying, she couldn't help but respect him for sticking to what he believed. Even if it meant he'd ditch her when he resumed his role as head guard.

It was probably for the best that their relationship was temporary. Although she didn't mind his strict adherence to the rules now, she might grow to resent it in the future. Their personalities just couldn't work together long term, could they? Alex needed certain things from her partner, and physical touch was one of her love languages. That didn't stop just 'cause they were in front of other people.

Not to mention the Earth-shattering information she'd gotten from Meg last night. If there was even the slightest possibility that she could return to her family, she couldn't lead him on. His refusal to open up to her about his life confirmed he felt the same. He allowed himself to be free with her, but only to a point.

No. They'd never work. But she could still enjoy his company for now and then spend the rest of her life fantasizing about what could've been. Hell, maybe in a few years if she managed to get home, this would all feel like a distant memory.

She made her voice cheery as she spoke. "Let's wait to see Gosten, and then we can leave. Gotta show our support."

***

Lucky for Auzed, Gosten was in the next group of contestants. Though he wasn't the fastest to answer his questions, he was the most deliberate, only answering when he was sure he was right. As such, his progress to the top was slow, but he managed to stay ahead of most contenders.

Auzed glanced to Alex for the billionth time, or so it felt, and tried to interpret her mood. Ever since they'd sat down, she'd been off. Stiff and quiet. Had he done something to upset her? Or was she still on edge because of Fierad?

The visit from the Sauven guard had been infuriating but also enlightening. It seemed as though the male had no solid leads and was trying to coax some kind of admission from Alex, by pushing the theory that she'd been confused when she'd agreed to be with Zed.

Was it really so unthinkable that she might pick him? He ran his eyes over her, now grinning and cheering Gosten on, and an angry part of him acknowledged that it might be. She was so full of life. So carefree and warm and open. All the things he wasn't. He'd never even considered there could be more for him outside of a prestigious career and occasional sibling bonding.

What if he could convince her to actually marry him? He took a long gulp of his drink and internally shook himself. What was he even thinking? He loved his job. He didn't want to quit. Give up the only thing that had ever made him feel worthy. Besides, if he wasn't a head guard or a soldier, what could he even offer Alex?

Maybe he could convince her to see him casually. The brief sexual encounters some Clecanians had in between marriages weren't ideal, but he'd take what he could get.

His chest warmed and bowed at the memory of her defending him to Fierad. Perhaps she did think he was a fine choice. But was she giving him too much credit? He was a mixed-breed Clecanian with a bad temper, no friends, and few hobbies. Fierad was right. She only liked him now because she didn't understand there might be someone better for her. Someone who enjoyed plays and allowed themselves to drink and have a good time. Her mate. Whoever that may be.

She was deep in thought again, a line forming between her brows.

"Is everything alright?" he asked tentatively.

"Yeah. Just a little tired." Her gorgeous mouth curled into a weak smile, and he couldn't contain his frown. That fake, forced grin didn't look right on her. He wracked his brain for a way to rekindle the internal glow she always seemed to have and landed on a thought.

She clapped and hooted as Gosten became the second male to reach the finish, but that tightness remained around her mouth.

He stood and pulled her up with him. "Let's go. I want to show you something."

20

After a meandering ride through Sauven, they reached the edge of the city. A wooden booth placed against a large tree contained an unenthusiastic male youth. His eyes were focused on a live projection of the games they'd just departed. A yellow kinyberry jelly hung halfway out of his mouth. Auzed cleared his throat to get the kid's attention while Alex glanced around curiously.

He hadn't told her what he intended to do here yet, and so far, it looked rather mediocre. Just a ramshackle hut at the edge of the city.

The young male glanced up. "Hello. Are you wanting to rent..." His eyes locked onto Alex and then widened in recognition. Immediately straightening and smoothing his hands over his loose, rumpled vest, the male sputtered, "Uh. Do you want a sky lounger?"

Alex's lips quirked as she noticed the boy's sudden fascination with her. She gave him a wide, warm smile that made the male blush from the tips of his ears down to his scrawny chest. "I'm not sure. Gotta ask the big guy," she said, tipping her head toward Auzed.

The male darted his gaze between them and finally wheezed out his question to Auzed.

"Yes. Do you have a menu?" Zed asked, trying to keep the humor out of his voice. The poor lad was already embarrassed enough as it was.

"Oh! Uh…of course." He fumbled around the small space and handed Zed a small cube that projected a menu screen.

"You're a human."

While scrolling through the options, Zed heard the male utter the words under his breath as if he hadn't meant to say them aloud at all.

"How could you tell?" Alex joked.

He glanced back up after making his selections to find the male had gone as purple as his dark, spiky hair. Zed coughed to hide his chuckle and handed the screen back to the boy.

"I'll get this ready right away." He backed up and slipped a little before righting himself and exiting through a hole in the tree.

Alejandra's real smile was back in place when Zed peered at her, and his heart seemed to skip a beat. "Looks like teens are awkward on every planet."

"I'd probably have tripped over my own feet if I'd seen you at his age too."

His compliment was immediately rewarded with a flush stealing over her cheeks. He could feel the purr build in his chest, but he squashed it.

"So, what exactly is a sky lounger?"

Before he could answer, the young male returned, out of breath and sweaty. "It's coming around now. If you'll follow me to the lift." He stepped onto the narrow walkway between them and guided them to the back of the tree, where a rail-enclosed platform waited. "Please use this if you have any problems or need anything else. We've got a few males working up top today, but we weren't expecting any visitors until tonight, with the games and all." Eyes glued to Alex, he handed Zed a sleek communicator.

She made a show of slipping her arms around Zed's bicep as they lifted into the air and gave the young male a small wave goodbye. The poor kid looked reasonably shocked, his yellow eyes becoming as wide and round as Wilson's.

Alex giggled, and when the male was out of sight, she gave Zed a playful grin. Then, for some reason, her gaze became apologetic, and she stepped away from him. "Sorry. I couldn't help it."

It took him a moment to understand what she was referring to, then a light clicked on. She must think he still didn't want her to touch him in public. Though he hadn't told her about his change of heart outright, nothing could be further from the truth. Based on his adamant urging otherwise only a few days ago, he could see how she might not understand. How was she to know that nowadays he felt cold and on edge every second between the moments they touched?

He recalled how wrong it had felt to move away from her earlier at the game. Was that why she'd been acting so strangely? When the camera had focused on her, he'd put distance between them on instinct. Years of experience told him a female wouldn't want to be seen engaging in an intimate act like that in public. Especially not while being broadcast to so many. He hadn't given it a second thought at the time.

Wrapping his arm around her waist, he pulled her close. "You've converted me. If I had it my way, you would never stop touching me."

A grin tugged at her lips, and she gazed up at him with a suspicious raised brow. "Really? But at the game—"

"I thought it would make you uncomfortable."

She gave a quick snort. Her focus strayed to the treetops they were quickly approaching, and her brows knit. "How high are we going?"

"Topside."

Her gaze bounced between him and the underside of the tree canopy. "You mean we'll be able to see the sun and the sky? Is there nice weather today? Oh my God, I don't even care!" She let out a little squeal.

Satisfaction shot through his bones, heating him from the inside out. Never had he gotten such gratification from being the cause of someone's happiness.

As they neared the highest layer of dense tree canopy, they saw a beam of sunlight shining through a carved-out opening. Too bright to look at, they both had to shield their eyes while they passed through it. The sudden heat and white light all around told him they were now topside. He pressed Alex's head into his chest, not wanting her to attempt to open her eyes sooner than was necessary.

"Oh no! Did Rew forget to give you glasses?" called a gentle voice from next to them.

Zed listened as someone rustled through a drawer or maybe a bin. Alex bobbed up and down excitedly, and he grinned.

"Here you go." The male pushed some glasses into Zed's hands. He slipped his on, then put Alex's on for her.

When he opened his eyes, he saw a sea of endless treetops in every direction. The tiny white vinasy blossoms that grew on crawling vines blanketed the leaves of the trees. The heat from the fiery-orange afternoon sun baked the flowers and made the air sweet with their warm scent.

A short older male waved at them, drawing Alex's rapt attention. Her mouth was hanging open in the most adorably satisfying way.

"I have your lounger all ready to go." He gestured toward a large white floating platform outfitted with huge, cushioned sunbathing areas, a small stocked kitchen, and a perfectly round shallow pool.

Alex spotted the lounger and put a hand to her heart, grinning from ear to ear. "It looks like the front of one of those fancy yachts or something. We get to go hang out on that?"

Anxious to get her alone so they could enjoy their day away from prying eyes, he gently urged her to board the lounger. "Yes, we do. Just you and me."

He tipped his head to the older Sauven male dressed head to toe in a protective sun suit and took the control the male offered.

"Anywhere particular you'd like to be placed?" the male asked while sneaking glances at Alex, now exploring the cupboards of the lounger.

"Somewhere with a nice view. You choose."

The male nodded and, after a last lingering look at Alex, retreated into a shaded floating hut.

Alex had decided to wear a soft pink dress today. As she bent to search the various compartments around the lounger, the hem of her skirt lifted, and he couldn't bring himself to feel bad for ogling her.

Realizing that if he was being graced with this view, others were as well, he activated the upgraded privacy settings. The faint flash of a shimmering bubble all around them was the only indication that their privacy shield was in place. Now he could relax, knowing no one could hear or see them from outside the lounger.

"It's too bad there isn't any sunscreen," she said, digging through a compartment of towels set in the floor.

Zed's brows drew together. Maybe she didn't realize he'd activated the shield. "I have our screen up. Do you want me to increase the shade?"

Sitting back on her heels, she cocked her head at him. "We aren't speaking the same language right now. I'm looking for lotion to rub on my skin so I don't get a sunburn."

Zed used the controller to shade one half of the lounger. She gasped and shot her gaze around like a startled bird. "The shield we have around us does what you're describing. I have it set to fifty percent, which should prevent us from burning while still enjoying the light. I can leave half of the lounger shaded, if you want."

She jumped up, spread her arms wide, and lifted her face to the warmth of the sun. "No! I can hang out in the sun without worrying about anything? Amazing!"

With an exaggerated sigh, she collapsed onto a plush floor-level cushion as wide as a mattress. A faint breeze ruffled her dress, and her upper thighs came into view.

After a small lurch, the platform began to move, gliding into whichever spot the male had chosen. Alex propped herself up on her elbows and watched as they slowly floated over the treetops.

"Would you like a drink?" He tore his gaze away from the luscious curve of her thigh and opened the stocked refrigeration cabinet.

"Maybe just a juice or water. I drank a lot with Meg yesterday." She'd laid back down and draped a forearm over her eyes.

He set her water down next to her and retrieved two yubskanis for himself, downing the first in a matter of seconds. Auzed had decided he'd be having many today. He could relax, dammit, and he'd prove it. They had two days left together, and he was determined to try and have a good time. How long would it be before he had an opportunity like this again? A day of sunshine and laughter with a beautiful female who was interested in him? Never, that was when. He would *never* have another opportunity like this.

Wiping his mouth and allowing his mind to wonder how her delectable cunt would taste mixed with the sweet yubskani, he relaxed onto a cushioned chaise across from her. The view of her basking in the sun, her bronze skin shining in the rich afternoon light, was a vision he'd never forget.

As the first hints of alcohol hit his system and relaxed his muscles, he understood why some people enjoyed doing nothing.

Nothing, if done with the right person, was like a balm for the soul.

***

Alex had no idea how long they'd been floating before the incredible luxe lounger finally came to a stop, but when she looked up again, the view before her stole her breath. They'd traveled to the edge of the forest, and the shores of a vast turquoise ocean spread out before them. Small neon-green islands dotted the crystalline waters here and there. They seemed close, but it could've been an illusion. The sky was an electric blue, so bright it almost hurt to look at.

Replacing the bulky sunglasses she'd been given, Alex flipped to her stomach and rested her chin on her hands, gazing out past the glittering pool inset in the lounger to the ocean beyond. Too bad she hadn't brought a swimsuit. The sultry air was the perfect temperature for swimming. She lifted the amber-colored bottle Auzzy had placed next to her and blinked. It'd been sitting out with her for a while now but was still cold to the touch. Taking an experimental sip, she found the water inside was somehow icy despite the blazing sun shining down. Now there were magically always–cold water bottles too? Could this sky yacht get any cooler?

Alex grinned ear to ear and stretched like a cat in a beam of afternoon light. Her body felt heated from the inside out the way it did whenever she laid out at the beach. As if she were becoming one with the hot air around her. The sweet smell of the flowers below tickled her nose and reminded her of her favorite body oil back home. *Mmm, vanilla sugar.*

She glanced over to Auzed and caught him polishing off yet another yubskani. Was he trying to get drunk? Absently, she wondered what he'd be like when intoxicated. Quiet? Angry? Touchy-feely? Alex herself was a happy drunk and would talk the nearest person's ear off if given the opportunity.

"It's hot," he rumbled, standing and curling his fingers under his shirt with clear intent.

Alex took a preparatory breath to no avail. When he slipped off his shirt, revealing the flat planes of his chiseled chest glistening in the bright sunlight, the stifled gasp that rose to her lips clogged in her throat. Before she could recover from the vision of a half-naked demigod strutting before her, he began to undo his pants. Her brain stuttered off.

He turned away from her to take in the view, seemingly oblivious to her interest. Alex bit her lip and watched him slide the loose black pants down his hips, letting them pool by his ankles. The gorgeous and pronounced curve of his lower back led to his perfect muscular ass and then down to thick thighs.

He *was* hot. Both figuratively and literally. She could see the sheen of sweat running over the hard ridges of his back. *Bet if I touched him, he'd be slippery.*

Now completely naked, he stretched his bulky arms to the sky, his muscles coiling and bouncing with his movements until she couldn't take it anymore. If she didn't stop looking at him, she'd jump him right here in plain view of whoever passed by.

"Aren't you worried someone will see you?" she called with her head turned away toward the much-less-impressive view of her water bottle. The thudding of her heart picked up speed in time with his approaching vibrating footfalls. *Don't look. Don't look. Don't look.*

"I activated a privacy shield. No one can see…or hear…in here."

The way he let his purr linger on the word *hear* had her sex growing instantly hot. For some reason, though, she was frozen. Glued to the cushion, her heart racing in her chest and her mind swimming. Was it the right time?

She wanted Auzed. Even the recollection of his solid, naked body from a moment ago had her feeling far too empty in too many places. But a spike of fear took her by surprise.

Would sex change things? They were supposed to head to Tremanta the day after tomorrow. Since the beginning, she'd made sure to remind herself their flirtation was temporary. Somewhere along the way, she'd naively convinced herself that if she kept their expiration date in mind, her feelings for him would never blossom past the point of no return. But the way her heart was racing now had her questioning how effective her mindset had been.

"What's the first thing you're going to do when you get back to Tremanta?" she asked, both hoping and fearing the hint would push him away.

She started as heavy steps traveled past her head, then away from her. When she peeked through her lashes, she found he'd waded into the bright-blue of their pool and was splashing water over his broad, defined shoulders.

Alex bit her lip. God, this was torture. She forced herself to look away. Flipping to her back, she flung off her glasses and shut her eyes against the bright light. *There, now I can't look.*

"I'd like to see my siblings. I've only been gone for a week, but..."

It feels like a lifetime, Alex finished in her head.

A bubble of resentment that'd been festering left a bitter taste in her mouth. She may never see her sibling again. It wasn't Auzed's fault, but envy that he was about to return to his perfect life with his family and his job and all that was safe and familiar to him coursed through her all the same.

"If you could have anything from Earth right now, what would it be?" His question was obviously an attempt to shift to a lighter topic, and she didn't mind.

The fact that he could sense her unease without her having

to say a word wiped her sour thoughts from her mind and made boiled honey drip down her scalp.

"Mmm. A warm tortilla with butter. Best snack in the world. Or hot Cheetos. Or Sour Patch Kids. Or a million other things." She twirled her mother's ring around her finger. If she really could have anything from Earth, it would be a photo album, but she wasn't going to dampen the mood by giving a real answer.

"Chee-toh," he murmured experimentally from somewhere overhead.

The echo and ping of an empty glass hitting the pool edge hit her ears. Another yubskani down. Without thinking, she tilted her head back and shielded her eyes to look at him upside down. Big mistake. Big. Huge.

Auzed had sprawled himself on a shelf only covered with a few inches of water. He reclined perpendicularly to her on his elbows, the alcohol in his system making his posture lazy and pliant. The turquoise water lapped around the muscles lining his ribcage and highlighted the light, luminous color of his skin and the glittering markings curving and crossing all over his body.

With his head turned to her, he roved his gaze over her upturned face and down the neckline of her dress. Similarly, her attention latched on to the rigid length between his bent tree-trunk-sized legs. She licked her lips, remembering the feel of him in her mouth.

A low rumble from his chest told her he'd noticed, and like a shot, she looked away. He was far too appealing for his own good. A hard, protective Auzed was one thing. The rough-hewn stone he often encased himself in called to her and made her feel safe. But this relaxed, tenderized sun god with his wicked, curving grin and halo of light hair glowing golden in the sunlight was something else.

She imagined this version of Auzed would leisurely bury himself in her core, pumping in and out of her in unhurried strokes until the cloudless sky grew dark and became speckled with unfamiliar stars. Heat bloomed in her sex, making her clench her thighs together.

"Thank you for this," she said, stretching her arms overhead. Sweat had begun to bead on her forehead, but she knew what would happen if she got into that pool with him. "I didn't realize how much I missed the sun. I can't remember the last time I laid out like this."

It amazed Alex that her voice was as casual as she'd wanted it to be, when the thud of her heart and the pulsing between her legs clamored for focus. Awareness of him blanketed her mind, though she was no longer looking at him. How could a person be so turned on and so rattled at the same time?

The slow swish of water filled her ears, and she squeezed her eyes more tightly shut. The sound of dripping water echoed on the firm, glossy floor as loud as hail to her ears. They both knew where he was headed and what he wanted. Electricity crackled all around, prickling her scalp. She didn't even attempt to hide the panicked, shaky rise and fall of her chest. She let him see it.

The bright light shining on the other side of her lids

vanished, and she knew he was standing over her, blocking out the sun. Small drops of water splattered onto her exposed skin and sizzled off her heated body. All her senses were laser focused on Auzed. Without looking, she knew what he was doing. The shifting air currents between their bodies told her he'd knelt.

The scent of him—crisp from the cool pool water yet retaining that underlying spice that was all Auzed—grew stronger. A drop of water fell onto her neck and trailed along her collarbone; she swallowed thickly. The heat was suddenly oppressive. She couldn't seem to get enough air in. Was she even breathing?

When scorching lips coated in chilled pool water slanted over hers, she sucked in a ragged breath, filling her aching lungs. He parted his lips and slid his delicious tongue against hers, slow and sweet and deliberate, making her toes curl and a desperate whimper ring in her chest. He swallowed the sound, rasping a low moan of his own and taking her mouth with a greedy hunger.

Without releasing her lips, he shifted above her. A rough knee between her legs wrenched her thighs apart, and he settled himself on top of her. One of his large palms slid up her inner arm still raised above her head, and his thick fingers threaded through hers, stretching them wide.

His body weighed her down, and cool water seeped into her dress between them. Droplets from his hair trailed along her temples and jaw, making her shiver despite the heat radiating from his smooth skin. No longer hindered by rational thought, Alex came alive underneath him. Her legs wrapped around his waist, her dress riding up to her hips. His warm erection pulsed at her entrance still covered by her panties.

Giving in to this drugged lust may prove stupid in the long run, but she no longer cared. All she could feel was him worshipping her with his lips and his tongue. They were here together now. She was his, and he was hers. And she was greedy. She might not be able to keep him forever, but she could have this perfect day. She'd regret it more if she didn't give herself to him now than if she'd held back for the sake of her heart. A part of it was already his anyway.

21

∾

Alex moaned and rocked against him as he ran wet kisses over her neck. Each kiss seemed to be placed with intention and consideration, as if he knew exactly where to press his tongue and teeth to make her shiver with pleasure. He was so damn competent.

The only thing that kept her from feeling completely inadequate was the occasional tremor that ran through his body and left a growl rumbling in his throat. He was hanging on to his control, but just barely. Could she push him over the edge? Did she want to? His methodical teasing was so wonderfully powerful.

Inhaling a ragged breath, he lifted off her and jerked his chin at her torso. "Take off the dress. I don't trust myself to do it."

An electric bolt built in her nipples and shot down to her clit at his rasped command. She fumbled in her haste to get the dress off. When it was halfway over her head, he yanked the underwear off her bottom so forcefully she wouldn't be surprised if they'd ripped.

She'd just slipped the damp fabric off her shoulders when his mouth came down hot and heavy on her sex and his firm tongue lapped in time with his deep groan. Alex couldn't catch a breath between her surprised gasps of pleasure. Her hips twitched in time with the firm passes of his tongue as he drank her in. He pulled her against his mouth so tightly, his finger dug into the tops of her thighs as if he couldn't get enough of her taste. She'd have bruises there, but a wanton part of her craved them. She'd be able to look at them for days to come and remember him naked and devastating under the bright Sauven skies.

Eyes rolling back, she sagged, melting into a puddle on the floor, and gave in to the overwhelming sensation of Auzed between her thighs.

With every lick, he stoked the blaze burning within her. He growled against her and clutched at her hips, seemingly unhappy about something. In a move that rent the breath from her lungs, he expertly flipped their bodies so she was perched on her knees above him, her thighs on his shoulders while he lay flat on his back. A moment of insecurity at the vulnerable position gave her pause.

She'd never received oral sex in this position. Was he really sure he wanted this? She had her answer when he impatiently wrapped his forearms around her hips, hands plastered to her low belly, and buried his tongue inside her. A moan tore from her throat, and she had to drop onto her hands, unable to hold herself upright any longer. She rocked her core against his tongue, and he growled his approval while suckling her clit.

Removing one hand, he buried two fingers inside her, making her lurch forward. Her body trembled all over, and her vision blurred around the edges. Her orgasm, steadily building before, now thrummed just under the surface.

Blinding ecstasy sparked over her skin when he purred, the vibration shooting straight to her core. As her orgasm rolled through her, white hot and violent, she tried to keep herself lifted. Her forearms shook with the effort.

Auzed dragged his hands over her ass in a firm caress as she continued to shudder against his mouth. Finally, when the world came back into focus, her body finally melted. She angled forward so she wouldn't collapse on him and sprawled onto her stomach instead. Lids heavy and breaths coming out stuttered.

Behind her, Auzed flipped back to his knees and slid large, rough hands down her back, applying pressure as the heels of his palms dipped into the curve of her spine. He leaned over her limp form, his thick erection settling against her ass, and pressed a kiss to her ear. "I'll have you now, Alejandra," he rumbled, sending shivers down to her toes and a blast of liquid heat to her sex again. Her core clenched as if shouting its agreement for her, since she was a bit too slow on the uptake at the moment.

Beyond words, she nodded and tried to rise to her knees. With a firm hand on her shoulder and a thumb at her nape, he kept her in place. As if she hadn't just experienced the best orgasm of her life, her body revved to life once again.

***

Auzed positioned his knees on either side of her thighs and took a moment to drink in the sight before him. His throbbing cock, flushed and swollen from watching her take her pleasure, settled in the glorious cleft of her ass. Her taste still lingered in his mouth; her cries echoed in his ears. But her scent—her sweet, warm arousal wafting off her every time he touched her—did more to muddle his senses then the many yubskanis he'd gulped down.

She tried to watch him over her shoulder, her lids heavy and her pupils dilated with lust. When she arched her back, attempting to move again, he pressed her down to the ground of the lounger with one firm hand clasping her hip and one on her shoulder. If she kept doing that, he wouldn't last long at all. He needed to be in control of this.

He'd lick and stroke and master her body until not even the idea of another male sparked interest. Then she'd have to come back to him. Maybe he could convince her to refuse to participate in the marriage ceremony. She could go on seeing him in Tremanta, and he could have whatever bit of her he could get. It was beyond selfish, but he no longer cared.

No one mattered to him more than Alex, and at long last he agreed with the avaricious roars of his Traxian half. He ran his shaky fingers along the beautiful dip of her spine, and raw ferocity spread through him. She felt like she was his, though she wasn't.

He seemed to *matter* to her, though. Really matter. Her eyes lit when he entered a room. Her breath caught when he kissed her. She actively worked to make him smile. And he found himself doing the same. What more connection could there be between mates? He couldn't even imagine.

Unable to reach anything else, she wriggled underneath him and slipped her hand over the one pressed tight against her shoulder, making his chest tighten.

With his other hand, he gripped his length and positioned it between her soft, rounded thighs, locked together under his spread knees. Alex clasped his hand on her shoulder more tightly as he slid between her legs and prodded her entrance. He stilled, letting her feel just the tip of him. She released a frustrated sound and tilted her hips, trying to get closer.

Auzed grinned and remained poised in place. He needed her to be desperate for him. As desperate as he was for her. Slowly he angled over her and pressed an open-mouthed kiss between her shoulder blades, then pushed forward, sinking into the wet heat of her sex.

A low, prolonged moan from deep in her chest rode on her exhale and caressed his senses. With her legs tightly clamped together as they were, the sensation of his broad head inching into her was almost too much. Letting loose a ragged groan, he lifted to his haunches and clutched the swell of her hips, ensuring he buried himself fully.

Alex's delicate fingers were balled into fists on either side of her head, and small moans escaped her lips with each breath. Angling forward again, he planted his palms on her shoulders. Sprawled over her like this, his pelvis tight against her ass, their size disparity was obvious. Lifting to her forearms, she curled up toward him, arching her back, and peered up at his face hovering above. He gazed into her amber-flecked brown eyes and gripped her chin with his right hand. Gently he guided her up to his mouth and kissed her upside down, sucking and nibbling her bottom lip from their new position. She whimpered and rocked her hips as if needing him to move but trying to wait for his lead.

Her chin still held in his fingers, their mouths still locked together, he slid out a few inches, then surged back into her. The feel of her silky core gripping him, flooding with liquid, snapped a piece of his control. He thrust into her again, a little more forcefully this time. The shaky moan she released into his mouth told him she liked the strength behind his movements.

That was just it, though, wasn't it? She liked him for the good and bad. Liked the spikes of emotion and his rough hands on her body. He didn't have to shroud himself in layers of etiquette and convention when he was around her.

Suddenly, they weren't close enough. He needed to feel every quiver of her body as he fucked her.

Releasing her chin, he lowered onto his elbow and wrapped his forearm around her shoulders. She sank her head back against his chest and clutched his forearm, scratching his overheated skin with her nails as his hips pumped faster. He matched each of her cries with growls of his own.

They were both slick with sweat; his chest glided over her

exquisite curves as he thrust, keeping his rhythm steady and forceful. It wasn't difficult to slide his fingers under her slippery pelvis. He rubbed the pleasure center at her entrance with quick swipes of his fingers. The choked cry she made and the feel of her teeth biting down on his forearm made the slight pain on his wrist buried beneath their bodies worth it.

"Yes, Auzzy. Right there. Please."

Goddess, that name. Her name for him. For as long as he lived, she would be the only one to call him that. He buried his face in her hair, tightening his forearm around her shoulders until her chest lifted slightly. His body was stiff and livid, aching for release, but he kept it at bay somehow. Alejandra was so close.

Her heels between his legs lifted and pressed into his ass just as her body began to tremble. Breaths shaky and stilted, every muscle in her body clenched. He couldn't decide whether he wanted to fall with her or watch as his beautiful female came apart for him, writhing and crying out.

The choice was made for him when her inner walls clenched, her palm rose to wrap around his neck, and her orgasm pulled his own from him. They exploded together, shouting their noises of pleasure into the empty sky. His, a booming bellow as he pulsed into the depths of her clenching sex. And hers a strangled cry followed by a breathy sob as her hips undulated against his fingers.

He relaxed against her, his breath coming hard and fast. With effort, he kept his weight from crushing her completely. She trailed kisses along his forearm, pausing every so often to gulp in a shaky breath. A purr of pleasure and contentment rumbled through him.

She jumped, releasing a harsh cry.

"What's wrong?" Auzed immediately rose off her, hovering close enough to see where he'd hurt her. Pain lanced through his chest at the thought, and his hand shook as he tentatively brushed the hair from her face.

Her wide smile and light giggling made him boneless with relief, and he collapsed onto his back next to her, one hand across his chest. "You scared me!" he barked with a smile.

"I'm sorry." She grinned and all but dragged herself to him, spreading her arms over his chest. "When you purred, I felt it inside me. I wasn't expecting it, and I'm very sensitive down there at the moment."

"Ah," he breathed into the sky. "Good to know." The weather was hot, yet now that their bodies weren't pressed together, he felt the ghost of a chill. Threading his fingers through her hair, he pulled her scalp toward him and planted a long kiss on her temple, basking in the faint hint of his scent that lingered on her skin.

They lay there in silence, softly caressing every inch of each other they could reach. The sun was lower in the sky now, casting the world in a peachy-gold tone.

Her fingers strayed down his abdomen and then his thigh and paused on the portion of his marks that were blackened. "What happened here?" she whispered against his chest. Her gaze caught his, and he could make out the apprehension in their depths. She didn't think he'd answer her. It was personal, and he'd been struggling to keep at least part of his being away from this creature. But it was no use. She wanted it all and, even more terrifying, he wanted to give it all.

He slipped his fingers over her hand, his thumb rubbing her palm underneath, and gently massaged. "You remember what happened to my mother and my brother?"

Alejandra gulped; her brows raised in surprise. "Yeah, the war, right?"

The corner of his mouth twitched. She was so adorable when she was trying to be subtle. He made a small sound of agreement. "Like I told you, my brother's marks were scarred beyond repair and he became a different person. People stared at him and whispered about the way he looked, and I could see the way it hurt him, changed him. I tried everything I could think to help but nothing worked. One day I decided that if I couldn't make him feel better, at least I could suffer with him. I snuck into our bathroom and tried to burn myself with a cetr torch so he wouldn't feel so alone. I was only able to char a small portion of my marks in private before my father caught me."

Alex's hand froze on his thigh. Her gaze flashed from the blackened marks back to his face. "How old were you?"

He stroked her hair and thought, but the sympathy and compassion for him shining in her eyes made it difficult to recall anything. "Mm, twelve, I think."

Her jaw slackened a bit, and she shook her head. "Your internal compass always points to *hero*, doesn't it?" She covered the area with her palm and rested her chin on his chest again. "What did your brother say about it?"

"Nothing. I never told him. To this day, anyone who sees it just assumes it's an injury I got from my days in the military. My father was the only one who knew…and now you."

She swallowed again, and the flutter of her heart quickened where their chests met. Had her pulse sped because she was overwhelmed? Should he have kept the story to himself?

Inching up his body, she placed a soft, healing kiss on his mouth. Without much effort at all, considering their bodies were still slick, he tugged her on top of him and deepened the kiss, cradling her skull with his palm.

"Can we stay here forever?" She sighed and relaxed against him. "How long do we have this sex raft for anyway?"

Auzed chuckled, inhaling her scent and trying to ignore the press of her core to his abdomen. "As long as you want. At least until your dress is dry, though."

She pulled her head up and searched around them until she found the garment. With a mischievous grin, she rose and collected her dress. He watched the sway of her hips and the jiggle of her small breasts as she sauntered to the edge of the pool. The softening sunlight bounced off her warm brown skin and glittered against the water of the pool. He was beholding a damn goddess; he was sure of it.

A dark freckle under her right breast caught his attention, and he chided himself for not giving her front half as much attention as the rest of her. Perhaps she'd let him pleasure her again before they returned to the nest, and he could remedy the error.

Her eyes locked on his when she reached the pool. She lifted the dress between her pinched index finger and thumb, then released it. The fabric fanned out over the water before darkening and sinking. "Oops."

22

Just as Alex had predicted, she and Auzed lounged in the golden light of the setting sun until faint stars twinkled in the lavender sky. He took his time learning her body, his hands roaming brazenly over her skin. Though she'd been pulsing with need for a while now, he hadn't pushed her any further.

She could tell he wanted her again. If his swollen erection didn't express it, then the blazing heat warming his pale-green eyes did. But he only stroked her body, occasionally focusing on one thing or another. A beauty mark here. The red imprint of his fingers on her hips there.

It was as if he were attempting to record every detail in his mind. *Because we'll be going our separate ways so soon?* Her heart fractured at the idea.

He was the sexiest man she'd ever met, but as she lay in the twilight examining her own reactions to him, she understood this clawing need was more than just lust. More than a need to have sex with the drop-dead gorgeous alien who made her see stars.

She wanted to bare herself to him and have him bare himself in return. No humor and lightness hiding the depth of her emotion. No thick armor hiding his. She wanted to *make love* to Auzed. She'd never craved that intimacy before and couldn't imagine ever wanting it with anyone else.

But she couldn't ask him to give up his life for her. It wouldn't be fair to him. Especially since she didn't know what she wanted for her future anyway. Last night, when she couldn't sleep through Meg's snoring, she'd called Lily.

They'd talked about so many things, including the fact that Lily had fallen head over heels for an alien of her own. Her mate, Verakko.

Lily, so closed off and impenetrable when they'd first met, radiated with warmth through the communicator. No doubts. No reservations about staying here forever with one man, who'd die before letting her go.

But Lily also didn't *want* to return to Earth. She had no one there worrying about her and wondering where she'd gone.

Alex's family, on the other hand, were probably putting up posters and searching for her even now. Which would be futile. Alex could just picture her tiny abuelita cursing out the police when the leads inevitably dried up.

And what if they ended up blaming some innocent person for her disappearance? What if they blamed Ray, her boyfriend—ex-boyfriend now. He was no catch, but Ray wouldn't lay a finger on her. He didn't deserve the scrutiny he was likely getting.

How could she just leave them all to suffer without at least trying to get back? She wished she could live two lives. One back on Earth surrounded by familiarity and family, and one here with Auzed.

She glanced down at his fingers, now lovingly circling the freckle on her ribcage near her breast. No marks lined those hands. He wasn't her mate. With her gaze, she traced the hard line of his jaw and the steady pulse thrumming along his corded neck. His eyes, pale green and framed by golden lashes, were so soft in comparison to the rest of him.

But no matter how alluring he was, they weren't spiritually bound for all time. A part of her was relieved about that. If his marks *had* appeared, she'd be trapped here. From what he'd told her, the consequences of abandoning a mate were dire. She could never...*would* never put him through that.

No. She couldn't ask him to give up everything he held dear just to watch her fight to return home. To leave him. She had to let him go.

The tenuous cord keeping her heart bound in her chest would surely snap when they finally separated, and he'd end up taking more of her along with him than he knew.

But it wasn't that time yet. And since her heart would be broken either way, there was no sense in holding back. His eyes widened when she drew up and planted a long kiss on his lips. His mouth split into a lopsided grin before he folded his heavy arms around her and turned their kiss into something scalding.

***

After a few more lazy hours basking in each other's company, the chill of the night air finally pushed them to return the lounger and venture back to the nest. So unlike their first few days here, Auzed remained glued to Alex's side, always touching her.

Any reservations he'd had before had dissolved in the wake of their intense day in the sun. When he wanted to smell her hair, he leaned down and buried his face in her waves. When the mere inch that separated them felt too distant, he'd pull her into his body, rejoicing in the immediate sigh she always released before leaning back against his chest.

Clecanian couples never did this, and he now truly understood why. It was addictive. Being able to reach out and feel your female in your arms whenever you wanted was like a drug. How would he manage going back to being alone?

"I'm exhausted." She yawned while halfheartedly covering her mouth with the back of her hand.

Auzed grinned, something he was having trouble *not* doing today. He bent his head to her ear, taking one hand off the bar of their travel platform to brush her hair away from her neck. "I'm not done with you yet, female."

The shiver that ran through her at his words sent a rush of blood to his cock. He rumbled a laugh and squeezed her against him more firmly, showing her what he was referencing. When they floated alongside the deck of the nest, Wilson was waiting for them.

She tooted her trunk as they approached, but the sound

was different than the normal trumpets of annoyance she made. They stepped into the nest and Wilson followed, wrapping her body around Alex's neck in an embrace. Then before he knew it, Wilson was scrambling toward him.

She pounced at his leg, and Auzed tensed for the attack. Alex would never forgive him if he hurt the creature, even if it had struck first. All he could do was brace for the sting of teeth and claws. But when he looked down, he saw the tuey had wrapped her little body around his ankle and was giving him a tight squeeze of greeting as well.

He remained frozen with his leg planted forward awkwardly. Looking up, he found Alex had pulled her lips between her teeth to keep the broad, teasing smile from her face.

His own mouth twitched. "Stop it. I thought she was going to claw me or something for taking you away all day."

"Oh, Auzzy. Were you afraid of little Wilson Phillips here?"

Wilson finished her affectionate assault and scampered out of sight.

"She's bonded to me, right?" Alex crooned, the tone drawing his focus in a snap. She stepped forward and gripped his hand, pulling him toward the lift. "Well, she can probably sense how happy you made me today."

Her bright smile was radiant, lighting him inside and out in her glow. She didn't belong here in the dark underbelly of Sauven. She belonged in the sun, where the world shone as brightly as she did.

His purr built in his chest, and he waggled his brows. "Give me some more time, and I bet I could become her new favorite person."

Alex burst out in melodic laughter. It rang through his chest, bolstering the intensity of his purr. He pulled her against him and took her mouth in a fierce kiss as they rode to the second floor and shuffled clumsily into her room.

She gasped when he gripped her around the waist and tossed her onto the bed, tearing off his shirt before she hit the mattress. She giggled as she bounced and tugged her dress overhead. He'd just spent hours admiring her naked body, but he still couldn't get enough.

He worked on the fastenings of his pants and internally thanked the Goddess for every square inch of her he beheld. Sliding off her underwear, she laid back, grinning and completely bared to him. That damn tightness squeezed around his chest again. Heat prickled down from his scalp to his shoulders at the sight of her wantonly parting her knees. A challenge glinted in her eyes.

Kicking off his pants, he braced his legs apart at the foot of the bed and took himself in hand, enjoying the view and the quick dilation of her pupils as she watched him stroke himself. Her small breasts, tipped with dark-brown nipples, jiggled as she took in a shaky breath. "Come here," she demanded.

His foot twitched to obey despite himself, but he stayed his feet.

She frowned, letting out a huff to show her frustration.

Four thin tree trunks rose to the ceiling at each corner of her bed, acting as bedposts. Reaching for the two at the foot of her bed, he wrapped his palms around them and waited, an unspoken challenge.

Never could he do this with a Clecanian female. If he was asked to give pleasure and refused, demanding his own instead? Well, it wouldn't turn out well for him. But Alex was not Clecanian. A fact he couldn't imagine ever despairing over.

She smirked at him, and her mind behind her lovely brown eyes worked, deciding whether or not to submit. Then finally, she lifted onto her knees and crawled toward him, holding eye contact as her body swayed side to side in time with her progress. He watched her inch closer with rapt focus. His heart bashed against his chest, and blood pulsed through his raised arms and his shaft.

Lifting onto her knees on the bed before him, she gazed up. "You think you're real slick, don't you?"

He rumbled a chuckle and bent his head until their breaths mingled. "Not *slick* yet, gorgeous."

She tried to smother it, but the grin that broke out over her face at the innuendo was too powerful. He loved that he could bring it out.

From his standing position, her eyes only reached his chest. She scooted a bit closer, purposefully brushing the head of his stiff cock over her low belly and causing him to hiss in a breath.

A hint of his precum glistened on her skin, and his grip

tightened on the trunks. The posts had been great for showing off his cocky, relaxed stance, but now they were the only things holding him back from forgetting their game and pouncing on her.

Lifting her palms, she ran them over his chest, brushing his nipple with her pinky finger. He sucked in a breath and exhaled, his purr mixing with a growl. Her lips quirked. She let her palms wrap around his back and pulled herself closer to him, trailing soft kisses along his pecs and down his stomach.

She gave a short groan of appreciation when she reached his abs, kissing each one in turn and spreading her knees wide to get lower. By the time she licked the blackened portion of his markings on his thigh, he was all but gasping for air. Maybe this had been a bad idea; he was going to explode as soon as she breathed on his cock at this rate.

As if she knew exactly what she was doing to him, she paused and caught his gaze. With a small grin, she took him into her mouth. The buck of his hips was unexpected, as was the string of curses he let out at the feel of her tongue swirling around his head.

His arms began to shake with the effort not to crush the trees under his hands into pulp, but he couldn't look away. Her dark brown hair fell in waves over her back, and her lashes were lowered, her cheeks hollowing as she sucked him deeper into her mouth. His fingers itched to bury themselves in her hair and feel the rocking of her head back and forth, but he didn't trust himself not to squeeze too tightly.

When her hands reached farther around his back and her nails sank into each side of his ass, he knew she had to stop. Like lightning, his hand shot down and speared into her hair just like he'd imagined, but instead of feeling her move on him, he tugged her away.

She released him with a pop, breathing hard. Color burnished her cheeks and chest all the way down to her nipples. Gripping her hair a little tighter at her skull, he angled her gaze to meet his. She flashed him a grin. "You taste like sunshine."

A harsh groan exploded out of him, and his mouth descended on hers with enough force to push them both into the soft mattress. He needed to be inside her, now. Snaking his hand between their bodies, he swirled his fingers around her core and moaned to find her already dripping and ready for him.

He sat up and grasped her hips, ready to flip her over, but she stilled him with a hand to his wrist. "No. Let's stay this way."

Confusion wracked his lust-dazed mind for a moment. "Really?"

She propped herself up on her arm and ran a thumb along his jaw, seeming entranced by it. Her brows drew together. "Yeah. Why? Don't want to look at my face while we do it?" She played it off like a joke, but he could see the flash of insecurity behind the question.

Gripping her face with both his hands, he caught her gaze. "If I could only look at one thing as I lay dying, it'd be your face." She rolled her eyes and grinned, clearly taking his heartfelt and very serious comment as an exaggeration. It was probably better if she thought of it that way, so he didn't correct her. "I've just never had sex this way before."

Her hand stilled while tracing the shell of his ear, and her eyes widened in shock. "Never?"

Heat raced up his neck, and the urge to explain away his inexperience flared. "Clecanian females have pleasure centers deep inside, not outside. The easiest way to reach it is from behind."

Understanding relaxed her expression back into serene arousal. "Oh. Well then…" She laid back, crossing her arms above her head and stretching. Lifting one leg and then the other, she draped them over his thighs, then scooched forward until he was poised at her entrance. "It's about time I blew your mind."

He barked out a laugh. She preened at the sound. His mind had been blown by her since that first day in the forest when she'd kissed him.

Rather than pushing into her right away, he remained on his haunches, admiring the view. He let his palms slide along her thighs and then higher, watching as her nipples pebbled into hard points and the flush returned to her chest. Covering one breast with his palm, he dipped his head to the other one. The small freckle on her ribcage called to him, so he bent and kissed it, nuzzling the underside of her breast along the way.

With patience he didn't know he had, he pressed into her core, tight and wet for him. She let out a moan of pleasure and buried her hand in his hair. Her grip tightened when he suckled her nipple into his mouth and swirled his tongue. She arched her back up to him so sweetly, rocking her hips to help bury him deeper.

When he was seated fully, he grazed his teeth over the side of her breast, nipping gently before moving to the other side. To keep her from writhing on his shaft any harder, he settled his weight on her, trapping her hips under his. But it didn't have the intended effect. Her cry only intensified, and he realized with a wide grin that in this position, the small pleasure center at her opening had direct contact with his body. No wonder she liked it.

He pulled away and then thrust back into her, curling his hips until she shuddered. He was propped on his elbows, her face below him. She beamed at him, and something shifted in his chest. The smile playing at his lips faded, and he stilled.

Alex's gaze grew concerned. Lowering to his forearms on either side of her shoulders, he framed her head with his hands and ran his gaze over her face, needing to look at her. Needing *her* to look at *him*. A wave of some astonishing emotion rocked him, but it took a moment to identify. It was love.

The feeling had always been there, just under the surface, yet something about this moment had caused it to roar to the forefront, no longer content to be ignored.

She must've seen it in his eyes because her grin faded too. They gazed at each other. Warmth and passion and tenderness sparking between them and turning the joining of their bodies into something…more.

He kissed her, a deep, slow kiss that had his throat tightening. Clutching at his neck, she kissed him back and wrapped her legs around his waist, pulling him closer. At length, he drew out of her and began rocking into her with slow thrusts, angling his hips so the pressure never left her pleasure center.

The purr that broke from his chest was deep and resonate. She whimpered into his mouth and shuddered underneath him, her orgasm already so close. Her body stilled, and her lips parted against his on an inhaled breath. The rocking motion of his hips became rougher as he felt her muscles clench around him. He gazed down at her, not daring to blink. Her eyes were squeezed shut, and her brows were drawn together in an expression that almost looked like pain.

Then her lids flashed open, and she cried out, holding onto his back, her nails scoring a path down his spine. His shaft swelled inside her, the convulsions of her core too much for him to take. Slamming into her with his head buried against her cheek, he quickly found his own release. He roared against her hair as he came, pulsing inside her.

His chest heaved against her breasts, and he kissed each of her closed eyes. Then her cheeks, her temples, the lines around her mouth. And finally, her lips.

After a while, when their breathing settled, he rose from the bed and retrieved a cloth. She grinned at him with sleep already glazing her eyes as he cleaned them both up, like she'd never seen anything sweeter. Climbing into bed, he pulled her against his chest and extinguished the overhead light.

He wasn't sure if this was how humans slept when they shared beds, but it was what he wanted. Her skin on his. The thrum of her pulse on his fingers circling her wrist.

He breathed in her scent and stared into the dark room. Whatever had just happened to him was indelible.

His career, his reputation. Did any of it matter to him as much as Alex did? The answer was clear. Her breathing deepened, and a surge of pride melted his bones, knowing she felt safe enough to fall asleep in his arms. That she *wanted* to fall asleep in his arms.

Movement was out of the question at the moment, but tomorrow he'd call his Queen. If sacrificing his job was what it took to be with Alex, he'd do it.

Deeper introspection gave him pause. He'd do it, sacrifice the life he'd grown used to…but only if it meant forever. He'd need to convince her to become a demskiv. To be shunned and sneered at by most of the Clecanian population for the rest of their lives.

He'd be treated even worse. Not only would he be considered a male who'd stolen a female away but one who'd stolen a human, someone else's potential mate. Unless she turned out to be his. But that was unlikely. Some sign of recognition should've shown up already. Still…it wasn't impossible.

The rush of emotion he'd experienced a few minutes ago felt like the mating pull—at least he assumed it did, but no marks covered his hands and his eyes hadn't changed. Alex would've told him if they had. She knew the importance.

What if he quit and she agreed to be with him, and then someone else recognized her? His arms, wrapped around her body, squeezed too tightly, and she squeaked. He loosened his grip, but the dread boiling in his gut didn't abate. Doubt rolled in.

He couldn't do this with her. Not if it wasn't forever. He could already see it now. What would the Traxian half of him do if another male came along, attempting to steal her away after they'd been together for months, years, decades? She could be recognized at any time.

And even if it never happened, if no one ever recognized her, he'd always be looking over his shoulder. Hiding her from view and urging her to stay inside, out of sight and scent of everyone else. What kind of life would that be for either of them?

Alex, so full of life and adventure, would grow to despise him if he cloistered her away. But what else could he do?

Let her go?

23

"Alex, wake up."

Gentle fingers brushed the hair off her face and traced a line down her back. Pleasurable goose bumps raced over her skin. She kept her eyes closed, hoping he'd do it again.

She was rewarded with a soft kiss to her bare shoulder.

"We slept through the morning. If you want to watch the last round of the games, you need to get up."

With a deep groan of indecision, Alex stretched her arms, still sprawled facedown on the warm mattress. She grinned; it smelled like him. "Okay, I'm up," she said without rising.

"I made breakfast," Auzed rumbled from above her, pressing another soft kiss to her shoulder before lifting off the bed.

She heard him walk out of the room and forced her eyes open. If she didn't, she'd accidentally drift back to sleep. Her body was stiff and sore yet boneless with satisfaction at the same time. They'd made love long into the night and few times in the early morning as well.

He was just too much. Too good. Too sexy. Too honorable. She'd already started wondering if it would be possible to see him every day and not be reduced to a sobbing puddle of tears and hormones. He was the head guard at the place she was expected to live after all. That wouldn't do. She wouldn't be able to look at the man she loved day after day and not have a breakdown.

She'd need to find somewhere else to live. Maybe a nice apartment—if those existed here—with a few of the other humans who wanted to get back to Earth. If it really proved to be too unbearable, she could always look into moving to another city. One where the marriage laws were similar to Tremanta and she could choose to remain single. No one would ever compare to Auzed. She was sure of it. He'd ruined her for all other men.

With a sigh, she rose and got ready. Love, fear, guilt, frustration, confusion. They all churned in her belly, creating waves. The warmth of love would crash through her and she'd feel lighter than air one moment, then a tide of heartache would wash the warmth away, leaving stark loneliness.

The only thing she could think to do at the moment was ignore it. As she ventured to the first floor and found Auzed exercising on the deck with Wilson rolling around his body as if his one-handed push-ups were the best type of game, she knew it'd be impossible.

After a hurried breakfast alone while Auzed cleaned off and dressed, they set out on their way to the final round of the marriage games. He held her close as they glided toward the arena, making her pulse quicken with awareness. At least Meg would be with them again today to help distract her.

Because they were late, their daily walk around the arena was more of a jog. She politely greeted everyone who came toward her, but, with a quick apology about the time, she forced each suitor to all but power walk alongside her if they wanted to say more than a sentence.

When they reached the entrance to their seating area, Alex was surprised to find Meg and Daunet hadn't arrived yet either.

Her shorts rode up as she settled into their familiar seats. She'd worn the white silky two-piece set she'd mistaken for pajamas their first night here. Auzed wore bright-blue pants and a tight vest of the same color that dipped low on his chest and exposed his magnificent body, now tinted with a hint of color from their day on the lounger.

The electric blue of his clothing reminded her of the cloudless sky from yesterday. Her body heated as other memories assailed her. He stilled, then turned to her with a raised brow and flaring nostrils.

"If there weren't cameras watching your every move, I'd take care of that need for you. But since I cannot, I'd kindly ask that you control yourself, female." He shot her a wolfish grin, flashing white teeth, and she blushed. She kept forgetting he could smell her arousal.

Crossing her legs to camouflage the scent, she reached over and slipped her hand into his. He squeezed her palm and purred.

"Who we rooting for today?" Meg cheered, skipping toward them with her hands raised.

Daunet sauntered behind Meg and shook her head in amusement. "This human never settles."

Both women relaxed into seats next to them. Daunet was wearing an outfit similar to Alex's, except hers was a butter yellow that enhanced the beauty of her pastel pink hair and pale skin. Meg, on the other hand, looked stunning in a fluorescent-pink dress that flowed around her shapely hips and chest.

Alex glanced around the whole stadium and saw that the bright neon colors were typical for the last game of the year. Auzed had explained it had something to do with old traditions involving games being played in relative darkness back on the old world. Bright colors were easier to see in the dim forest.

"Gosten is still in the game, so we're rooting for him," Alex called.

"Ooh, nice. What about enormous Sparta man?"

"Him too." Alex grinned, recalling how enthralled they'd both been with the large brute who'd bowled through opponents that first day.

Auzed's grip on her hand tightened a fraction and lines appeared around his mouth as he contained a frown. Her chest expanded at the slight show of restrained jealousy. She didn't particularly gravitate toward jealous men, but in her mind, there was nothing wrong with a person getting a bit peeved when their partner showed interest in someone else.

She ran a soothing hand along his forearm, and his shoulders relaxed. He shot her a quick look that said, *You're killing me.*

"The Queen allowed you to be off duty?" he asked Daunet.

She grinned. "Yeah. I'm not going to relax completely, but she made it clear that my trip here with Meg was more of a test run than strict guard duty."

"Test run?" Alex questioned loudly above the sound of horns announcing the game was soon to start.

Meg leaned forward in her seat and beamed. "Yeah! A while ago, the Queen announced she wanted to send a few humans out traveling so the rest of the Clecanians could get to know more about us. Not many wanted to sign up, but—"

"But of course *you* did." Alex chortled.

Meg rolled her eyes in exasperation. "It's an all-expense paid trip around the world, where I get to meet new people and be fawned over. *Of course* I signed up! I was the *first* to sign up, and I've been nagging the Queen's aid, Metli, about it ever since. I wouldn't be surprised if the trip was finally approved because Metli threatened to murder me otherwise." Meg chuckled.

Daunet chimed in. "The Queen wants each female to have a chaperone. I'll be able to enjoy my time as well, but I'll need to keep an eye on her. Explain customs and money and help keep the suitors at bay."

"Oh yeah, that's right," Alex said, her brows knitting together. Meg sought to enjoy life in whatever ways she could, and that included lots of talking and drinking…and flirting. How was that going to work with the reserved cultural norms of this planet? "Aren't you worried some person will recognize you as a mate? I'm sure that's half the reason they're sending you out at all. They probably assume it'll happen."

She let out a breath. "Not really… I wouldn't say I'm soul-mate material." At first, Alex assumed Meg meant she wasn't cut out for long-term relationships because she preferred the single life, but the brief glint of insecurity shining in the woman's eyes had Alex questioning that assumption. Did Meg think she was undeserving of a soul mate?

Before Alex could question her, Meg eyed Daunet and said, "But just in case, we're working on a plan to deal with that little inconvenience."

Daunet's expression went sour, her lips pursing. "*You* are working on a plan. I want no part in it."

Meg waved her away. "It'll probably be fine anyway, though, 'cause from what I've learned, all the couples were mated after spending a bunch of time together. Ipso facto, I limit my dalliances to one night—" she clapped her hands together as if performing a magic trick, "no marks!"

Alex shook her head. Meg was going to leave a wake of heartbroken Clecanians wherever she went.

Daunet leaned back in her seat and crossed her arms.

"That is not how things are done here."

Auzed turned to Alex and smirked at the comment. He'd said almost precisely the same thing to her countless times. She narrowed her eyes at him and stuck out her tongue.

Meg continued to argue with Daunet as if they'd discussed this many times over already. "Well, the reason I'm going around the world is to show everyone how humans do things, right? Are you—" Horns, louder than normal, blared through the arena, cutting her off, so she shouted over the noise and continued, "Are you going to be a buzzkill for the entire—"

Meg and Alex screamed as the seating suddenly dropped. She clamped onto Auzed, holding on for dear life. When she heard the warm rumble of his laugh, loud and hearty, she opened her eyes.

The seating was indeed moving downward, but it appeared only she and Meg had been surprised by it. She caught sight of Meg, and laughter wheezed out of her. Meg's arms were spread wide, one hand gripping the table in front of her and the other hand clawing Daunet's forearm. The look on her face was not dissimilar from that of a cat being scared by a cucumber.

Face pale and eyes bulging, her gaze flashed to Alex now clutching her sides. "Not. Funny."

Alex shook her head and covered her mouth with her hand but could not form any words through her laughter.

Meg leaned back in her seat, a small chuckle escaping past her resolutely annoyed expression.

"You could've warned us," Alex said when her laughter

finally fizzled out.

Daunet and Auzed grinned at each other. "Where would be the fun in that?"

"What's going on anyway?" Meg said through tight lips.

As they'd descended, a column of ropes, platforms, and various items Alex couldn't identify came into focus and stretched up toward a large golden ring the size of a semi-truck.

"The third round is an obstacle course. Competitors start on the ground and have to climb to the top. Whoever makes it first wins the most points."

"Whoever has the biggest arms, you mean? For the climbing?" Meg muttered, leaning over the rail to get a better look at the lower section of the obstacle course.

"Not necessarily," Daunet replied while fiddling with the view on her screen. "There are traps and mental obstacles you have to complete along the way. Some platforms require you solve a puzzle to move them. Some ropes are not attached as securely. The course is meant to be a test of both strength and intelligence."

Without asking, Auzed brought Gosten up on their screen.

Alex pouted. "Aw, he looks nervous."

The massive sections of seating came to a halt near the bottom of the forest, where the competitors crouched, waiting for the signal to start. The air was thicker down here. Cooler but heavier too. And the herbal smell of lush foliage and dew was more concentrated than it was in the high city.

It was odd being so low to the ground, not seeing the

emptiness below and above. After spending a week in the treetops of Sauven, it felt almost claustrophobic to have the impenetrable ground so close.

Alex searched the faces of the men, all ready and waiting, and found Gosten hovering near the far side of the stadium. It was difficult to see him between all the items hanging along the course, but she could make him out.

"Ooh, there's Hulk." Meg sighed, pointing to the large man they'd gushed over earlier. She propped her hand on her chin. "I bet he wins."

"Not likely," Auzed said without malice but like there was something he knew that they didn't.

"Why not?"

"The competitor listing says he's competing for eligibility." When both humans shot him confused glances, he went on. "It means he got into trouble and his marriage eligibility was taken away. If the crime was minor enough and the allotted time has passed, some males can petition to compete for reinstatement of their eligibility. But they rarely win. The other competitors are expected to try to knock him out—sabotage him if they can."

Meg's wide eyes turned back toward the man, and she grinned dreamily. "So, he's a bad boy on top of everything else? I might not want to marry him, but I could definitely make him feel better if he loses."

A sharp blast sounded, and the men all jumped into action, leaping superhuman distances to snatch the hanging ropes. The men who were smart grabbed multiple ropes, but a few only grabbed one. Just one rope proved to be a phony, though. The man holding it roared as it snapped free. He fell, shouting obscenities as an invisible net caught him.

Just as Auzed had said, a group of five began swinging in a coordinated attack against the solitary giant, who was attempting to dodge his way past flashing tails and legs aiming to knock him off. Meg and Alex both stood and booed.

Luckily, Gosten didn't seem to be interested in knocking out any other player. He was slowly but carefully jumping from rope to nearby platform to hanging bar, his actions as calculated as they'd been in the last round.

He leapt for a bar and missed, falling in midair. She let out a gasp, her heart fluttering to a stop as he fell. With his tail and a flailing palm, he caught a nearby rope and slid for a few feet before coming to a halt, his teeth clenched. She hissed. The insides of his palm and tail would be raw.

She hadn't realized how tightly she'd been gripping Auzed's hand until he tugged his fingers out of hers with a chuckle. He shook out his hand with an exaggerated wince of pain. She slapped at his arm and rolled her eyes.

"Careful. I need that hand for other things," he whispered into her hair while wrapping an arm around her shoulders and pulling her against him.

She caught Meg's joyous gaze and grinned when the woman gave her a ridiculously nerdy thumbs-up.

The seats in the arena rose in time with the climbing men in order to keep them in view. One by one, the competitors fell until ten remained. Unfortunately, under the pressure of four against one, the large hulking male had finally been knocked out. The roar he released rattled the audience, and some spectators applauded his ferocity even though he'd lost.

They were only a few feet from the golden ring now, and a lanky forest-green man with an exceptionally long tail was in the lead. Gosten was second.

"If Thren gets to the top first, he'll win," Daunet said, leaning in toward her and Meg and staring at the lanky man. "He has enough points that the bump in score would put him far in the lead."

The other six men had been delayed below, trying to work out a projected puzzle not unlike an Earth Rubik's Cube.

The lanky man paused when he reached the top of the attached ropes. They ended short of the golden ring. In their place were two shining metal hoops spaced too far apart to be of any use.

Everyone in the crowd seemed to lean forward as the lanky man in the lead tensed to jump. He sprung toward the hoop, airborne, and the crowd sucked in a collective inhale. He'd never reach it.

At the last second, he flipped in midair, catching the hoop with his tail. Using the momentum of his swing, he propelled himself up toward the final hoop. With an unnecessary flourish, he flipped onto the stage above the golden ring and raised his arms in triumph, taking in the booming cheers that thundered all around him.

A loud jangling sounded from the crowd rather than applause, and Alex looked around to find the source. The

Sauvenians, now on their feet, had begun to swish their tails rapidly like rattlesnakes, creating a cacophony of jingles from the rings circling them.

From a pocket under the table, Auzed pulled out a collection of gold rings bound by a leather rope and handed a bundle to each of them. They shook the bundles in the air, joining in the applause.

The sound only grew louder when Gosten, using pure power, propelled himself directly to the hoop, not needing to use his tail, and climbed onto the stage with the other man. He smiled and waved. Meg put her index finger and thumb in her mouth and whistled loud enough to make both Daunet and Auzed flinch. The boisterous cheering carried through until the fifth man climbed onto the stage with a slight limp.

The bride, dressed in a gorgeous multicolored gown, floated to the stage, smiling at the man who'd won. His grin was wide and infectious as he watched her approach. She walked up to him and demurely wrapped her tail around his. The cuteness of the gesture sent Alex's brain into overload, and her heart fluttered. Meg had much the same reaction, releasing a squeal and pressing her hand to her chest.

After a while the stage was cleared, but the loud chattering of the crowds continued as people filed out of the arena toward various gatherings around the city.

"You guys ready for a party?" Meg shouted, excitement lighting her grin.

24

Auzed watched Alex from across the room as she chatted with Meg and two other Sauvenians he didn't know. The heart-pumping game they'd witnessed earlier today had helped to distract him, but it was no match for the turmoil charring his insides.

All night and day he'd thought about what he should do. Should he ask her to stay with him forever? Should he *really* forget everything he ever valued, change his core beliefs in order to be with her?

He was using this party as a test for himself. As soon as they'd entered, he'd been on edge. Males and females peered at her and Meg, covertly attempting to sniff them as they walked by or pushing their way into their conversations. Every muscle in his body was strung tight.

He was barely able to carry on any conversations of his own because his heart always leapt into his throat every time a new person approached her. Would this one be the one to recognize her and take her away from him forever?

He'd wanted to see if he could handle the constant scraping against his Traxian side, and he was finding out he couldn't. Mild annoyance continued to build and morph into something far more dangerous. The next person to clasp her hand for too long when she taught them her Earth greeting was going to lose it.

"How are you doing tonight, Auzed?" His attention shifted to Relli, who had at some point walked up to him. Her brows were lifted in a mixture of curiosity and concern.

"I'm well, Relli, and you?" His head snapped to the side at a flash of movement near Alex, but it was only Meg, returning with drinks for herself and Daunet. He exhaled.

"*Are* you well?" Relli asked.

It took Auzed a moment to process her question. He looked back at her and saw in her expression that she already knew the answer.

She let out a long sigh, and he saw a glimmer of understanding light her yellow eyes. "How far gone are you?"

He clenched his jaw and drank deeply from his glass, forcing his attention to remain on Relli. "I don't know what you mean."

She pursed her lips at him and raised a brow.

His shoulders fell with his deflating exhale. "I am consumed," he muttered finally, not knowing quite how to describe the overwhelming feelings he had for Alex. How could any emotion simultaneously lift you higher than you've ever been and smother you in weighted blackness?

Relli nodded, a knowing smile playing around her lips. "That's how I felt for Jut."

"But…" he trailed off, not used to speaking so personally to near strangers, especially female ones. "But isn't it difficult, the way everyone treats you two, and…well, what if more humans come? What if he recognizes somebody else?"

Relli's face paled a fraction, and guilt swamped Auzed. He should've never put that thought into her mind. It'd been unintentional, but it was cruel all the same.

She peered over to where Jut stood, politely listening to a very drunk and very happy Gosten, retelling the same story he'd been barking about since he'd arrived, and smiled gently. "Say it did happen." She turned back to Auzed. "If he recognized someone else. It would break my heart, but it wouldn't change all these happy years we've spent together. At least I'd have that. When I think of where I'd be if I hadn't stayed with him…" She gulped. "I would still be miserable and alone. Floating through marriages and pretending that each time I had to leave a new home, I didn't feel hollow."

Her words hit him hard, constricting his chest, because that was exactly right. When Alex wasn't around, he felt like a shell of himself. She'd brought him to life.

"But," Relli added with a pitying look, "I will admit this isn't quite the same. I didn't have females beating down my door to speak to Jut. And being recognized was never a concern. With so few humans, it still isn't. I understand it's different for you. And I can sympathize with your apprehension."

And he was back to where he'd started. Auzed took another long gulp from his glass.

"Have you talked to her about it?"

"I decided to wait until I knew what I wanted myself. It'd be no good to come to her with more problems. She's been through enough."

Alex caught him staring and beamed. She gave him a small wave from across the room. Meg looked between them, then leaned toward Alex to whisper something. Alex's grin faded a fraction. She tilted her head toward the balcony, and they walked away, disappearing through the sliding glass.

"Auzed!" Gosten boomed, stomping over to them and weaving slightly. "Did you and Alex watch the game today?"

Here we go. "Yes, we did."

"Did you see that ending? Yeeshutu was incredible!"

"And so were you." He grinned, slapping the male on the back.

Taking that as his opening, Gosten replayed the game from his perspective. "I was halfway up when I saw…"

Auzed couldn't help but grin and listen to the male repeat his story of success. It was no wonder he was so elated. The points he'd received would likely double his overall scores. He was almost guaranteed a wife in a few weeks.

Auzed pushed down the spike of envy and forced himself to be happy for the male.

***

"So, what is going on with you and the hunky ice ball?"

Alex smiled, but it was forced. "I don't know, really."

Meg raised her brows in surprise.

"Let me ask you something," she said, tucking her leg under her and facing Meg. "How realistic…or, I guess how likely is it… Ugh I don't know how to ask this." She sighed. "Is it possible? That they'll let us go back to Earth, I mean?"

"Ah." Meg nodded. "Worried to start something you can't see through to the end?"

Alex grimaced. Like an idiot, she'd already started it. "More or less."

"You want the truth?"

"Yes," she groaned.

"I think it's a real possibility. Maybe not soon, but soon enough." Meg tipped her head and stared through the forest. "If it were just us humans complaining about it then I wouldn't give it a second thought, you know. But it isn't. Everyone and their mother wants humans to come here. Every city, every leader, *every* Clecanian. A whole planet of evolved, powerful, space-traveling beings are all working together to make this happen. I can't even begin to imagine how quickly the red tape is going to get cut with everyone fighting desperately for the same cause."

Alex deflated. Part of her had hoped the notion of going home would be so farfetched that she could give up on it. But if there was any possibility at all, she had to try…didn't she?

"From what I've heard in the meetings the Queen has at the Temple, the only thing she thinks will hold us up are the other planets within the Alliance. They don't give two shits about revealing themselves to humans, mind you," Meg added with irritated pursed lips. "They just want to use their votes as bargaining chips to get other resources from Clecania. Or so the Queen thinks. She's a smart cookie. Fair and firm. Doesn't spew the bullshit we'd expect."

Alex gazed at the lights twinkling around the hanging nests of Sauven. They were brighter tonight, and colorful. If only she felt the same.

"Is that what's been bothering you today? You miss home?"

"Of course I do. I miss my family and my friends. I miss movies and familiar food and sunlight. I miss not worrying about how I act every. Single. Second." She threw her hands towards the sky. "I need to find a way back home. I can't imagine what my family is going through."

"What about Auzed?"

Alex had to take a steadying breath; the tears that sprung to the surface just imagining leaving him burned. "We've known from the beginning that this was temporary. He has his job to go back to, and he can't be married while he's head guard. If I'm just going to leave him to go home, then what's the point anyway?" She needed to start resigning herself to this. Bitterness at how unfair it all was rose in her throat. "Besides, he's so rigid. We would've never worked long term. He barely tolerates the idea of demskivs as it is."

The clearing of a throat behind them had them both turning. Alex's heart stopped.

Auzed stood in the doorway to the house, muscles tensed and eyes as hard and cold as ice.

Meg cursed under her breath and aimed an apologetic glance at Alex. Then she hissed through her teeth. "Maybe I should…go."

"That's a good idea," Auzed all but growled. "King Bet would like us to meet him at the nest to discuss our departure tomorrow. Now."

How much had he heard? Alex took in a shaky breath. It wasn't as if anything she'd said was untrue, though.

Meg pulled her into a hug. "I'll see you tomorrow morning, alright?"

Alex nodded thickly as Meg scurried by Auzed and out of sight.

He held her gaze for a long moment, a nerve twitching in his jaw. "Go inside and say your goodbyes." Stalking past her, he headed toward the herd of travel platforms waiting to be used.

Heart still thrashing against her ribs, she dashed inside. They'd made a point of saying goodbye to their new Sauvenian friends throughout the night, knowing they wouldn't be seeing them again before heading out the next morning, but she couldn't leave for good without a final goodbye.

Her mind was half gone, focused on the furious, hurt male waiting for her outside as she forced a smile and shook Fenut's and Calep's hands. "It was so wonderful to meet you. I hope I can see you again someday."

"Maybe you could come back when I compete in a few years." Calep grinned.

"Yeah, maybe," Alex replied. She hoped one day she'd feel comfortable enough to visit Sauven again, but her forced imprisonment here for the last week might take more than a few years to get over. She peered over to Gosten passed out on a low couch with a huge grin curling his lips. "Can you tell Gosten I said goodbye? And tell him congratulations for me again. He was stunning."

Next, Alex found Relli and Jut exchanging heated glances in a corner and paused, wondering if she should interrupt.

Relli spotted her before she could decide. "Alex. Are you leaving?"

"Unfortunately." She sighed. "Thank you both so much for everything. I want you to come visit Tremanta as soon as you can, okay?"

Jut grinned. "We'll have to wait until winter to avoid the sun."

Alex tipped her head, "Huh, that's right. Well then, I can't wait until winter." She clutched Relli's biceps with both hands. "And you. You are an amazing, spectacular unicorn of a woman, and you really need to find another job."

"Tell me about it. Though I don't know what a unicorn is." Relli chuckled. "The problem is I love being a ranger. And at least if I'm a ranger, I can make sure people like me aren't treated poorly. Fierad is difficult to work with, but I can manage him."

"Good." Alex pulled Relli into a big hug and said her final goodbye, then moved toward the porch. She took in a steadying breath before walking outside. At the sight of

Auzed fuming on a travel platform, a shudder rolled through her. She didn't want to have this conversation. As soon as they did, whatever they had between them would end.

He angled his body on the board to make room, a silent request for her to get on. As soon as both her feet were on the board and her hands touched the handle, he took off.

The warmth that usually radiated from his body and into her back felt different, like a thousand small pricks against her skin. "Auzed, about what I said…"

"Which part?" he rumbled.

She sighed. "Nothing I said was untrue, Auzzy."

As soon as the nickname had left her lips, he twisted the platform, heading to a nearby nest still being built, judging by the half-finished roof. Pulling up to the curb, he leapt onto the wrap-around porch and paced, hands on hips.

He refused to even look at her.

She swiped her sweaty palms on her shorts and searched for the right words to say. "We were talking about the future, and she asked me about you…about us. I didn't know what else to say."

"Because we always knew this was temporary?" he spat.

Alex scanned the smooth wood he paced over. "Well…isn't it?"

"How long have you been planning on returning to Earth?" he fumed, halting and facing her.

Alex blinked. "Is that what you're mad about?" She'd just assumed her jabs at his personality were what had sparked this anger in him.

"Why else?"

A spike of irritation shot through her worry. "Auzed, that's not fair. You can't be mad at me for wanting to return to my family. I don't understand why that comes as such a shock to you. You have your job back in Tremanta. What did you expect me to do, sit around and be alone forever on an alien planet until you decide to retire?"

His chest heaved, but he said nothing. Yet his gaze was still accusatory, pushing her to say more.

"And what then? Get married for three months?" She raised her brows at him. "I may have said it a little more harshly than is true, but you *do* have a problem with demskivs and breaking with traditions and all that. You care what other people think. I don't want to have a temporary relationship…not with you."

His eyes softened, and he took a step toward her. "What if I quit? We could move outside Tremanta and be married."

"And extend the marriage indefinitely?" Alex couldn't believe her ears. Was he really offering this?

"Yes." He took her hand with both of his. The sincerity in his expression was genuine, but there was something else there. Uncertainty? Fear, maybe?

An image of her family gathered together at Easter, unable to be happy because she'd gone missing without a trace, popped into her head. "Auzed…" Her voice broke.

His mouth thinned, and he stepped away. "You'd still want to leave, wouldn't you?"

"My family…I can't just abandon them." She lit on an

idea. "You could come back to Earth with me." Her voice wavered even as she said it, knowing he couldn't.

He shot her a humorless smirk. "Oh sure. I can try to inhabit Earth as soon as they learn aliens exist." He shook his head. "I'd be captured and locked away in an instant, or I'd put you and your family in danger."

Alex wanted to argue, but she'd seen too many movies and knew what humans were like. He could *almost* pass for human, but he was just different enough that it wouldn't be long before someone caught on.

"Well, that's it, then." He shrugged, an aggressive hike of his shoulders.

What else could she say? He'd offered her everything he was able to offer, but she couldn't take it. The guilt would eat her up inside. If she stayed with him, she'd spend every day thinking about her family, imagining their suffering.

When she remained silent, he rushed past her and boarded the travel platform. Alex's eyes were glued to her feet for the whole ride back. Her heart seemed permanently lodged in her throat, and she didn't dare say another word for fear of dissolving into tears before they came face-to-face with the king.

Two guards and the king were waiting for them when they arrived. Inside the house. Not outside like any other respectful guest. She reminded herself that despite how it felt, this wasn't their home, though. This was temporary lodging provided by the regents. He had every right to be inside.

"Sir," Auzed greeted.

She glanced up to Auzed and saw his disposition was passive and stony, the same way it had been when they'd first met. Somehow, seeing him like that, as if the warm, grinning man she'd grown to love was gone, sliced through her more than anything else had. This was her fault.

She barely heard any of the conversation about transportation and timing. All she could do to keep from breaking down was stare ahead and listen to the buzzing in her ears. It could've been after minutes or hours of conversation, but at some point, King Bet moved and her attention snapped back to the present.

"It was wonderful to meet you, Alejandra. Are you positive we can't do anything to get you to stay?"

Alex tried for a polite smile. "No, sorry. We have to get back for our...you know...marriage."

The mention of their fake marriage had Auzed tensing next to her.

"Yes. I do hope the events of this week haven't put a strain on the two of you. Dasa regretted not being here to see you off, but she had to travel to the council seat for a meeting concerning your kind." The king nodded to both of them and made his way toward the door. "I was informed earlier today that your resignation has been finalized. I hope you two have a very happy marriage."

Alex and Auzed both stilled. Had all the air been sucked out of the room, or was she just not breathing? The swoosh of the door closing behind the king sounded, and they turned to each other, eyes wide with disbelief.

307

Auzed dug into his pocket for his communicator and walked away. He didn't need to tell her who he was trying to contact, but his quiet, "This is Auzed trying to reach the Queen," confirmed it.

Alex stood frozen as he paced, clutching the communicator to his ear. A sudden weight on her shoulder made her jump, but she quickly realized it was only Wilson. The tuey gripped her face and looked at her with round, worried eyes.

"Hello, my Queen. The king of Sauven just mentioned something to me, and I wanted to confirm that it was false. It's about—" He paused, waiting. "Yes, about that."

His brows drew together as he listened. His features gave nothing away. He was once again impenetrable.

"Yes. I understand." He nodded. "I'll see you tomorrow, then."

He lowered the phone with deadly calm.

"Wh…what did she say?" Alex forced herself to ask.

Auzed looked up at her, and his green eyes seethed with barely contained fury. "I'm no longer head guard."

***

Auzed grappled for control. Liquid fire boiled in his gut. Alex's face had grown two shades paler in the moments after his announcement.

"Can they even do that? How are they allowed to do that?" she asked in a small voice from behind him.

He spun. "A ranger brought the fact that I was still listed as the active head guard to Queen Dasa's attention. She

308

contacted my Queen this afternoon and requested my resignation papers as proof that we are, in fact, getting married. My Queen had no choice."

"A ranger? Fucking Fierad. But why would Queen Dasa care when you—"

"I told you before! She dislikes my Queen. She didn't have to ask for my resignation to be official. She pushed for it, knowing it'd be a blow since the Queen appointed me herself. It's a petty, inconsequential power play, but Queen Dasa could've argued for you to remain in Sauven if the request wasn't met!"

This was Alex's fault. Never listening. Never caring about their customs. And all the while content to leave him and never return. He'd thought their biggest problem was him. That he was too rigid. Too opposed to leaving his career and settling into an unconventional life with her. He'd thought his fear of her leaving him for another male was the only thing holding them back. How stupid he'd been. She'd never intended to give him a chance.

Turning away, he crossed to the lift, no longer able to look at her. The female who'd made him fall in love, all the while knowing she'd eventually leave.

"Auzzy!" She caught his arm.

The surge of warmth that tightened his chest at the contact made him boil over. "No!" He flung off her hand. "Au-zed. We are nothing to each other anymore, right? So you don't get to use that name."

"I…" She struggled to find words, mouthing as her eyes

309

grew glassy and pleading. "I'm so sorry. What can I do?"

"What can you do?" He advanced, and Wilson trumpeted at him, pressing herself between them.

He glared at the little creature, then stalked back to the lift.

She whispered, "Stay here," to Wilson, setting her on the ground, then hurried over to him, catching him on the lift just before it rose. Her scent invaded his nostrils, so he breathed through his mouth. "Please talk to me."

"Talk about what?" he barked. "How you forced your way into my life and are leaving it a smoking pile of ash?"

"Hey," she cautioned, anger coloring her cheeks.

"You talk about how I'm rigid—what about you? You don't think anything through. You wanted me, so you had me. You didn't care how this would end."

"Hey!" she said again more forcefully. "This isn't all on me. You weren't an inactive participant. And you were planning on leaving me too! Don't think I didn't notice your hesitation when you offered to quit your job. You would've resented me eventually, resented our life. It's not what you really want. And all because you can't see past what you've been told to believe. Not even enough to realize that the only time you've been happy is when you were with me. I saw it! You changed."

Her words settled over him, and the truth he heard ringing back only added to the pyre of flames in his gut. "That was a fantasy. An act. One *you* provoked. This isn't real!" He gestured between them. "You want to *leave*! I fought with myself every second since the day we met not to wrap my arms around you, and I should've fought harder! You know why?"

Alex stood back, crossing her arms over her chest defensively and swiping a stray tear. She bit the inside of her cheek but didn't answer.

"Because that's not how things are done here!" he roared, enunciating every word. "I don't get to sleep in a bed with my wife. I don't get to stroke her hair or lose my temper or laugh with her. In three months, she'll be gone, and all I'll have to show for it is whatever she's left me with. I was content in that knowledge! Then you showed me differently. You made me want things I can never have again, all the while knowing you'd leave."

Fat tears rolled down her cheeks. He felt pain and pleasure in equal parts because they meant she agreed on some level. Knew what she'd done.

He crowded her. "And yes, I hesitated, but not because I'd be married to a demskiv. It's because if we were together, I would worry about losing you every single day. So, thank you. You showed me I was spot on. I was going to lose you no matter what I did."

The pain shining on her face tore at his insides until he couldn't stand it anymore. Forcing his feet to move, he retreated into his room and sank to the floor, head in his hands.

25

The light glowing from the ceiling in the nest hallway told him it was morning, but it might as well have been the middle of the night. The passing of time no longer felt normal.

His eyes were swollen and itchy as he stared at her door, working up the courage to hand her the container she'd need to pack up her things. They were scheduled to leave soon. Back to Tremanta. Back to isolation.

Should he knock? His fists clenched around the soft packing cube. He could just barge in and drop the cube onto the floor. He'd be in and out before she had a chance to say anything, which was preferable. He didn't feel capable of listening to her voice at the moment.

He hadn't slept a wink. Only tossed and turned until his skin was sore from the friction. His boiling rage would occasionally settle into a sour gurgle, but the pain constricting his throat melded with the fury. It was easier to be angry.

He held on to it for dear life, knowing when the anger subsided, only grief and crushing loss would remain in its place. The worst part of all was that he understood where Alex was coming from. She'd been abducted. Had had her whole life ripped from her. It made sense that she felt an obligation to return home to her family. Her career. Yet he couldn't stop the bitter jealousy from invading his mind.

It was selfish and arrogant to a sickening degree, but the knowledge that he wasn't more important to her than anyone or anything else tore at him. More so because she *was* the most important thing to him.

Bile rose in his throat. The most important person, and yet he'd hurt her. The look of anguish on her tear-streaked face from the night before flashed in his mind.

Her accusations of his hesitancy to quit his job and be with her came back to him. She hadn't been wrong about that either. But somehow being the one who was confused, the one who needed to make the call about whether or not they could be together had been preferable to this. At least when it'd been his decision to make, his career to sacrifice, his reputation to tarnish, he'd had control. Now he was powerless. If the laws changed and she was allowed to go back to Earth, he couldn't stop her. Not legally anyway.

His baser half, the half that was currently reveling in his emotional turbulence, locked on to that idea. He had money. He had knowledge. Hell, he could pilot a small ship and take her off-world if he really wanted to. Settle on some barren planet and hope she'd come to accept it over the years. But he'd never do it. *She'd hate me, and I'd hate myself.*

Steeling himself, he pushed her door open without knocking, praying to the Goddess that she'd be asleep. His breath whooshed out of him when her puffy, bloodshot eyes met his. She sat on the bed, stroking Wilson, who was curled in her lap and whose flattened ears and droopy eyes made her look just as tormented as Alex.

Her gaze widened and brimmed with tears as he walked in. His whole body clenched in an effort not to cross to her and pull her into his arms. He dropped the cube onto the ground. "Pack your things. We need to leave within the hour." His voice sounded strained to his own ears.

Her mouth parted, but before she could speak, he bolted through the door, like a coward. His chest rose and fell, not able to take in enough air.

***

Alex choked back her sobs as she packed up her few belongings, mostly clothing. Remorse and shame had battered her until she felt lower than dirt. She knew that everything she'd said was perfectly reasonable, but she couldn't help feeling guilty for the part she'd played in this situation. Auzed had made some fair points. If she'd held back instead of flirting and pushing, none of this would've happened.

She'd treated him like a boyfriend on a planet where boyfriends didn't work. And though she hadn't been plotting her escape back to Earth like some mustache-twirling villain set on breaking him, she couldn't deny that leaving was her goal. Not because she didn't *want* to stay. She did. The urge to remain on Clecania and forget everything else was so strong, she almost wondered if she could do it. Almost.

It wasn't just the pull of her family and all the things she loved back on Earth that kept her from agreeing to be with him, though. It was also this world. A cowardly part of her didn't know if she could handle being a demskiv. And what if he grew to resent their life together?

What if he didn't? How could she ever have a child with him here? Could she watch their child be subjected to the demands of this place? Watch her little boy go to husbandry school or her little girl grow reserved and distant the way they'd teach her to be? She'd always imagined her children surrounded by love and family.

She'd only known Auzed for a week, and though she trusted her feelings toward him, she also knew intensity like this often fizzled out over time. Going back was the safest option. And if she planned to go back at all, she couldn't spend any more time leading him on.

Hefting the cube stuffed with clothing, she waited for Wilson to hop on her shoulders, then took a deep breath. When she lowered to the first floor, she spotted Auzed already waiting on the porch, arms crossed over his chest and shoulders bunched up to his ears.

A piece of pink bread waited for her on the counter, and her chin wobbled. She clenched her jaw to stop it, then joined him. Her stomach was in too much chaos to eat anyway.

"Meg and Daunet will be arriving shortly. They went to

retrieve a cruiser from the sky stop."

She didn't know what a "cruiser" or a "sky stop" were and couldn't bring herself to care. His expression was hard again. Impassive and stony. No emotion, good or bad, lit his eyes, and his voice was professional...civil. Was he trying to act like nothing was wrong? Or was he simply trying to become the man she'd met a week ago? The man who didn't let silly emotion dictate his attitude or his choices.

She held in a sigh. She supposed it was for the best. He'd had years of practice feeling nothing and remaining distant. Maybe it wouldn't be so hard for him to revert to a normal life. Alex would never go back to normal. She'd think about Auzed every single day of her life and what could've been. Wilson nuzzled her head under Alex's chin, and her little claws tightened around her messy braid.

From the corner of her eye, she noticed people floating toward them, but neither Meg nor Daunet were among the group. Ice sluiced down her spine. Fierad led. The king traveled behind, flanked by two soldiers. And there was one other person...Relli?

"What do they want?" she whispered to Auzed.

He stared in the direction of the quickly approaching group with furrowed brows and a tense jaw. "Nothing good."

"Oh, good! We caught you before you left," Fierad said, stepping off his platform in a flourish. His grin was wide, his white teeth flashing dangerously.

Alex focused on a confused Relli, who gave a small shake of her head, indicating she didn't know why they were there either.

"Let's get this done with, Ranger," King Bet drawled as he too stepped onto the nest porch.

Fierad plastered his hand to Relli's back and all but shoved her toward Auzed.

"Ranger!" the king barked. "Do not dare touch a female like that again."

He barely flinched at the king's scolding tone. "Apologies, I'm just excited to see justice served. Auzed, I have a signed order here to have you *swayed*."

Silence reigned as Auzed glared. He didn't appear perturbed or anxious. Had he known this was coming?

Fierad continued to speak, seeming to find joy in explaining the situation. "See, when the regents confirmed your resignation papers were in order, I realized that since you aren't head guard anymore, there's nothing stopping us from *swaying* you."

"I have places to be, Ranger," King Bet grated from behind them.

He shot a glance over his shoulder. "Yes, of course." Fierad caught Alex's eye. "I wanted to make sure he was here as a witness. Relli." He just stopped himself from pushing a furious-looking Relli toward Auzed again. Instead, he waved forward, urging her to start.

Back turned to the king and Fierad, Relli raised her brows at both of them, and Alex knew. Relli was going to try to lie. Going to fake the *sway*. Would Auzed go along with it, though? He hated lying, but surely he'd do it now. Sweat gathered in the small of her back. Was he angry enough with her to throw it all away and tell the truth? She didn't think he would, but she'd also never seen him as enraged as he'd been last night.

"Auzed." Relli began swaying from side to side. "Look at me." Her voice, smooth as velvet, held a surprising amount of power. Enough so that everyone on the porch shifted their gaze to look at Relli.

Just as she had before, Alex shook the *sway* off as soon as it curled around her mind. She saw from the small head shakes of the king and of Fierad that they'd experienced the same thing.

"You will answer Fierad's questions." Relli swayed in front of him for a moment longer, but her gaze grew worried.

Pushing his way past Relli, Fierad placed himself in front of Auzed. "Now you'll see, Majesty. They've been lying from the beginning."

King Bet crossed his arms, and his gaze darkened. "I'll give you one more minute before I leave, Fierad."

Alex tried to catch Relli's gaze. Relli gave a small shake of her head. Had Auzed not broken out of it?

"Did Alejandra say she'd marry you?" Fierad asked with a wide smile.

Alex sucked in a breath. What could she do? Was there some kind of diversion she could make?

"Yes, Alejandra said she'd marry me," Auzed answered in a monotone.

Fierad's jaw dropped. Alex just stopped her own jaw from

dropping. Was he faking it? He must be.

"Alright. Now that we've settled that, let's let our guests leave in peace," the king grumbled as though being dragged here had been the last thing in the universe he'd wanted to do.

"No. Wait!" Fierad found his voice. "I don't understand…" He spun on Relli. "Is this your doing? I've had my reservations about you, demskiv, but if you'd stoop to that level—"

Relli let out a squeak as Fierad lunged at her. Fury flared through Alex white hot, and she stepped forward too.

"Ranger!" the king boomed, directing his guards toward Fierad as well.

But before any person could reach him, Wilson had propelled herself off Alex's shoulder and buried her tiny claws into Fierad's face. She scratched and blasted shrill trumpets into his ears.

He tried to pry her off, clawing at her and swatting her with his tail while stumbling around. All hands reached toward him as one as he took one step too far and toppled off the nest porch with a bellow.

Alex raced to the ledge. "Wilson!" Her heart resumed beating when she spotted the tuey gliding toward a tree to their left. Fierad continued to fall away from them until a bright-blue electric current illuminated in a wave all around him and caught him. He bounced into the air once, then settled. He was too far away to hear clearly, but she'd bet he was down there turning purple with the string of curses he was letting out.

"Well, perhaps that was for the best." King Bet sighed, staring down at Fierad, who kept attempting to rise only to fall back down again.

"Auzed, wake up," Relli gently called, pulling him from the *sway*.

Like a shot, Auzed's body tensed. With an emotionless nod to the king, he turned on his heel and strode back inside the nest.

The way he avoided her gaze while brushing past was like a kick to the gut.

"You'd better go retrieve him." The king got back onto his travel platform and waved toward Fierad far below with his tail. As his guards took off to do as he'd asked, he faced Relli. "Relli, is it?"

"Yes, Majesty." She nodded with wide eyes.

He gave her a small, restrained smile. "A superior treating a subordinate like that is unacceptable. I assure you, Fierad is in for a demotion as well as relocation. As I'm in charge of the rangers in Sauven, I'd like to formally apologize for his actions as well as his bias toward you."

Relli let out a shaky breath, but a small smile appeared on her face and her tail swished from side to side. "Thank you, Majesty. I appreciate it."

"Would you mind joining me so we can discuss who a suitable replacement may be?"

Relli inhaled a large breath and beamed while trying to keep her grin at bay. She gave an excited nod, then ran over to Alex and wrapped her in a tight hug. "I don't know what happened. I tried to distract everyone so he could break out of it, but I don't think he did. Get out of here while you still can," she whispered with a final squeeze and a smile.

"Go nominate yourself, girl!" Alex whispered back, then watched her hop onto Fierad's vacated travel platform.

"Have a safe trip back to Tremanta," the king said with a quick nod toward Alex. He and Relli glided away, not waiting for the guards, who were far below retrieving Fierad.

Alex let out a relieved breath. It was done. King Bet didn't believe Fierad, and Relli was finally rid of him. Wilson glided over from the tree she'd been climbing and landed in Alex's outstretched arms. "Good job, you little hero."

Steps behind her told her Auzed had emerged from the house. She turned to look at him, and any bit of good mood she'd gained from watching Fierad make a fool of himself faded. He stared ahead, refusing to meet her gaze. Wilson let out a sad whine that matched the choked whimper clogging Alex's throat.

"How did you do it?" she asked." Did you break out of the *sway*?" Her attention caught on a large floating silver orb approaching them.

Auzed seemed unperturbed by the enormous ball, so she relaxed. She looked back at him, waiting for an answer. His Adam's apple bobbed. Gaze shifting to the ground, then back to the orb, he cleared his throat. "I was under the *sway*. I didn't lie."

"But—"

He focused on her, and his green eyes hardened. "You *did* offer to marry me. Once. You may not remember, since it clearly wasn't sincere, but *I* do. A Clecanian male would never forget an offer like that."

Alex remained still as he strode past her to meet the large orb pulling alongside the porch. Memories of their time together flew through her mind. In the kitchen of the nest on their first night here. She'd been a moment away from breaking down, and she'd offered. But he'd turned her down. *If I married you, it wouldn't be to get out of a lie. And it wouldn't be because you pity me or feel indebted or because you're desperate.* His words replayed through her mind, and they stung all the more because he'd asked her to marry him last night and she'd refused.

A long section of the shiny ball slid open, revealing a comfortable, cushioned interior. Meg waved from inside, as did Daunet. Their expressions faltered as they gazed between her and Auzed. She could only assume what the two of them looked like. Not to mention the pulsing tension between them.

Since Daunet and Meg were seated next to each other on one side of the cruiser, Alex and Auzed were forced to crowd in on the other. The confined quarters made it so the sides of their bodies touched and, selfishly, Alex was grateful. While it might have been the last thing in the world Auzed wanted, the simple press of his thigh against hers was electric. She greedily luxuriated in the heat of his body and his scent, knowing she'd never be this close to him again.

The reminder had her throat closing up, and she held in a swallow to keep the sob from pouring out of her mouth.

"Happy to be leaving?" Meg asked awkwardly, gaze ping-ponging between them. She'd been present when they'd left the party last night and could probably guess what had happened.

Alex knew she looked terrible. Puffy eyes and pale skin from crying all night instead of sleeping. It made her feel fractionally better to see that Auzed wasn't looking his best either. His green eyes had dulled and, though she could've been imagining it, it seemed like the markings that decorated his body weren't shining quite so brightly today.

Daunet, who'd placed her hands on her knees and locked her arms in the most stiff, unnatural way, was doing nothing to ease the awkwardness in the confined cruiser. The door slid shut, and a gentle shift told Alex they were moving. "Sir, I've gotten word that a house has been prepared for Alex at the Temple. We should be arriving in about an hour. They gave her a house on the far East, but, as I told the Queen—"

"I'm not your superior anymore, Daunet. You don't need to address me as sir. Whoever the Queen assigns as Heard Guard can deal with whatever the problem is," Auzed interrupted in a clipped voice. Not impolite, but not soft either.

Alex stiffened. Her jaw grew sore from grinding her teeth. Meg caught her eye and raised her brows in question, trying to have a silent conversation. It was a conversation Alex couldn't handle at the moment, so she dropped her gaze to her lap, head hanging.

Daunet's jaw was still hanging open midsentence. She studied Auzed with disbelief. Then stammered, "N-no. That can't… But, sir," she implored.

He raised a hand to silence her. "Not now, Daunet."

She snapped her mouth closed and glared into the floor of the cruiser.

Alex peeked over at Auzed's lap, not brave enough to sneak a glance at his face, and found his fists balled tight on his thighs. God, how she wanted to reach for his hand, grasp it, and soothe him. But that would be cruel.

She squirmed in her seat, attempting to give him a bit more space, but all she managed was to make their legs not press together quite so tightly. His knuckles turned white.

After a moment, Auzed shifted. If an outsider looked at the microscopic movement of his legs, they'd assume he was simply getting comfortable, but the pressure that returned to her thigh made her wonder if he'd done it on purpose. Needing the contact as much as she did before they said their goodbyes.

Meg and Daunet both took the hint and remained silent for the entire ride. Daunet had said the trip would take an hour. It felt infinitely longer than that.

The heavy air in the cab of the cruiser was muddled. Across from her, Meg pulsed with curiosity and concern. Daunet with irritation. Waves of grief, doubt, and barely contained longing rolled off Alex. But from Auzed? Nothing.

He didn't appear to feel anything at all. Which was the

reason the cruiser felt so crushing. Like walking into one of those scientifically soundproofed rooms. She'd watched videos of people trying to remain in those places. None of them could for very long. The oppressive silence was so unnatural, it could drive a person crazy within hours.

That was what Auzed's aura added to the mix. Nothingness that was louder than anything else and made each of the women in the cruiser itch with stress. Alex twirled her ring around her finger, polishing the inside with the repeated motion.

When they came to a halt and the side of the cruiser slide open, Meg released a harsh, "Oh thank God," and all but dove over Daunet to get outside.

"I brought a token and pads for Alex," Daunet said softly, dropping a small purple circle into Auzed's outstretched hand, along with rubbery thin ovals. "I'll wait by the lake to take her to her house."

"I'll see her off, then take the cruiser to my lodging on the West end," he rumbled.

It seemed like Daunet wanted to say more as she stared between them. Instead, she resolutely set her jaw and climbed out.

Alex and Auzed remained frozen. He was blocking the exit. She watched the vein in his neck pulse while he stared into the empty seats across from him. His thigh twitched.

Finally, with a deep inhale, he stood and climbed out of the cruiser. She and Wilson followed, the tuey still wrapped tightly around her neck, attempting to contain the waves of sadness with her little body. They rounded the large orb, and she spotted Meg and Daunet speed-walking toward an incredible sight. A lake topped with blossom-like floating houses glittered in the sun before her. The Pearl Temple. He'd described it to her. How the water was guarded by glowing creatures, and how only those with a token and approved access could cross it.

She couldn't seem to appreciate the beauty of the Temple, though. Everything felt wrong. The ground under her feet was too firm, giving her the odd impression that her legs hurt. And Auzed was wrong too. He wasn't himself anymore.

They stood facing each other, but their gazes were both shifted away. She should say something. Anything.

"I…" She cleared her throat. He lifted his eyes to her, and tight lines formed around his mouth. She tried again. "I want you to know I didn't always plan to try to go back to Earth."

He studied her face, his spine straight and his shoulders impossibly solid.

"I didn't even know it was an option. It was only three days ago that Meg told me the Queen here was working toward it and that it might be possible," Alex said in a rush. She gulped. "Leaving you isn't something I *want* to do. You know that, right?"

He flinched as if she'd slapped him. "I do," he whispered, almost too low for her to hear. Reaching forward, he gently lifted her wrist. The contact sent a bolt of heat up her arm, goose bumps breaking out all over her body. He swept her long, baggy sleeve up and turned her wrist over until her inner arm was pointed up. With an odd suctioning motion, the purple token he placed on her inner wrist attached to her skin.

Though the token was in place, he didn't let go. His thumb swept over the sensitive skin of her inner arm just above her wrist, and he gazed into her eyes. "I hope you get back to them, Alejandra. And I hope you'll be happy."

Tears burned behind her eyes. She choked on her own words and could only nod.

Suddenly, Wilson squeaked. With a small leap, she jumped the short distance to Auzed and wrapped herself around his neck, sliding her eyes shut and squeezing.

Alex draped an arm around her belly, the hollowness in her stomach gnawing at her. Even Wilson knew this was a mistake. Maybe the biggest of her life. The sudden urge to plead for more time built in her. But that wasn't fair. More time would only mean more pain down the road, and the last thing she wanted to do was cause either of them more pain.

Auzed let out a sigh and stroked the little animal's fur before peeling her off despite trumpeted objections. He placed her in Alex's arms.

With a stilted nod, he held Alex's gaze for a tense moment, then turned and strode away.

She remained stuck in place, lead seeping into her soles. As he climbed into the cruiser without looking back, the tears came.

26

For over a week, Alex had been adrift. She'd met a dozen other humans, all excited to befriend her. Lily had been inundating her with requests to visit as well. But the buzz of activity around the Temple held little appeal. She didn't want to see Lily, happy and settled with her fucking soul mate.

The progress toward returning to Earth was now more important than ever, and she put every ounce of strength she had into learning all she could about intergalactic law. As if trying to prove that the choice to be apart from Auzed was justifiable.

She'd even petitioned a meeting with the Queen in order to volunteer her services in whatever way she could. Maybe the Queen would send her away somewhere to be a human representative. Off to an Alliance meeting in the sky to plead on behalf of humans, perhaps. Anywhere would be better than here.

The seat under the large front window of her house had a

permanent divot in it from hours spent kneeling and looking through the glass, hoping to spot a glimpse of Auzed. He didn't work here anymore, but she'd heard whispers from the other women that he'd been taking care of a few unhandled duties around the Temple until a new head guard could be assigned.

It also smelled strongly of pineapple in this section of the house, since Wilson tended to occupy the seat whenever Alex wasn't. The abundant sunshine that blazed across the sky when she actually left her house only worked to sour her moods. She found herself indoors whenever possible, curled up with Wilson in a dark corner.

No matter how many times she went over their crash-and-burn ending, she couldn't get rid of her guilt. It wasn't entirely her fault that he'd lost his job. Sauven had pushed for it, but she still felt bad that after all they'd been through, she was left with some hope of returning home and he was left with nothing. Would he find another job somewhere? Would she ever see him again?

There'd been so many times when she'd almost gone searching for him. Almost asked Daunet to send him a message. Almost caved and considered lying about wanting to go home. But she loved him too much to hurt him like that.

She gazed out the window and stroked Wilson's soft, illuminated fur that had dulled a shade each day they'd been in Tremanta. With a depressed toot of her trunk, Wilson got off her lap and rolled toward the open patio door. She often went out at this time, the dim sky of twilight the most similar to the light in the forests of Sauven. The sun had just dipped below the horizon, painting the sky a gorgeous deep lavender, the same color it'd been their night on the lounger. Alex's chest tightened. Unable to look, she started to turn away.

A large man in normal Clecanian attire standing motionless a few houses away caught her eye. Odd, she'd rarely seen men who weren't guards walking around the Temple. Pressing her face to the window, she squinted. Were the broad shoulders on this man the ones she'd dreamed about nearly every night? The build was right and the hair was a light color, but he was too far away. The man remained motionless except for his hands, which he balled into fists. Was he staring at her house? Was it him?

Alex's blood pounded in her ears. The wall between them felt like the bars of a cell. She wanted to run outside but knew she shouldn't. *Please come here. Please.*

The sky darkened as she watched him, praying he'd move closer of his own accord. She wouldn't go outside. If he changed his mind, she'd let him walk away. He spun, retreating, and a short wail burst from her lips as her heart sank into her belly.

He took a few steps away but then abruptly paused and turned back, moving toward her home with deliberate stomps. As his face came into focus, butterflies erupted in her stomach. *Auzed.* He was even more handsome than she'd remembered.

He stopped a few feet from her house and stared at her

door. All the windows were tinted, so while she could look out, he luckily couldn't see her pressing her face to the glass like a lunatic.

Hungry for the sight of him, her gaze roved over his body. Cold seeped down her spine when she noticed the dark circles around his eyes. Had he lost weight as well? It killed her to know he was in pain. He pulled something out of his pocket and examined it. It looked like a card. Black and thin. A bit larger than a credit card.

His eyes were hyper-focused on the card in his hand, but she suspected he wasn't really looking at it. Rather, he was using it as his locus as he worked through something else in his mind.

Finally, he let out a long exhale, his shoulders slumping. She angled her head to the side, pressing roughly against the glass to follow his movement, and saw him place the card down at her door, then step back. *No. No. No.* He wasn't going to knock. He was just going to leave whatever it was and walk away.

When he spun to leave, just as she'd expected, all sense fled. She couldn't have stopped her sprinting feet if she'd tried. Before she realized what'd happened, she'd burst through the door. "Auzed!"

He turned to stone a yard away with his back to her. Long moments passed. She almost thought he'd keep walking. But then he spun. When his gaze landed on her, his green eyes flared and his chest heaved a singular deep breath.

Alex's whole body responded to that eye contact. Her

heart thrashed inside her chest, and her skin tingled all over. He stepped toward her and bent to retrieve the card. His scent hit her like a bag of bricks. Spicy and warm. It took all her concentration to keep herself from throwing her arms around him.

"I…" He peered at the card, a muscle twitching in his jaw. "I thought you might want this." He handed it to her and made sure their fingers didn't touch when she took it from him.

"What is it?" Her voice was breathless. Normally she'd be embarrassed by how desperate she sounded.

"I happened to see there was a new play coming to Tremanta. We…ah…we'd talked about it, so I figured—" He gestured to the card flippantly, as if the incredibly thoughtful gesture was no big deal. "There are two passes on there, so you can take someone else." He caught her gaze. "Meg or Lily maybe."

She just managed to contain her frown. The words behind the suggestion were clear. She could take *Meg* or *Lily*. Not *him*. She couldn't find the right thing to say. She stared at him dumbfounded, looking him up and down with greedy sweeps of her eyes.

"It's pretty dark in there," he said, gesturing into her almost pitch-black house.

I can't be in bright light without thinking about you. "Wilson is still getting used to it being so bright here," she said instead. Not a complete lie.

He rumbled a low, noncommittal sound.

"How are you doing?" she blurted.

His tight lips turned down in a frown. *¡Idiota!* she berated herself. Of course he wasn't doing okay. "I have to go." He spun on his heel.

Not knowing what she would say or how she'd explain herself, she caught his arm.

Angling to the side, his gaze slid down to her hand on his bicep. A muted growl reverberated through him. It didn't sound threatening. The tone was something else entirely.

Liquid heat flooded her core. She snatched her hand back as though burned. His heated gaze landed on her, and his nostrils flared. Shit. He knew what the touch had done to her.

Quicker than lightning, his arm flashed out and wrapped around her. He slammed her tight against his body, his lips crashing over hers in a frenzied kiss.

After a moment of stunned paralysis, she moaned and threw her arms behind his neck. He backed them into the house and slammed the door behind him. As soon as it closed, he pushed her down to the ground.

His firm hands flashed over her body, squeezing and rubbing more roughly than they ever had before. Her tongue slid over his, and he groaned, taking her mouth in a punishing kiss. This wasn't like before. There was no slow build, no whispered words or tender caresses. This was desperation incarnate.

Two people who'd been starved of each other for far too long. Alex clawed at his shirt, pulling him on top of her with her legs locked around his waist. The walls of her sex clenched the empty space where he needed to be. Now. He lifted off her body only long enough to hike up the short, flowy, pale-green dress she liked to sleep in.

He pulled it up to her chin and delved his fingers between her thighs. She cried out and pressed her forehead into his shoulder, whole body going tight as a brutal orgasm rapidly built. With his free hand, he gripped a handful of her hair and tugged her head back and to the side, baring her neck. When he ran his tongue over her pulse, inhaling deeply and groaning, she came apart, the shockwaves of her violent orgasm dotting her vision.

At some point, while the pulses of her orgasm burned through her, he'd freed himself from his pants. The broad head of his shaft probed her opening, and she spread her knees farther apart, needing him inside her. Needing to feel that connection with him again.

In one harsh thrust he buried himself, stretching her wide, almost to the point of pain. His forearms slipped beneath her skull, pillowing her head. His height put her face at chest level, so she buried her nose into the valley between his solid pecs and breathed in his sweet, spicy scent.

One hand fisting her hair, he thrust into her again, pressing his mouth to her forehead and growling with pleasure. With her arms clutching his waist and her legs wrapped around his hips, she basked in the knowledge that he was in her arms, loving her in his own wild way.

His pounding hips reverberated through her, building her orgasm at a furious pace. Thrusts growing frantic, his arms encircling her head tightened. He'd made love to her before, but now, he was claiming her. No matter where she went, she'd always be his.

She stretched her face up to kiss the cords of his sweat-coated neck. He moaned and rocked his hips in exactly the right spot. Her orgasm crashed through her, inner muscles convulsing around his cock, still deep inside. He pressed her face into the crook of his neck and bellowed, pulsing inside her and coating her core in hot liquid.

They stayed wrapped up together as they caught their breath. Unexpected tears burst to her eyes from fear. Fear he'd leave. Fear he'd stay.

He lifted his head and gazed down at her, his expression masked. Maybe if it were a bit lighter in here, she'd be able to search his eyes. Catch the signs of emotion she'd learned to pick up on.

Shifting his forearm from under her head, he cupped her face and used a thumb to brush away a tear from her cheek. Words didn't feel right. What was there to say anyway? She placed her hand over his on her cheek, and his eyes locked onto it.

Slipping his hand away, he gripped her fingers. He kept his eyes locked to hers as if asking for something. Slowly, he tugged the gold band she wore from her finger and wrapped his fist around it.

Throat clogging, she nodded, knowing what he wanted. She loved that ring, but it would bring her so much warmth knowing he had it. Maybe he'd stare at it on occasion and remember her.

He placed a soft kiss to her lips, then pulled away from her. After dressing in silence, he was gone. The soundless tears that streamed down her cheeks didn't stop until finally, she curled into a ball and fell asleep right there on the floor.

27

Auzed couldn't recall ever feeling worse. He couldn't eat. Couldn't sleep. All he did was lie around and argue with himself about whether or not to throw out caution and beg Alex for a finite relationship. They'd been together temporarily in Sauven, and it was the happiest he'd ever been.

His fantasies of ways in which they could be together were growing more and more outlandish. Maybe he could pilot a ship and abduct the rest of her family. Then she wouldn't have to worry about them going on without her. What if he found the most powerful Swadaeth and forced them to *sway* her into forgetting about her family?

Every solution that popped into his head was cruel and selfish and impossible. He fiddled with the gold ring on a leather string around his neck. It'd been a week since he'd broken down and gone to see her. He'd only planned on giving her the tickets, but he should've known he wasn't strong enough to stop at just a delivery. It was a good thing his access to the Temple had been deactivated since, or he knew he'd have gone back.

"You look like a dying guarsil." Maxu poked, handing him a cold mott.

Since he'd returned to Tremanta, Maxu was the only member of his family he could bear to see. Luka and Theo made his insides burn. Even seeing the blue mating marks covering their hands was enough to make him want to pummel them. His sister, Asivva, was married and busy. And his youngest brother, Izor, was almost as mopey as he was. The relationship between him and the human female he'd been following around like a pup had hit trouble, though Auzed hadn't delved into precisely what the problem was.

He shrugged at Maxu's jab, knowing perfectly well how wretched he looked.

Maxu pushed. "You look as if a young male just out of husbandry school beat you in a fight."

He frowned.

"Like you just crawled out of Pearl Lake after being stung by a thousand bilom." Maxu raised his glass and cheered.

"I get it!" Auzed barked, not at all amused. "Terrible. I look terrible." He took a swig of his mott and pointed at Maxu. "Don't you have somewhere to be? There's a ceremony tonight, isn't there?"

Maxu grinned a wide, evil grin. "Yes, but I still have three more ceremonies left before they force me to participate—or rather until I decide which law to break to render me unsuitable."

Auzed rolled his eyes but found he didn't care about his brother's rule-breaking quite as much as he had before. Why should he have to wed a female? He'd do everything he could to make her happy, only to have her leave him. Auzed took another swig of his drink, feeling that thought hitting too close to home.

As soon as Maxu's ass touched the chair, a chiming sounded from above. His brother let out a lazy snarl and rose again to see who was requesting entry at the gate. "Did you ask someone to come here to see you?"

Auzed frowned in answer. There was only one person he wanted to see.

Since losing his job at the Temple meant he'd also had to vacate his onsite house, he'd moved in with his younger brother. Maxu, an ex-mercenary and all-around loner, had built the house with isolation in mind. Warnings and booby traps, along with a thick fence and invisible shield that bubbled the house, lined his property high on a hill outside of town.

At least everyone had finally started to leave Zed alone now that he'd taken up residence here. Most people knew that venturing to Maxu's house—and actually getting let in—was too much of a hassle.

Maxu shuffled back into the large room, his lips curled in irritation. "It's the Queen."

Auzed sat up straighter, surprise breaking through his haze of self-pity. "Why?" he said stupidly, knowing Maxu would never have invited her here himself.

"I doubt it's to see me," Maxu growled, leaving again to get the door.

He hadn't spoken to the Queen since handing in his credentials the day after visiting Alex. The loss of his job, his life's work had been surprisingly easy to stomach. In fact, he rarely thought about it at all. Hadn't even tried to look for another job yet. It stunned him how insignificant something he'd thought he valued above all other things would end up being after experiencing true happiness.

Auzed patted down his rumpled clothing and tried to smooth his hair. He stood, picked up some stray trash lying on the table near him, and swore when he knocked the bottle of mott onto the ground.

"Auzed," came the Queen's regal voice.

"Majesty." He rose from his crouched position over the bottle, only to bow low and then stand back up again. Up, down, up, down, Like a damn child's toy.

The Queen eyed Maxu as he shuffled by her and collapsed into a chair. They knew each other well enough, seeing as Maxu was always getting into some type of trouble. Neither liked the other.

"I wanted to come by and formally deliver my message," she said, still standing along with her guards rather than sitting in the chair Auzed had cleared for her. Her maroon dress was plain and covered her from chin to toes. Her white hair was neatly twisted into a design at the back of her neck. And her lavender eyes were clear and calm.

No crisis, then. So why had she felt the need to see him in person?

"I am reinstating you as head guard of the Pearl Temple." She smiled with tight lips.

Auzed couldn't stop his jaw from going slack. He studied her face, his confusion warring with...indifference. "My Queen?" Where had this come from all of a sudden? Had she made a deal with Sauven? What had she traded in return?

Ice slid down his spine, and his stomach clenched. He stepped toward her in his worry, something that was not done. She lifted a delicate brow, and he stopped.

"Alejandra? Did you... Where is she?"

The Queens lips twitched. "She's here in Tremanta. I didn't swap her for your job if that's what you're worried about."

All the air rushed from Auzed's lungs as he released the breath he didn't know he'd been holding. The flood of relief was interrupted by curiosity. "So how, then?"

"Well, Alejandra came to see me a few days ago."

And just like that, the tension shot back into his body.

"She wanted to make a deal to get your job back for you. Very persistent, that one."

Auzed let out a humorless bark of laughter.

"We came to an arrangement. I spoke to the regents of Sauven and explained that the strain of your time together in Sauven had soured you toward each other. They conceded that your forcible detention may have been excessive and agreed to let you resume your duties. I also promised to send a few willing humans to visit Sauven when the time came."

341

Just like that?

"Since Alejandra will, in fact, be marrying another Tremantian instead of you, they agreed you've suffered enough."

Buzzing sounded in his ears, and he blinked, unseeing. What had she said? When her words finally registered, he roared, "What?"

The guards, who'd been positioned behind the Queen, sprang in front of her. With a wave of her hand, they backed away.

"I explained to Alejandra when she came to see me that giving you your job back and allowing her to remain unmarried would be like a slap in the face to Sauven. I told her if she agreed to participate in the ceremony and choose a husband, I'd reinstate you. She wasn't thrilled, but anyone could tell how guilty she felt that you'd lost your career helping her. So, she agreed."

"The ceremony!" he boomed, gaze frantic. "The ceremony happening tonight?"

The Queen lifted her brows in surprise. "Yes." She peered at her hand clock. "In a few hours."

Auzed became a whirlwind of movement. Gathering his communicator and searching for his identification pad containing all his scores and his eligibility. It'd be tight, but if he got there in time and registered himself quickly, he might make the cut.

"Whatever are you doing?" the Queen asked with furrowed brows.

"I'm going to the ceremony. I refuse your offer." With a wince, he turned and gave a quick bow. "Ma'am."

She shook her head, perplexed. "If that's what you wish."

He dashed past the guards stiff and ready to aim an attack at him, then bolted in the direction of the ceremony building.

***

Maxu studied the Queen's face for long moments after his brother fled. She caught him assessing her and stared back, unflinching.

"Sauven would've never agreed to that deal. Queen Dasa hates you," he remarked coolly, draping his arm over his chair and taking another sip of mott. He'd always loathed authority and politics. The society they resided in could burn to the ground for all he cared. But the twitch of the Queen's mouth had him curious.

She tipped her head at him as though he were a child. "No, they wouldn't."

A slow smile spread across his face. "Mm. Not bad, Majesty." He nodded approvingly. "Do either of them know that?"

"They do not." She turned to him, clasping her hands in front of her and tilting her chin up.

"Why didn't you tell him days ago when Alex agreed to it?"

She pursed her lips and thought for a moment before answering. "Do you think your brother would've done well with more time to agonize over his decision?"

Maxu shook his head. His brother had always been a rule

follower. Always working a problem based on what the *right* thing to do was. "No, he would not." He stood and rolled out his shoulders. "Still, a bit risky, don't you think?" He lifted his brows and gave her his most charming grin, the one that either made females run or melt.

She blew out a sigh and cupped his chin. "So young. Someday you'll understand."

He jerked away, irritated by the patronizing tone.

The Queen tipped her chin to him and turned to leave, her ever-present guards shifting to protect her back. "I'll be interested to see how you get out of the ceremony this year, Maxu. You don't have long."

Maxu grinned at the door as it closed behind her. He'd already formulated his plan.

28

Alex instinctively moved to twirl her ring around her finger but only touched bare skin. She sighed and wrapped her arms around her waist instead. Her ceremony aide, an older, reserved woman named Blina, had explained each round of the ceremony to her. In this round, something they called the Viewing, she'd look at a parade of men and pick out the ones she liked.

Emptiness echoed in her heart, thinking about the only face she wanted to see. Ever since her and Auzed's passionate encounter, she'd begun to hollow out. No more tears sprung to her eyes. Nothing made her laugh. Even the idea of her family back home no longer warmed her like it used to. She was dead inside. Stone.

"Hey there, scaredy cat."

Alex turned at the voice and spotted Vanessa. Had she been living at the Temple this whole time?

Months ago—it now seemed like lifetimes—she and

Vanessa had broken out of their underground prison together. Battling their way to the surface past their Insurgent abductors.

She and Vanessa had only spoken briefly once they'd escaped, but the memories Alex had of the woman weren't fond ones. She could accept that perhaps neither had been in a completely rational state of mind at that time, though. Their actions had been spurred by terror, too wrapped up in the scramble to figure out what to do next to be polite to each other.

When Alex and Lily had wanted to take their chances in the forest, fearing they'd be re-captured if they didn't—a reasonable reaction which she would argue for to this day—Vanessa had scoffed, calling them insane.

"Hey…you." She nodded as the woman approached. She was almost positive her name was Vanessa but it'd been so long, and she didn't want to be wrong.

"Vanessa." The woman smiled.

Alex studied her and noticed that despite Vanessa's confident attitude, she looked worn and unhealthy. Her skin was waxen and drawn, and her slight frame, which at one time would've made any model jealous, was gaunt. What had happened to her?

The lights dimmed, and the hallway on the other side of the glass illuminated.

A small man with a warm smile and bright excited eyes sped toward Vanessa. "You understand what you're supposed to do, yes?"

"Yes, Zikas, you're a doll."

Alex smothered a smirk. She could tell from Vanessa's tone that she was actually trying to be nice, but a hint of sarcasm colored her words anyway.

The man seemed to hear it too because his brows drew together briefly, but then he grinned again and walked away.

One by one, men filed in front of them, stopping at planned intervals to gaze through the one-way glass. Alex tried to concentrate, but what did it even matter? She should just pick one and be done with it. She'd already made it clear to the Queen that she'd be doing nothing with her husband at all. A part of her felt bad for whomever she picked, knowing how important being selected for marriage was, but if this was what it took to give Auzed even a bit of happiness, she'd do it. When the marriage was over, she'd just lie and gush about how amazing the guy was at everything. Hopefully that would make him more interesting to women for the next time he signed up.

A sharp needle pierced her heart as she wondered what Auzed would say about her plan to lie.

Suddenly, she spun to Vanessa, their setting finally registering in her brain. "Wait. You?" Alex sputtered. Obviously, Vanessa was *here,* wasn't she? But her brain still had trouble computing. "*You're* getting married? Voluntarily?"

Vanessa's jaw clenched as she stared at a new man who'd just started posing behind the glass like a swarthy playboy pirate. "Yeah, to that arrogant, cocky, overdressed meathead."

Alex snorted. "Sounds like you two are really in love."

She studied the man to understand why Vanessa wanted to choose him despite her obvious irritation. He was good-looking enough, that was for sure. Broad-shouldered and tall with smooth, bronzed skin and a dark messy mop of hair—almost as black as Vanessa's straight hair. He was dressed in a heavily embroidered plum coat with pounds of jewelry dripping from his throat, ears, and hair. More jewelry topped his fingers as well as the soles of his boots. His thousand-watt smile practically lit up the room all by itself, not to mention his single dimple rakishly popped whenever he smirked wide enough.

Alex glanced back at Vanessa. It was clear she knew him. Nobody could be that irritated by someone they didn't know. "He seems like trouble—but the sexy kind," she said matter-of-factly.

Vanessa watched as he sauntered down the line, then, with a quick glance over her shoulder at Zikas, she leaned in close and whispered, "He's my ticket out of here."

Alex's gaze flew back to the handsome stranger. "Really? What do you mean?"

Vanessa raised her brows. "He has a ship and spends most of his time off-planet. And does some underhanded stuff. Like going to planets he's not supposed to." Vanessa lifted her brows, forcing the consequence of her words to register in Alex's mind. "He's supposed to leave for another trip this week, and so help me, I'm getting on that ship." She gestured around the room. "This seemed like a better plan than trying to sneak on. I'd probably fuck it up and end up in the trash room or something and get sucked out into space when they dump it."

Heart thudding in her chest, she digested that. If Vanessa was going home, that meant…could she go too? Sneak onto the ship with Wilson in Vanessa's luggage or something? A slice of pain, sudden and crippling in its intensity, tore into her heart at the idea of leaving. She probably wouldn't even be able to say goodbye to Auzed. He'd spend his life wondering, and…

Shocking clarity overcame her. Now, confronted with the real opportunity to go back to Earth, she couldn't do it. Physically couldn't stomach it. Even thinking about the possibility of hopping onto a ship next week made her roil with nausea.

She'd assumed when the opportunity to leave finally arrived, she'd be so stricken with homesickness and concern for her family that, although sad, she'd also be relieved and excited to go home. She didn't feel that way at all—just the opposite. The thought made her skin crawl.

The knowledge that her family was suffering and would continue to suffer stole her breath, but to her surprise, leaving Auzed felt the same way. He was her family now too. One day, Earth would be accessible again. Until then, her family would survive. They had each other after all.

She'd make it her mission to change the laws protecting Earth. If she had to annoy every last politician on this planet each day of the rest of her life, she'd do it. But she wanted to do it with Auzed by her side.

Suddenly all the reservations she'd had were washed away. But then…despair roared to life in its place. She'd turned him down, and now she was here. Required to pick a man to marry. A man who wasn't Auzed.

Her gaze darted around the room, searching for an escape. How the fuck had she let this happen? A door against the far wall caught her eye, but so did Zikas and Blina, who were gazing at her warily.

"God, he looks like shit," Vanessa grumbled from nearby.

Out of instinct, Alex glanced at the person Vanessa was talking about and did a double take, staggering back a step. She stared hard, not quite believing her eyes.

Haggard, out of breath, and more than a little furious, Auzed stalked into the hallway. He glared at the glass as if he could crack it with only the power of his mind and blind fury.

She grinned, a goofy, lovesick grin. Her heart throbbed at double its usual pace, and happy tears blurred her vision.

"God, don't tell me you want that one. He's a guard at the Temple, and he's so uptight."

"And you're a bitch." Alex chuckled and elbowed a shocked Vanessa in the arm. "But I still like *you*." She shot her a wink. Then as if on a cloud, she floated to the glass, wishing she could reach through it and squeeze her disheveled mountain of a man.

In the distance, she heard Vanessa chuckle. "Touché."

Before Alex knew it, the Viewing was over, and they were

taken to a separate but identical room for the Choosing. Blina reminded her she'd need to remember the numbers of the men she wanted to test in the next round. Alex kept her eyes peeled, not trusting herself enough to even blink.

Vanessa sidled up to her again and whispered, "I'm collecting letters with addresses from as many humans as I can. Want me to try to get something to your family?"

Alex's eyes flashed to Vanessa, and she threw her arms around her in a crushing bear hug.

"Okay. Alright. I get it." She shook out her limbs when Alex released her. "Write it and give it to me as soon as you can, and if I get to Earth, I'll make sure it finds your family."

If? "Didn't he agree to take you back to Earth?"

Vanessa's shoulders slumped. Her lips pulled to the side in annoyance. "Well, not exactly. He doesn't even know I'm planning on bagging him. But he's my ticket out. If I can get onto his ship and off Clecania…" She shrugged. "Even if he doesn't agree to take me, I'm still off this planet and one step closer."

Alex wanted to point out the many ways in which that plan was doomed to fail, but the desperation in the woman's eyes had her snapping her mouth shut. It was unlikely Vanessa had planned all this without coming to that realization herself. If she still wanted to take the risk? Well, that was her decision. Just as it'd been Alex's to run into the forest after escaping from that bunker.

The knowledge that she'd never actually had a shot of going back to Earth rang through her mind. She grinned. That fact changed nothing. The way she'd felt when she thought she could leave told her everything she needed to know.

She pulled a stiff Vanessa to her and wrapped her in a tight hug again. "Thank you." She sniffed.

With an awkward pat on the back, Vanessa muttered, "Yeah, no problem." Her eyes lit on the flashy man entering the hall, and she squirmed out of Alex's hold.

She chuckled when Vanessa walked away and in a firm voice directed at Zikas said, "That one. I want that one."

That poor guy had no idea what was about to hit him.

***

Alex was practically bouncing as Blina led her to the Testing room. They passed Vanessa, who gave a small wave while barring the entrance to the room the man she'd picked was presumably in. "Keep moving, he's spoken for!" she hissed to an annoyed teal-haired beauty who tried to enter, apparently having picked the man as well.

Alex chuckled. She'd checked and rechecked with Blina that no one else had selected Auzed. She supposed his bedraggled appearance worked in her favor because she wouldn't need to fight off any women of her own.

They reached the door, and suddenly her nerves got the better of her. What if he didn't want her to choose him? What if he was doing this to get back at her or something?

She shook off the worries as soon as they entered her brain. Her deal with the Queen had been very clear. Alex had to get married, and then Auzed would get his job back. If he was here, that could only mean one thing. He'd turned it down. Not only that but he'd turned it down and come here. Laying himself bare to her again.

The last time he'd offered her a life with him, she'd crushed him. She inhaled a deep breath. Not this time.

"Remember," Blina said in a rehearsed tone. "He'll be blindfolded, and he won't know who it was who picked him."

"I can take the blindfold off, though, right?" Alex asked, smoothing the drab russet romper-like garment she'd picked for the day when she'd been miserable and wanted her attire to match her mood.

"Take it…" Blina reared back and stared at her as if she had two heads. "Why would you want to take it off?"

A slight annoyance that she was spending one more second talking out here when she could be in that room reuniting with Auzed made her words a bit more clipped than necessary. "Can I? Please, just yes or no."

Blina grimaced at her and stepped away, rustling through a low cabinet. She produced an odd handheld tool and dropped it into Alex's upheld palms. "Press the button on the left to soften the covering," she drawled.

"Whatever that means!" Alex beamed, giving an appalled Blina a quick hug before rushing to stand in front of the door.

She took a long, shaky breath in and out. Butterflies bombarded her stomach, and her cheeks hurt from grinning so hard. *You got this.*

She swung the door wide. There, in the middle of the room, was Auzed. He paced with his hands slammed onto his hips. The clunking of his shoes vibrated through the whole room. He must've been lost in thought because he didn't immediately hear her come in until the door shut behind her.

He paused and sniffed at the air. Checking to make sure it was her? The black tar-like substance covering his eyes would make spotting her impossible. She now understood what Blina had meant about softening it.

As soon as he identified it was her, he erupted. "What were you thinking? I didn't ask you to offer yourself up to some stranger for me. Being impulsive...*again*! After everything we went through!"

He continued to bark and blunder, but all Alex could do was grin. He looked so cute standing there like a blind volcano of a man. Angled just far enough to the right, not quite facing her, to undermine his furious tone.

"Alex. Are you listening to me? How dare you choose to marry—"

She ran and leapt at him, wrapping her arms and legs around his body as he let out an *oof* and took a step back. Before he could say another word, she kissed him.

He stood still for only a second before he came alive underneath her, crushing her against his body and devouring her kisses. She slid her fingers through his shaggy hair, now longer than she remembered.

"No! Stop. We aren't done." He forced her down, gripping her biceps and setting her away.

Quickly, she wiggled out of his light grasp and retrieved the tool needed to remove his eye covering. "I'm so glad you're here, Auzzy."

The hard lines marring his face with anger flickered, then softened. He shuffled in place, unsure how to act now that he wasn't still brimming with anger. She gently guided his head down and held the tool over his eyes.

"Really?" he breathed.

Damn, she'd wanted to wait until they could look at each other to say what she needed to say, but the hope shining on his crinkled brows and parted lips broke her.

"I love you, Auzed. More than anything in all the universe. I want us to be together. Whatever way we can be."

His mouth remained open as he digested her words. She pulled at the odd tar, but it was still too hard. He winced.

"Sorry."

"But…what about Earth? What about your family?" She could hear the pain in his clipped words and hated it.

"Long story short, I thought I had the opportunity to go home today, and I just couldn't." She cupped his cheek with her free hand. "I love my family. I always will. But I *can't* live without you."

The corner of his mouth twitched. Then, a handful of different emotions flitted across his face. A flash of doubt, anger, then pure joy, then reserved joy. He still didn't quite believe her. "What if they let humans go back?"

"Unless you go with me, I'm not going. But I'll do whatever I can to let my family know I'm safe and that I'm completely"—she pressed a kiss to his right cheek— "perfectly"—she kissed his other cheek—"and incandescently happy."

His purr rumbled through him in time with his wide grin. "I love you so much, Alejandra."

Dragging her grinning mouth to his, he kissed her slow and deep just as the tar over his eyes softened. She peeled it off and pulled away to look at him fully.

With a shriek she stumbled back, falling hard on her ass.

"What?" he roared, crouching into a fighting stance and blinking around the room in the bright light, searching for the danger.

She stared, unable to process what she was seeing.

His attention focused on her still on the ground where she'd fallen, and he knelt. She gazed into his eyes. His worried eyes. His *black* eyes.

"Alejandra, what's wrong?" he rasped, taking her hand.

She gave a shrug and beamed at him. "Looks like we don't have to get married, after all."

A moment of hurt flashed over his features before he registered her grin. His brows drew together.

She peered down in wonder to where he clasped her hand in his and, sure enough, bright-blue markings started to appear, twining their way around his wrists and up along his fingers.

Following her gaze, he stilled. He muttered something under his breath that she couldn't quite make out.

"What, Auzzy?"

He peered up at her, grinning like an idiot. "You're mine."

He said it as if he didn't quite believe the words himself, and she wanted him to believe them. Needed him to because somewhere deep down, she'd known it all along.

"What was that?" she goaded with a hand to her ear.

"You're mine," he said again, crawling over her until she was forced to slowly lie back.

She wrapped her arms around his neck. "One more time for the folks in the back!"

"You're mine!" he bellowed, then descended on her in a hard, passionate kiss that vibrated along with his deep purr.

He pulled away and shot a disbelieving glance back to his hands, then back to her.

Alex stroked his cheek, tucking his hair behind his ears, and marveled as the black in his eyes faded to the soft mossy green she loved.

"I'm yours," she whispered, her chest so full it could explode. "And you're mine."

Epilogue

Two Months Later

Alex wiped her sopping face as the lights came on in the traveling dome theater. She peered to Auzed, who grinned with raised brows. It was clear from his eager expression that he wanted her to tell him how she felt about this world's version of a play.

"It was indescribable. So amazing, honey."

Auzed's chest bowed with pride, and he flashed her a smug, toothy smile. "I told you. Better than movies?"

She chuckled. "Well, I wouldn't go that far, but it was definitely a more intense experience." Every question he'd had for her about movies now made sense. "How can people do that every day?" She sniffed, watching the actors on the floating platform stage disappear from view. They looked exhausted, and rightly so.

Auzed leaned over and helped her unfasten the clasp of the bodysuit she'd been given. Apparently, on Clecania, plays were a completely immersive experience. Actors weren't expected to *pretend* to feel whatever emotion was written—

they were expected to *actually* feel those emotions. The audience members, all connected to the actor of their choice, were clad in head-to-toe suits that allowed them to feel exactly what the actors were.

Alex couldn't wrap her mind around how it worked, but a combination of incredible electric currents, temperature controls, and spritzes of particular chemical combos made it so Alex actually felt the female actor's raw pain, joy, and grief in time with her. The experience was overwhelming and yet satisfying in a way she'd never thought possible. No wonder plays were few and far between. The amount of skill needed for each role alone would be enough to make them rare. Not to mention the toll it took on the viewer. She'd loved the experience, but she'd need a bit of downtime before signing up to live in someone's body again.

"I told you you should've picked Rahe your first time. He isn't as good of an actor, and his role was less emotional according to the guide." Auzed removed his own suit and hung it nearby in their cube seating area. The small space allowed the scents, holograms, and temperatures choreographed to the scene to feel real. For a second, during the climax, Alex had lost herself and actually believed she'd been Weduta, kneeling in the snow with raw, wet knees, her heart breaking a thousand times over as her family boarded a separate ship leaving old Clecania.

Alex leaned against him as they wound their way through the crowds, using Auzed's nearness to wash away the last vestiges of sadness. He wrapped his arm around her and proudly nodded at the passersby who stared. They loaded into a cruiser and made their way toward their new home on the outskirts of Tremanta.

"It's a good thing Wilson is off in Sauven looking for a mate right now, or she'd have broken down the door to get to us." Alex grinned, twining her fingers with Auzed's and curling into his big body on the double-wide cushioned bench in the personal cruiser they kept near their out-of-the-way home. Ever since that fateful ceremony day when Auzed had recognized her, Wilson had begun treating him the same way she treated Alex. Though Relli had confirmed what was happening on one of their frequent calls, Alex had already worked it out.

Auzed was her other half. They were bound by whatever magic lurked in a Clecanian's veins, and as such, Wilson was bonded to him as much as she was to Alex.

The memory of Relli's explanation jogged something in Alex's mind, and she sat up. "Oh, I forgot to tell you. I talked to Relli yesterday, and guess what?"

Auzed pulled her back against his body, purring at the contact. "What?"

"They finally made her head ranger!"

"Should've been made official a while ago," Auzed grumbled, fiddling with her hair the way he often did.

Alex shrugged. "Obviously, but at least it's done." She gazed at his thoughtful expression and, with some difficulty, pulled away. She tucked a leg under herself and ran her hands up his arms, letting them rest at his shoulders. She'd meant the gesture to be caring, but the hunger that blazed in his eyes showed her he'd taken her touch a different way. She chuckled. "Wait. I want to ask you something."

He pursed his lips and narrowed his eyes at her suspiciously.

"Are you really okay? I mean, does hearing about Relli's promotion make you jealous or anything? 'Cause we could always move—"

He flung his head back and swiped a palm over his face. "This again!"

Alex pursed her lips. "It's just...you got so many prestigious offers off-world, and I don't want you to not take them because of me, you know?"

He gave her a long-suffering look, then broke it with a lopsided grin. The view of his face transformed by a smile still stole her breath.

"I love my new job," he crooned, angling his body so he reclined along the bench seat. He pulled her on top of him, and she went without a fight. "I prefer working short hours these days so I can be home with you when you aren't meeting with the Reclassify Earth group."

She and a group of humans and Tremantians had formed an official group to handle the human presence on Clecania. In addition to their many hours spent researching intergalactic law and drafting arguments in favor of reclassifying Earth, they'd also started documenting their history and culture for the archives, guessing that if human civilization was more well-known and present in records throughout the Alliance planets, Earth would feel more familiar. They were counting on that familiarity when the time came to decide if Earth was ready to be reassigned.

Alex had begun uploading detailed movie summaries of the greatest films from Earth, while other women outlined famous novels or works of art. Bonny, who'd turned out to be a historian, had been pouring all she knew into the archives for months and still hadn't made it through prehistory.

Seeing the sheer amount of effort the humans were putting in and the benefit of their hard work, the Queen had decided to make their group official and pay them as employees of the city. Alex got so much fulfillment from her unexpected job, and she worried that Auzed didn't, though he told her differently whenever she brought it up.

"Yeah, but—" she started to argue.

"No buts. I'm still doing important work. I'm personally training the soldiers who protect my family." He grinned and tucked a lock of her hair behind her ear. "It feels good. Every time they're able to land a punch or every time their strategy-exercise scores go up, I feel useful. That's all I need."

She folded her arms on his chest and pressed a quick kiss to his chin.

"Besides," he continued, "remember how excited Wilson got when she saw the forest behind our house? We can't move her now."

Their small home with its shady forest backyard and panoramic views of the sunset was the best of both worlds. They often spent their afternoons stretched out by their shielded front-yard pool and their evenings wrapped up together on their large floating bed.

In the mornings when they weren't working, Auzed would explore new hobbies, trying to find the ones he truly enjoyed. After much experimentation, he'd decided cooking, tinkering with electronics, and reading all failed to hold his interest. But Alex wasn't complaining because until he found something that appealed to him, he reverted to his favorite pastime of pulling her into their room and making her toes curl.

Over the last week, he'd been experimenting with building, however, and seemed to enjoy it enough. He'd even built Wilson her own special nest area with an entrance on the roof. He insisted on constructing a connecting sheltered tube that would protect her against the sun as she rolled back and forth between the dark forest and the house.

"If she ends up finding a mate, she may return with a litter," Auzed said, his mind wandering and his brows drawn together. "Do you think she'll need a bigger nest?"

Love bloomed in her chest at his serious expression. Her family was gonna love him. The thought of them back on Earth still ached, but she forced herself to remain positive these days. They would fall in love with Auzed, just as she had, *when* they met him. Not if. When.

Still deep in thought, he added, "We'll have to teach Laura and Cebo not to mess with the litter. They'll be gliding all over the house in no time." His brother's child, Laura, and their alien hound, Cebo, loved to play with Wilson, chasing her all over the house while she rolled and dodged. Whenever

Wilson trumpeted from her short trunk, Cebo would howl and Laura would break out into squealing laughter. Unfortunately for Alex's eardrums, Wilson loved Laura and Cebo as much as they loved her and would try to spur on the laughter and howling whenever she could.

Auzed's brows were still drawn, and he appeared to be far away, working through how to protect everyone and everything under his roof. Alex bit her lip as electric excitement sizzled through her veins. She hadn't told him yet, was waiting for the right time. But the warmth and love she felt whenever his family and her human friends got together had stoked a long-forgotten fire in her belly. She wanted to have a child with him. Wanted to see him dashing about like a madman trying to contain a toddler and keep them from getting hurt.

"Could we section off the ceiling for gliding, perhaps?" he murmured under his breath.

Sliding up his body and making sure to rub against every rigid part of him, she snaked her hands around his neck. "I've never met such a softy."

He smirked and clicked his tongue. "You lie."

"Never to you, Auzzy." Alex pressed a kiss to his curling lips and let his rumbling purr wash over her.

About the Author

Victoria Aveline has always enjoyed immersing herself in a good romance. Alpha males are her weakness but, while possessive dominating heroes have always been titillating, she craved something more. So she decided to create a world in which devastatingly sexy men could be aggressive and domineering but still bow down before the matriarchy.

Victoria lives with her husband, dog, and about sixty thousand badass honey-making ladies. When not writing or fantasizing about future characters, she enjoys traveling, reading, and sipping overpriced hipster cocktails.

victoriaaveline.com

Made in the USA
Coppell, TX
11 November 2021

65557312R00215